Dark is the

An Inspector Carruthers novel

Tana Collins

Print ISBN978-1-912986-26-2

Also By Tana Collins

This book is dedicated to Allison (Ally) Brady.

Prologue

Hearing footsteps behind her, she clutches her canvas bag tighter to her chest. As she picks up her pace she feels the moisture of sweat on her hands and tastes it on her top lip. A sudden sense of claustrophobia comes over her in this dark, cobbled, medieval alley with its high stone walls. The light barely penetrates here and everything is in shadow. Her heart hammers in her chest. It is almost painful.

Greyfriar's Wynd is empty except for her and the person behind her. She is wearing red wedge sandals but can still hear the other person's footfall, measured and deliberate. All her senses are on alert. Why did she take this short cut? She descends three worn steps quickly. She always takes this short cut from the library, that's why, and nothing has ever happened before. But she's never been followed before. And with the recent news of that girl being attacked, what is she thinking?

She doesn't dare turn round. She can't. She stops abruptly and the footsteps behind her stop. Hairs prick up on the back of her neck. She hears a strange tuneless whistling. She feels a sudden shiver. Panic threatens to overwhelm her. She tries to scream but can't. She can't turn back, there's nowhere to hide, so the only option is to keep going forward. Thank God, she's not wearing heels, although the wedge sandals are bad enough on cobbles.

A sudden noise behind her. The sound of heavy shoes. *Oh my God.* The man is running. She starts to run too, cursing as her tight denim skirt impedes her progress. Why does she think it's a man? He's getting closer. He's closing the gap quickly. She can hear his breathing, smell his sweat. She's a fast runner, but not in this skirt. Another couple of seconds and she knows she's not going to be able to outrun him. A large hand grabs her shoulder, swings her round. Her shoulder bag slips to the ground, the contents spilling out.

It is then that she sees the mask and the knife.

Chapter one

An eerie artificial light bathed the alley. The lighting system was already set up and the scene of crime officers had cordoned off the entrance and exit. Dr Mackie knelt by the body in the ancient close. A strobe flash signalled another photograph from Liu, the diminutive Chinese photographer.

Mackie tilted his head so he was looking up at Carruthers. 'It's a nasty one, Jim.'

DI Jim Carruthers, all kitted out in his paper overalls, ducked under the tape and entered the close. Dark-haired DS Andrea Fletcher followed closely behind him.

Mackie tried to straighten up. Carruthers looked at his shock of white hair and worn face and wondered fleetingly how long the pathologist would keep going. He must be getting close to retirement age.

'She's been slashed across the face, laddie. It's no' pretty. My estimate is that she's only been dead less than an hour.'

'So about three in the afternoon then.' Although Carruthers felt butterflies in his stomach his professionalism kicked in. 'And the perpetrator had some kind of knife or sharp implement. Any puncture wounds elsewhere?' He leant into the slim body lying still in its last repose.

'Not that I can see. I'll start the PM as soon as it's possible.' Mackie's voice sounded husky to Carruthers – was that emotion clouding his voice, or did he have a head cold? The detective knew Mackie hated violence, especially violence against women.

'However, look at this.' Mackie leant over the corpse of the young woman, gesturing at the neck. 'We may have our cause of death.'

Carruthers could see bluish marks on the neck and what looked like fingerprints. 'Manual strangulation?' He turned to Fletcher. 'We need to find out who she is.' He gazed back at the slim figure and blonde hair of the dead woman.

'Can you tell me anything with any certainty?' asked Carruthers.

'All I can tell you at the moment is that she didn't take her own life.' *Mackie's standard response to a suspicious death,* thought Carruthers.

'Reckon she might be a student. She's about that age,' said Fletcher. 'Any ID on her?'

Fletcher nodded her thanks to a scene of crime officer, or SOCO, who offered her the bagged possessions. Carefully, Fletcher pulled a pair of latex gloves on. She opened the clear plastic bag and rifled through. 'Looks like our victim's name may be Rachel Abbie. There's a jotter with that name on it on the front. But no student ID, which is unusual, and no purse or bank cards.' She gave Jim the bagged possessions. 'There's also a library book in here.' It was a slim paperback. She looked at it. 'David Hume. *A Treatise of Human Nature.*'

Carruthers raised his eyebrow. 'David Hume? As in Scottish Philosopher?'

Fletcher looked at the blurb on the back of the book. 'The one and same. Maybe our victim's a philosophy student?'

He frowned. 'Anything with her address on it?'

Fletcher shook her head.

'Get over to the philosophy department. The David Hume book is our only lead. See if they have a student by the name of Rachel Abbie.'

He watched the younger Fletcher shiver. Despite the fact Scotland was in the throes of spring it was a cold, windy day. What was the expression people used? "Ne'er cast a cloot, till May be oot." He smiled as he thought of the translation he'd have to give his English DS. "Don't throw away your clothes until May is over". There'd been an unexpected frost that morning. A reminder that winter wasn't long behind them.

'Nobody saw or heard anything apparently, which in itself is strange.' He was thinking that this was a busy university town in the East of Scotland. The area was also popular with golfers and tourists. And the local RAF base was just six miles down the road in Edenside.

'Who found the body?'

'A couple of male students walking back from the Earl of Fife.'

One of the better frequented student pubs in the centre of town.

'Okay, don't let them leave without taking a statement from them.' He asked hopefully, 'Do either of them know the deceased?'

Fletcher shook her head. She was very quiet, Carruthers noticed. Unusually so.

'Pity. Was worth a long shot.'

He'd noticed Fletcher's mood had plummeted the last couple of weeks. Wondered what was wrong. He thought she'd managed to put her relationship breakup with Mark behind her. But what about her miscarriage? How could she put that behind her?

His eyes trailed back to the prostrate figure of the young woman lying on the ground. What was she? Eighteen or nineteen? Too young to have seen much of life. Not long out of childhood herself; on the verge of adulthood. Once again, he silently cursed the fact that someone could take another human being's life. He added her to the growing list of the dead who would haunt his dreams.

* * *

Fletcher wrapped her coat protectively around herself and walked the ten minutes to the philosophy department through the ancient streets of Castletown. She could smell the fresh sea air in her nostrils and hear the cry of gulls as she crossed the cobbled street by the Quad. She looked up at the turreted gothic building against its backdrop of the North Sea as she walked across the tarmacked road. It wouldn't look out of place as Hogwarts on a film set. She ran up the worn stone steps and through the open blue door. Fishing in her handbag she brought out her mobile, glanced at it to see there were no new messages and slipped it back in the bag.

A few minutes later she was up two flights of steps and in the secretary's office. As the middle-aged woman with the silver coiffured hair busied herself going through the student files, Fletcher stared beyond her out through the second-floor window at the sparkling blue sea. A thunderous noise signalled two low-flying Tornados from nearby RAF Edenside.

'Rachel Abbie, you say? Yes, here it is. I thought she sounded familiar. We do have a second-year student by that name. If you hold on, I'll just get her term-time address.' The secretary tapped at her computer with her short, manicured nails, opened her desk drawer, brought out a sheet of paper and wrote the address down for Fletcher.

The door opened and a young woman with shiny black hair came in, carrying a black shoulder bag. She looked ready for a night on the town in a little red dress. Fletcher wondered if she'd come to work looking like that or if she'd made a quick change in the toilets. It looked as if she'd just brushed her hair and put on a slick of red lipstick.

'Can I get off? I don't want to keep Dave waiting.'

The secretary checked her watch. 'Go on then. It's nearly five anyway – see you tomorrow,' she added as an afterthought as the woman closed the door.

She rolled her eyes at Fletcher. 'Temps.'

'Do you have an out-of-term address for her too? Rachel Abbie?'

The secretary nodded. 'Pateley Hall, Pateley Bridge, Nidderdale, North Yorkshire.' She scribbled that down for Fletcher too.

'You wouldn't have a photograph of her, would you?' Fletcher asked hopefully.

The secretary pulled a face. 'I'm afraid not. And to be honest I wouldn't know what she looks like. They're mostly just a sea of faces to me. I don't get to have much personal contact with the students on an individual basis. Can I ask what this is about?'

'Just making some enquiries,' said Fletcher, privately wondering if any woman was safe in Castletown at the moment given recent events. This was the second attack in days. She wondered where the temp was heading. Wherever she was going she hoped she'd take care. 'Can you tell me anything else about her?'

Two more Tornados flew low overhead, drowning out the secretary's answer. The woman stood up and walked over to the window. 'No, like I said, I don't know her personally.' She pulled on the sash window and shut it. 'I'm very sensitive to noise. Sometimes you can't hear yourself think with those jets. I once knew a student who had to ask for ear plugs during her exam in this building. I did feel for her. Even more sensitive to noise than me, poor dear, although I'm sure stress played a part.'

'Did the student pass the exam?'

'What? Oh yes. With flying colours.' Smiling, she turned and faced Fletcher. 'You could ask her supervisor, Professor Mairi Beattie. She will have had more personal contact with her, although she's not in the department at the moment. I believe she's coming back later. She sometimes stays late marking students' papers.'

'Mairi?' asked Fletcher, frowning. 'Is Beattie her maiden name?'

'Why yes. I believe she's recently returned to it. Do you know her?' said the secretary.

Finding she was holding her breath, Fletcher asked, 'Just out of interest, what was her married name?'

'Carruthers.'

Mairi Carruthers. Oh shit. Jim's ex-wife.

Chapter two

DS Andrea Fletcher leant over DI Jim Carruthers' desk. He looked up at her, and taking his glasses off, put them on his prematurely greying head. He rubbed his face with his hands. 'How did you get on at the philosophy department?'

Fletcher read from her little black notebook. 'There *is* a Rachel Abbie registered. I managed to get her term-time address. It's over at Strathburn Halls. But there was nobody home when I went round. I put a note through the door so I'm hoping someone will ring soon. I've also been given a home address for her. It's in a village in Nidderdale, North Yorkshire, called Pateley Bridge. I've been in touch with the control room at Bilston and they're going to get hold of the local constabulary and dispatch someone to the property.'

An image came into Fletcher's head of the picturesque market town in the middle of the Yorkshire Dales. She'd seen it recently in a magazine that celebrated England's natural beauty. There'd been an article in the magazine about a Dark Skies Festival in North Yorkshire that she'd been interested in. She frowned, wondering what she'd done with the magazine. She wanted to pass it on to Carruthers. With his love of the outdoors she could imagine a Dark Skies Festival would be right up his street.

'Good work.' Carruthers picked up his polystyrene cup and drained the remains of his cold tea. She knew he was trying to drink less coffee these days. He pulled a face. She also knew he wasn't much of a tea drinker. 'Andie, I want you to get Dougie to pull all the files on crimes involving similar MO in Scotland in the last few years and get on to the CCTV, will you? See if we can pick anything up of her last movements.'

She nodded, privately wondering if it wasn't a massive waste of time to try to pull all the files on previous similar crimes. Her gut instinct told her that they had no bearing on recent events. But then it was nothing more than a gut feeling and, in the end, nothing beat good old-fashioned police work.

With no leads or motive she wasn't going to voice her thoughts to her DI. They both knew they were currently clutching at straws.

Her thoughts turned to Dougie Harris. That man usually needed a rocket up his backside to get him motivated to do any proper work. However, this year she'd seen a more conscientious side to him, although sadly it hadn't been work-related. He'd recently returned from taking some leave to look after his sick, disabled wife.

As for the CCTV, they'd found nothing that had been of any help in the search to catch the attacker of Serena Davis, the first victim. Fletcher couldn't make up her mind whether she'd prefer it to be the same attacker or not. Of course, one person would be easier to catch, in theory, than two, but then a single perpetrator of these crimes meant it was more likely to be a serial attacker. She sighed. If the situation had been different and Serena Davis had died they could now be searching for the killer of two women, not one. They certainly didn't want a serial killer.

As if to voice her thoughts Carruthers said, 'At least the last one's still alive. Two girls in five days. What do you think the motive is?'

Fletcher shook her head, her eyes dull. 'Does there have to be one?'

Carruthers placed the empty polystyrene cup back on his desk. 'Few serious crimes are random. Most are committed by people the victim knows, which is why we need to start the investigation close to home for both women. But it's interesting. Thankfully, he didn't rape her. He didn't rob her. But he did slash her. Just like the first one.'

Fletcher picked up the photograph that had been lying on Carruthers' desk of the most recent victim. 'Except it looks like he finally killed Rachel Abbie by strangulation, if that's who our victim is.'

She listened to Carruthers as he continued to speak. 'He slashed her right across her face. Then he throttled her. Why slash and then throttle?'

Fletcher sighed. 'This act was committed by someone who hates pretty women? Perhaps someone who just hates women in general? There's enough of them about. It's a very intimate attack without being sexual. To slash someone across the face you physically need to get close enough to them.'

'And using a knife on a victim… there's not that disassociation between victim and perpetrator you get with a gun. On the other hand, guns aren't as easy to get hold of as knives.'

Carruthers nodded. 'Whatever the reason, he's got to be caught, and soon. We'll also have to handle the press very carefully. I don't want them to cause widescale panic.'

Fletcher put the photograph down carefully. 'Do we have a potential serial killer on our hands, Jim?'

'I don't know, but two similar attacks on two girls in five days doesn't look good. One of the first things we need to do is to find out whether the two girls knew each other.'

'I wonder if these attacks have been committed by a student?' Fletcher mused. 'I mean, assault on female students is rife.'

Carruthers looked at his watch. 'Yes, but those sorts of assaults are usually of a sexual nature, aren't they, including inappropriate touching or groping. This appears to be something very different.'

Fletcher nodded her agreement, but she wondered about the number of attacks on female students. She knew there was an epidemic of sexual violence at British universities, which she found really depressing. The police statistics were only the tip of the iceberg; most attacks still went unreported. She couldn't imagine being the mother of a teenage girl nowadays. There were just so many perils.

Carruthers jumped up. He grabbed his jacket and mobile. 'I want a quick word with our new DCI, then let's head to the hospital. I want to go over Serena Davis's statement again.'

'Jim, there's something you need to know about Rachel Abbie's supervisor…' She really did have to tell him before he found out from someone else that Rachel Abbie's supervisor was his ex-wife. But typically, Carruthers had already left.

* * *

Carruthers felt himself tensing as he approached his old office. He lifted his hand to knock on the door, hesitating only for a fraction of a moment, before giving a sharp rap.

'Come.'

The voice was curt. And female. He opened the door and walked in, closing it softly behind him. An unfamiliar smell greeted him, something vaguely flowery. The figure sitting behind his old desk stood up and smoothed her navy skirt before sitting down again. Carruthers didn't kid himself that she was standing for him. Why would she be? Since his demotion he was just a DI now. She was wearing a long-sleeved cream blouse. It looked like silk. Her navy blue jacket had been neatly placed over the back of the chair. A lock of hair fell over her face. She swept it back with an impatient air, looking harassed. Carruthers couldn't help but feel a small sense of satisfaction as he looked at his new boss, DCI Sandra McTavish.

She glanced up at him, a frown settling on her attractive face, making her look older than she actually was. 'What is it Jim? You can see I'm busy.'

He looked into the brown eyes of the woman who was barely older than him, before glancing at the files laid out neatly on her desk. It had never looked like that in his day. He thought of the midden that was his own desk – the empty polystyrene cups and messy piles of paperwork. He and Harris always vied for the title of untidiest cop. He ventured forward, standing closer to her desk. He felt a moment not just of resentment but also of jealousy before he forced those unwanted feelings to the back of his mind.

'I want to interview Serena Davis again.' He avoided looking at the framed photograph of her husband and kids on the desk.

McTavish's frown deepened. 'For what purpose?'

'Victims can remember important details of their attack or attacker days later once the shock wears off, and to be honest, she wasn't up to much during her first interview.'

'I need you here. Send someone else.'

Carruthers bristled but remained calm. 'We've not got much to go on, Sandra. We've barely got a description of her attacker. I'm happy for Fletcher to go but I'd like to go with her. I'm pretty sure I could get more from Serena about the attack.'

Sandra McTavish appeared to be thinking it over, steepling her hands in front of her face. Finally, she nodded. 'Okay. Stay close to your mobile. I'm waiting to hear back from the Procurator Fiscal. I'll ring you when I get word from them. I want the PM done as quickly as possible. We need to know what we're dealing with which means we need to contact next of kin urgently.'

'Understood. I'll head to the hospital in the next few minutes.'

She adjusted her glasses as she spoke. 'Jim, we need to catch this person and quickly. I don't need to tell you how serious these attacks are—'

'I know.'

'Keep me informed, will you?' She picked up a pen and bent over her paperwork once more. Carruthers took the hint that he had been dismissed. Briefly, he congratulated himself on keeping his superiors better informed of his actions, and his temper in check. If he'd done this a couple of years ago, perhaps he'd still be a DCI with his own office. He retreated to gather his car keys and collect Fletcher.

Chapter three

Fletcher hated hospitals and this one in particular. It was where she had lost her daughter, Lara. She tensed as she stepped through the door Carruthers opened for her, averting her eyes from the maternity unit as she walked straight to the lift.

'Are you okay, Andie?' She could see that Carruthers was looking at her and wondered if he knew what she was thinking.

'Yes, I'm fine, Jim. Don't worry about me.' She was still going to counselling. It was helping, and she was learning to be more open about her feelings, but she wondered if she would ever get over her late miscarriage. At least it wasn't a problem to talk about it now, but she still had one painful secret that hadn't been shared with anyone and she knew that at some point she would need to talk about that. She pushed those unwelcome thoughts out of her head and replaced them with concern for her DI. Not only had he a new boss to contend with, but his ex-wife was now back working in her old department. She glanced at him, wondering how he would feel about that.

Carruthers pressed the button for the lift.

'Jim,' said Fletcher, 'I need to tell you something a bit awkward.'

He looked at her. 'Spit it out. You know you can tell me anything. I knew there was something wrong. You haven't been yourself.'

'It's not about me. It's about you.' She pushed the words out. 'The thing is…when I spoke to the secretary of the philosophy department, she suggested I talk to Rachel Abbie's supervisor…'

She saw Carruthers stiffen. *Perhaps he's already worked out what I'm going to say.*

'The girl's supervisor is your ex-wife, Mairi. She must be back working at the university.'

'I know what my ex-wife's name is, Andie.'

'Of course you do,' Fletcher said quickly. She stole a glance at her boss. It hadn't been her imagination that she had seen him wince. It was almost imperceptible, but it had been there. As far as she knew, Carruthers hadn't seen his ex-wife since she'd walked out on him. Would he have told her if he had, though? He was an extremely private person but the two of them had become close and she liked to think they were friends as well as colleagues. Yes, Fletcher decided that he would have told her. So he hadn't seen her. But then he must have known he would run into Mairi at some stage. Fife could be so small and there weren't many places you could teach philosophy. And his first response and the fact he nearly bit her head off frankly spoke volumes.

Being naturally inquisitive, she wondered just how much she could push with the personal questions before he snapped at her. She decided to push her luck as her burning curiosity overcame both her politeness and sensitivity. 'Your wife? Didn't she leave academia to write a book?'

His Adam's apple bobbled and she watched him swallow. She felt momentarily bad that she was asking these personal questions but she really wanted to know the answer.

'Yes, she wanted to write a book on how to make philosophy accessible to the masses.'

'Did she manage to write it?'

He shrugged. 'No idea. As you know, she didn't keep in touch.'

Did he really have no idea or had he said that for her benefit? If your ex had written a book would you go to the bother of finding out? Granted it was an academic tome and not a work of fiction, but still... Fletcher looked up at her boss, watching, imagining a myriad of fleeting thoughts going through his head. He certainly seemed lost in thought. And for a moment he looked wistful. Despite his nonchalant response to her question she realised he must still care for his ex-wife. And it was obvious to her that he wasn't happy Mairi hadn't kept in touch. Once again she wondered why they'd split up. She struggled with her conscience, finally deciding she didn't want to be the one to make him remember sad thoughts, so she put the conversation on more of a professional footing. 'Jim, how do you want to play it? Do I go ahead with the interview or do you want to do it?'

The lift arrived and Carruthers let Fletcher go first before he joined her. She pressed the button for the fourth floor. 'Jim?' He hadn't answered.

'Happy for you to interview her,' he said casually. A bit too casually for Fletcher's liking, but if she was honest, she was dying to meet the woman who had so obviously broken her boss's heart. 'Take Gayle with you.'

Fletcher thought of Gayle Watson, the no-nonsense woman, who had stood in for her when she'd been off during her miscarriage. When she had come back there'd been a fair amount of friction between the two of them, mostly from Fletcher's side to be honest, but they'd got over it after she'd apologised and they'd gone on to form an unlikely friendship. Fletcher was relieved. Life was hard as it was. She didn't want any tension at work.

She glanced up at Carruthers again and this time he smiled down at her. 'Don't worry about me,' he said. 'The marriage has been over a long time now. Water under the bridge – but I don't feel a particular need to see her or conduct the interview myself.'

Fletcher nodded, not entirely convinced. She wondered when his divorce had come through. He had never said, despite her probing. *Best left alone,* she thought. *Don't poke the bear.*

'Just do me one favour,' he said, looking up. 'Don't mention my ex-wife to Sandra or anyone else at the station. They don't need to know my personal business.'

Fletcher pictured tall, black-haired DCI Sandra McTavish and wondered how Jim really felt about her appointment. She then thought of the rest of the team and the likelihood that a gossip like Detective Constable Willie Brown had already filled McTavish in on Jim's private business.

The lift doors opened and the two officers got out. They made their way down the sterile corridor to the private room housing Serena Davis. Fletcher knew, in all likelihood, Serena would be on her own. Her parents, who were trekking in Borneo, still hadn't been located. She had no siblings or extended family as far as they were aware.

Fletcher's shoes made a squeaking noise on the linoleum floor. She wrinkled up her nose, smelling disinfectant. Fletcher tapped on the door and opened it. Serena Davis was lying in bed, eyes closed, her pale face turned towards them. Her blonde hair fanned out around her. She snapped her eyes open as they entered the room. Fletcher put her handbag on the floor by a chair. It made a scraping noise as the bag fell against the floor. Serena Davis started. Fletcher noticed that there was a polystyrene cup containing coffee dregs on the table beside Serena's jug of water. And next to that, a book by Ayn Rand. It looked like she'd had at least one visitor, after all.

'Sorry,' said Fletcher, smiling, only half meaning it. After all, they were here to interview the student and gain more information about her attacker, but still, she didn't want to scare her. The poor lassie had been through more than enough. Fletcher took a seat and moved the chair closer to the girl. The legs of the chair once again made a scraping noise on the floor. Fletcher tried not to stare at the dressing over the girl's cheek. *Bastard,* she thought. *Who would want to slash this beautiful young woman?*

Carruthers remained standing.

'Do you feel up to answering some questions, Serena?' asked Fletcher. 'I hope you don't mind that I've brought along Detective Inspector Jim Carruthers.' She nodded in his direction.

Fletcher saw Serena glance warily at Carruthers. The student addressed her answer to Fletcher. 'Why are you back?' Her voice came out in a rasp. 'I've already answered your questions. I didn't see anything. He was wearing a mask.'

Fletcher thought of the clown mask Serena had said her assailant had been wearing and the killer clown craze that had been sweeping the UK the year before. She knew that creepy clown costumes had been blamed on Stephen King's horror novel *It* which had been released in the mid-1980s. Unfortunately for the police there'd been a recent film adaptation of the book with the consequence that criminals and pranksters were using the disguise. She wondered what, if any, connection there was between the two attacks and the recent terrifying craze.

'But you said in your last interview you had managed to pull the mask partially off the face.' They had taken swabs underneath Serena's fingernails in the hope they might get some DNA from the forensics. Fletcher made a mental note to chase the results up.

'I hardly saw anything. Just the bottom of the chin really. He managed to get the mask back on.'

'And we have it in your notes that the man was wearing a clown mask?'

'That's right.'

But you're sure it was a man?' Carruthers joined the conversation.

It was obviously a struggle for Serena to speak. 'I think so. He was big. Tall. Had the build of a man.' She closed her eyes.

Fletcher wondered for a moment whether the assailant could be a woman. She would have to be a big woman. And strong. It was possible but, given the build and the fact most assailants who attacked women were men, unlikely.

'Can you just go over what he was wearing again?'

Serena sighed. 'I can't remember much. I think he was dressed all in black.'

'When you say black, was he wearing a black suit or was he more informal, like in black jeans and a black top?' urged Fletcher. 'Were his arms bare or was he wearing long sleeves? These details are really important. Please try your best to remember.'

Serena swallowed painfully. She shook her head. 'No, he wasn't wearing a suit. At least I don't think he was. I think he was less formal.' She shut her eyes.

Fletcher hoped this was a bid to try to recall the details of her attacker rather than switching off from the conversation. But who could blame her if she did want to switch off? The last thing this young girl, any young girl, would want to do would be to relive the moments she got attacked.

She opened her eyes. 'But not black jeans either. I think they were a bit baggier.'

'More like the trousers of a shell suit?' Fletcher was a bit more hopeful. 'Were they shiny?'

'Oh, I can't remember. I've got a headache.' There were tears in Serena's eyes.

Fletcher didn't want to keep pushing but she knew she had to. 'Perhaps more like black jogging bottoms then?'

'Yes, that's right. Jogging bottoms.'

This was hopeless, thought Fletcher, feeling frustrated. The poor girl is just saying what she thought they wanted to hear.

Chapter four

Fletcher leant in closer to Serena before asking her next question. Her notebook was poised in her hand. 'Last time we spoke you couldn't remember how old you thought your attacker might be. Can you give us anything to go on? Anything at all?'

'I don't think he was old.'

Fairly young then, thought Fletcher. After all, pretty much anybody over the age of twenty-five would be considered old to an eighteen-year-old.

'Do you think he might have been your age? A teenager?'

'Might have been. I don't know how old he was, except…' She hesitated and looked intently at Carruthers before pointing at him. 'I don't think he was as old as him.' Fletcher managed to resist a smile.

Carruthers pulled up a chair and sat down. 'And you got attacked on Marshall Place?'

'I already told you this. Why are you asking me again?' She swallowed. Even the attempt to swallow looked painful.

Fletcher referred to her notes. 'We're just trying to establish the facts. And sometimes mentioning place names jogs the memory. You said in your statement you'd been to the library and you were on your way home when you got attacked?' Fletcher thought of the location of the attack. Marshall Place was about five minutes' walk from the central library. And it was another quiet street often used as a short cut between the central library and Serena's halls of residence. She thought of the dead girl, Rachel Abbie, if that's who she was, and the fact she'd been found with a library book on her. No big deal in itself. After all, this was a university town, but still… She made a mental note to follow up the connection.

'That's right.'

'And it was the university library rather than the departmental one? The one on King James's Way.'

'Yes. Do we have to go through this again?'

Fletcher leant into the patient's bed. Before speaking, she glanced at Carruthers, who nodded for her to carry on. 'Serena, do you know a student by the name of Rachel Abbie?'

The girl opened her eyes once again and lifted her head slightly. Fletcher tried not to recoil at the sight of the angry red marks across her throat. She was lucky to be alive. Fletcher knew Serena was eighteen, but she looked so young, and with no make-up on, she looked even younger. Of course, Fletcher reminded herself, they start university a year earlier in Scotland.

There was a flicker of her eyes before she answered. 'No, I don't think so. Who is she?'

There was something about her response that made Fletcher wonder if she was telling the truth. But then again why would she lie? Fletcher exchanged another quick glance with Carruthers before she broached her next question. She brought her voice down to little more than a whisper. 'Can you remember anything else about the attack? Anything at all, however small? It mightn't be significant to you, but it could help us find the person who did this before they—'

'Before they attack again, you mean?'

That's exactly what Fletcher was going to say and it wasn't like her to make such an uncharacteristic gaffe. But Serena's words had stopped her just in time.

'Before they get away, I was going to say.'

Serena tried to sit up in her hospital bed. Fletcher helped her. The girl motioned for the beaker of water on the table beside her. Fletcher moved the beaker towards her and Rachel sucked at the straw. She took three or four sips before she spoke.

'This girl, Rachel Abbie, has he attacked her too?' The girl sounded like she had a bad case of laryngitis but Fletcher knew it was because the attacker had tried to strangle her. 'There's been another attack, hasn't there? Tell me.'

Fletcher once again cursed herself for her clumsy choice of words.

'Another girl has been assaulted, yes,' said Carruthers, throwing a warning look at Fletcher to be more circumspect. 'But we can't tell you any more than that.'

Serena's eyes were wide and staring. Fletcher patted the girl's cold hand. 'It may not even be connected to what happened to you. You're perfectly safe here in hospital. Don't worry about that.'

'What if he comes back? Comes into the hospital I mean? Attacks me here?' Her hands were scrunching up the bedding. 'He hasn't been caught. He could be anywhere.' Her voice was rising in panic.

Fletcher lay a reassuring hand on Serena's bare arm. 'He isn't going to attack you here. You're safe.' But even as Fletcher said this, she thought back to the last big case she and Carruthers had investigated. She thought of the day she'd so nearly been kidnapped while visiting a suspect in hospital. Her mind turned to the police officer who had been shot by the assailant who had been posing as a cleaner. It was the fact he had been wearing a Rolex that had given him away. That, and his accent. It could so easily have been her who had taken a bullet. She'd found out the officer who'd been shot still wasn't back on duty. A shiver ran down her spine.

Dragging her mind back from these disturbing thoughts, she focused on the case. Whatever she'd just told Serena, it certainly wouldn't be the first time an assault victim had been attacked in hospital. And this girl wasn't just a victim of assault, was she? She was a victim of attempted murder. She decided to have a word with Carruthers after the interview. Perhaps they could get a uniform put on the door. But would the police budget stretch to that? Carruthers didn't call the shots any more. Sometimes she forgot that they all had a new DCI. Fletcher's thoughts turned to the dead girl. 'But you're sure you definitely don't know a student called Rachel Abbie?' she pressed.

Serena shook her head and turned away from Fletcher. A wall had come down. Her eyes filled with tears once more and she touched the side of her face that had the dressing. 'They can't tell me how bad the scarring's going to be. I have to keep the dressing on.'

'Doctors can do amazing things, Serena,' said Fletcher. 'And scars fade with time.' Even as she said it she hated herself for it. It sounded trite and patronising. How would she cope if she was the one lying there? She looked at the pursed lips of Serena Davis. *She's trying to be brave. I bet she feels like sobbing.*

Once again, Fletcher got the feeling Serena wasn't telling the whole truth about knowing Rachel Abbie, but it was more her copper's instinct. She made a mental note to mention it to Carruthers to see if he had come to the same conclusion. She looked at Serena, hoping that this poor young girl would get all the help, both physical and emotional, that she needed. How could she have thought this girl was lucky?

Outside the room they heard voices. *Perhaps doctors doing their rounds,* thought Fletcher. Or cleaners. She shuddered, remembering once again how close she had come to being shot. She had a sudden flashback to the feel of the cold hard gun pointing to the side of her head as he marched her down the corridor. She heard someone whistling, and then footsteps receding. The noise brought Fletcher out of her reverie but also it seemed to disturb Serena. Her eyes were wide with fear. Fletcher realised the girl was shaking.

Fletcher touched the girl's arm once more in what she hoped was a reassuring way. 'What's wrong? Should I get a nurse?'

Serena's face was ashen. 'Don't let him in. The man who's whistling.'

'You've remembered something. What is it?'

'Yes, I have. I have remembered something.' She swallowed painfully.

Fletcher was starting to have a sore back and shoulders with all the leaning forward she was doing, but she ignored the discomfort and moved a little closer to Serena to be able to hear what she had to say. She felt it was going to be important.

'Just before I got attacked–' She motioned for the water again. Speaking was clearly an effort and she was down to a whisper.

Fletcher picked up the beaker, moved the straw closer to Serena, who tried to sit up to drink from it.

'What do you remember?'

Serena took a couple of sips and then lay back on the pillows. 'Someone whistling. I heard someone whistling. Just before I got attacked.'

Fletcher put the beaker down, sat upright and dug into her handbag for a pen. 'What sort of whistle? Was the person whistling the tune of a song?'

She exchanged a look with Carruthers. This was the first solid lead they had had. It might mean nothing but still, it was a start.

With difficulty, Serena shook her head. 'Not a song. No.'

'A wolf whistle? That sort of whistle?'

'No, nothing like that. It sounded strange. Almost as if it was done through the teeth. It wasn't tuneful and it was just for a few moments. I can't remember anything else. I'm sorry. Then I got attacked.' She shut her eyes once more and turned her head away from them.

The door to Serena's room suddenly opened and in walked a stout woman carrying a polystyrene cup. Fletcher could smell the rich aroma of coffee. She wouldn't have minded a coffee herself right now.

The woman stopped short. 'Who are you? You're not medics. What are you doing in Serena's room?'

Both Carruthers and Fletcher took out their police IDs.

Being senior in rank Carruthers introduced himself first. 'I'm Detective Inspector Jim Carruthers.'

'DS Andrea Fletcher.' She watched the woman put her coffee cup down next to the empty cup and fold her arms. She clearly wasn't happy and Fletcher could already hazard a guess why. She just hoped the woman wouldn't cause a disturbance in front of the young victim. And who was she? What was her relationship to Serena? She hadn't yet introduced herself.

'Excuse me, can I ask you who you are?' Fletcher found herself saying.

The woman faced Fletcher. 'I'm Clare. Clare Stott. I'm best friends with Serena's mum, Yvonne.'

'Well, I'm glad there's someone here looking out for Serena.' Fletcher tried to smile.

'Which is more than you're doing.'

Here it comes, thought Fletcher glumly. *She's going straight for the jugular.*

'It's been five days since Serena's attack and I take it you still haven't caught the bastard?'

Serena tried to prop herself up on a pillow, failed, and sank back into the bed. 'There's been another attack,' she rasped.

Bugger, thought Fletcher. *Bugger. Bugger. Bugger. But then again, the news would get out soon enough.*

'Oh my God. There's a potential serial attacker on the loose.' Clare Stott's voice rose a pitch. 'And you're doing nothing to catch this lunatic. What are you doing in here talking to Serena? Why aren't you out trying to catch this nutter?'

Fletcher tried to display a calm she wasn't feeling. She was starting to feel increasingly annoyed by this woman's lack of thought around the patient. She kept her voice level. 'We have nothing to suggest the perpetrator of these two crimes is the same person.'

The woman's eyes widened in fright. 'Jesus, that's even worse. There are two potential serial attackers on the loose.'

Carruthers cleared his throat. 'Mrs Stott – Clare, it's not helpful to refer to the person who attacked Serena as a serial attacker. And it may not actually be true,' he added.

Fletcher was happy Carruthers had decided to chip in. She listened to him as he continued to speak, reassured by his calm manner. 'And we certainly don't have two serial attackers on the loose, as you put it. And to be honest I think you should take this conversation outside with my DS. We don't want to be upsetting Serena any more than she's already been upset, now do we?'

Carruthers' words seemed to have got through to Clare as she fell silent. As Fletcher steered the older woman to the door, she didn't voice what she was thinking. She was biting her lip. She was so close to pointing out that the older woman could be a damn sight more helpful if she was doing something useful like trying to trace Serena's parents to their current location herself. They needed to be at their daughter's bedside.

Fletcher opened the door, but before Clare Stott had even left the room, she had turned on her. 'So, what *are* you doing to catch this maniac?'

'We're following up various leads at the moment and we're hopeful we'll make an arrest soon,' said Fletcher, keeping her breathing even. This seemed at least to placate the woman, even though it was clearly untrue.

'Have you managed to trace her parents yet?' Suddenly, the woman seemed full of questions. She also seemed to have decided she wasn't leaving the room after all, despite the door being held open for her. Her feet were firmly planted wide apart and she had her arms folded. Her aggression no doubt masked her fear.

Fletcher sighed. 'We're still working on it. Can we take this outside, please?'

The woman tutted. 'God, you really are useless.'

Fletcher bit her tongue, but this woman was seriously doing her head in. She glanced at Carruthers. He was rubbing his hand over his short, stubbly grey hair – a habit he had when he was aggravated. This woman had got them both rattled.

'No, I'd like Clare to stay in the room,' said Serena. 'I feel safer with her here.'

Clare Stott gave Fletcher a smirk, as Fletcher, struggling not to show how frustrated she was, closed the door. She didn't trust herself to speak, so she let Carruthers once again take up the reins.

'We would appreciate it if you kept the news of this other assault to yourself for a while. It's not yet in the public domain. And, as I said to Serena, there's no reason to think at this stage the two incidences are connected.'

Fletcher couldn't imagine Clare Stott doing that for a moment. *I'm sure she would love nothing better than to tell the whole world just how shit the police are at doing their job,* she thought.

Carruthers obviously thought the same, as he added, 'You don't want to be the one to reduce our chances of catching this person, do you?'

That seemed to have got through to the woman. 'No, of course not.' She walked over to Serena's bedside, picked up both coffee cups from the table, and turned on her heel, mumbling about needing to make a call.

Who's she gone to ring? wondered Fletcher, as the woman left the room, shutting the door firmly behind her.

'Not much chance of Clare keeping it to herself, by the way,' rasped Serena.

Fletcher's heart sank. 'Why not?'

'Clare's a journalist. She's probably gone to phone her boss.'

Oh fuck, that's all we need. If Fletcher's heart had sank earlier it was now well and truly on the bottom of the ocean.

Chapter five

Carruthers and Fletcher left the hospital. Walking to the station car, a huge gust of cold wind knocked over a wheelie bin. Fletcher wrapped her coat around her and shivered as Carruthers righted the bin. 'What is it about the weather up here?' she said. 'It's gone back to being winter again.'

'That's the Scottish spring for you. Strong winds can come down from Scandinavia. There's a weather warning in place. I think it's a depression coming in from the Atlantic. They're expecting some local disruption to transport tonight.'

Fletcher looked less than impressed but remained silent. She seemed to be in a world of her own. Carruthers knew she had something important on her mind.

'Are you okay?'

'I was just thinking about Clare Stott. I can't believe that woman's a bloody journalist.'

'I know. What are the chances? Well, we're going to have to tell Sandra. She won't be too pleased.' Another gust of wind almost took Fletcher off her feet. She stumbled.

'As much as I love Scotland, if there's one thing I would change, it would be the weather. I really miss the south east of England this time of year. You can actually sit outside and get a suntan.' She removed a lock of hair that had partially obscured her face. 'It's funny. I always feel most homesick in April and October.'

'Well, look at it this way. You're probably saving your skin from becoming leathery from too much sun. Anyway, you've no time to sunbathe,' said Carruthers, looking fondly at his DS. His expression then became serious. 'We need to catch this person before they strike again.' Before Fletcher had a chance to answer, Carruthers' mobile rang.

It was Sandra McTavish with news of the response from the Procurator Fiscal. 'We've got the result we wanted, Jim. Green light to carry on with the PM.'

'That's great, Sandra. I'll get hold of Dr Mackie. See if he can clear his decks.' He finished the call, punched in a number and held it to his ear. He spoke swiftly to John Mackie. The pathologist was as keen as any of them to get on with the PM.

Carruthers cut the call and put his mobile away. 'He'll do the PM within the hour.'

Fletcher had to increase her stride to keep up with him. 'Great. We're finally starting to move on this. So, *do* you think we have a serial killer on our hands?'

Carruthers spoke slowly. 'Serena Davis is lucky to be alive, but for someone to be classified as a serial killer they need to have killed at least three people.'

'It's just pure luck Serena Davis wasn't killed. If there hadn't been a noise of that car backfiring in the next street that scared the attacker off, she'd more than likely be dead. Do you think the fact she heard whistling's important?'

Carruthers wondered about this. 'Well, it was most likely her attacker whistling. Do you mean is it part of this monster's modus operandi? No idea at this stage.'

'It's a bit creepy though, isn't it?' Fletcher persisted. 'To hear tuneless whistling just before being attacked?'

Carruthers did indeed think it sounded creepy.

'I got the feeling Serena wasn't telling us everything.'

Carruthers' hand shot out and grabbed Fletcher's arm. A car was reversing out of a space and the driver hadn't checked to see if anything or anyone was behind him.

'Oh thanks, Jim. Idiot driver. Did you not think Serena was keeping something back from us?'

'How do you mean?'

Fletcher was almost running to keep up with Carruthers' long strides. 'I don't know. Didn't you notice how she responded when we asked her if she knew Rachel Abbie? Her eyes flickered almost as if she knew who I was talking about.'

Carruthers stopped abruptly and turned to Fletcher. 'Do you think she was lying? What reason would she have?'

Fletcher pulled herself up short. She'd nearly walked into the back of the DI. 'I've been asking myself the same question. I honestly don't know. But the biggest problem is the description she gave us of her attacker. It was so vague it could have been anyone. I mean, she couldn't tell us what he was wearing at all, except that he was dressed all in black. And she's not even sure about that. Or that he was even a man.'

Carruthers pulled a face. 'Mackie thinks the two attacks were most likely to have been inflicted by a man, although I agree that it would have helped if we had a better description to go on.'

'Well, we know he was wearing a clown mask so that's a starting point. Mind you, we've already exhausted the possibility of it being bought locally. Nothing's turned up on that score which means it was more than likely bought online.'

'Or just not bought in this area.' Carruthers groaned. 'God, policing used to be so much easier in a lot of ways in the old days. If you wanted to find out if someone had bought a mask that had been used in an assault or a robbery you'd just go into a joke or novelty shop.'

'You wouldn't be without your advancements in forensics, though, would you, Jim? And you can't have it both ways.'

He thought about what Fletcher had said about the likelihood of the masks having been sold online.

'True. Okay, well, we'll just have to hope that those checking with online sellers will have some joy that somebody's sold that sort of mask to someone in this area.'

Fletcher unlocked the car but didn't get in. 'At least Serena is alive to give us some sort of description even if it's not very detailed.

You never know, she may start remembering more, although I don't actually think she wants to. She's trying to block it out.'

Carruthers leaned against the car. 'Brain's a funny thing, especially in a stressful situation. It might have partially shut down to protect her.'

'Do you think it might help if we get a hypnotist in? Try to regress her? Perhaps under hypnosis she'll remember more about her attacker.'

'Can't see either her or Clare Stott going for that, can you? And we'd need Serena's permission. And then there's the budget to think about.'

Carruthers watched Fletcher's face fall. 'But it's worth keeping it in mind. Depending on how the investigation goes I might run it past Sandra. But I don't think all leads have been exhausted yet to use hypnosis.'

Fletcher pulled a face. 'But that's just it, Jim. We don't seem to have any leads apart from the assailant wearing a mask and whistling. And anyway, even if we did, exhausting all leads takes time. Serena Davis is clearly very upset. You said yourself she could be trying to block the events out. Wouldn't that be reason enough? Then there's the fact I feel she's withholding information. Surely hypnosis is also used where the subject's very upset about the crime or where he or she is considered to be withholding information from the police. The former is certainly true in the case of Serena Davis and I strongly suspect she's also withholding some information from us. Anyway, there's heaps of instances where forensic hypnosis has been used to help jog the memory along.'

Carruthers knew that Fletcher could be like a dog with a bone once an idea sprung into her mind. He wondered what Sandra McTavish thought of forensic hypnosis. It wasn't a subject they'd had cause to discuss. 'It's purely conjecture on your part though, Andie, that Serena isn't telling us the whole truth. I'm not sure that's the impression I got from talking with her.'

Fletcher frowned. 'Really? Like I said, I thought it was pretty obvious she wasn't telling us everything.'

Carruthers could just imagine how the comments about bringing a hypnotist in would be greeted by the old school brigade like Dougie Harris or Willie Brown. Fletcher's mobile rang. She fished it out of her bag and answered it.

She mouthed the words, 'North Yorkshire Police' to Carruthers. He listened to the one-sided conversation. A few moments later she finished the call. 'Did you get most of that? Nobody at home. They've spoken to the neighbours. There's only a Mr Abbie. Mrs Abbie died a few years ago. Car accident. Apparently, Mr Abbie's on holiday and nobody knows how to reach him.'

Carruthers frowned. 'Oh God. Not another one. Haven't they heard of social media?'

'Well, it's not helped us locate Serena's parents.'

'True, but then it's unlikely Mr Abbie's trekking anywhere as remote as Borneo.'

Fletcher grinned. 'Apparently, he's only gone to the Borders. The local police are on to it. They're finding out if he's on Facebook or Twitter. It's just going to take a bit longer than we would have liked, that's all. I did discover one interesting thing, though.'

Carruthers looked up.

'They're not short of a bob or two. Mr Abbie and his daughter. Their house is a three-hundred-year-old mansion.'

Carruthers whistled.

'What now?'

Carruthers climbed into the driver's seat. Fletcher jumped into the passenger side.

'I'm going to head off for the PM after dropping you at the station.' Carruthers shut his door as he spoke. Fletcher followed suit.

Fletcher snapped her seatbelt on. 'Sounds good. I'll pick up Harris or Watson and pay the halls of residence a visit. And I'll set up a meeting with your – with Mairi Beattie, I mean.'

Starting the engine, Carruthers said, 'Take Gayle with you to the halls. And keep an eye on Dougie. He's meant to be pulling the files on any recent slashings and strangulations Scotland has had, but his mind's clearly elsewhere.'

'How's his wife, do you know?'

'Not great.' Carruthers took the handbrake off and he started to manoeuvre out of the hospital car park. He glanced at Fletcher. 'I think Dougie's going to have to get more help in for her. He can't manage it all himself.'

'I never thought I would say this, but poor Dougie.'

Carruthers joined the short queue to exit the car park. 'I think he's surprised us all, hasn't he?'

'Do we actually know what's wrong with his wife?'

'She's never been in the best of health but I believe she's just been diagnosed with Alzheimer's.'

Chapter six

Fletcher drove herself and Gayle Watson in her green Beetle over to Strathburn Halls. It was situated close to the cathedral by the outer walls of the town. The wind had increased in intensity and Fletcher wondered if the weather had started to affect the local transport links after all. She was glad of her Beetle. When she'd been a student here, she hadn't had a car. Some of the weather she'd had to walk into and from her department had been atrocious. They parked in the student car park, Fletcher locked up, and they started walking towards the building. Fletcher's hands were numb.

'It's only five degrees today,' said Watson by way of conversation. 'It still feels like winter.'

Fletcher rubbed her hands together once more, thinking of the summers she'd spent down near Rye. 'Doesn't surprise me. It's bloody freezing. And I've already had Jim telling me about Scandinavian winds wreaking havoc in Scotland in springtime. Not hard to believe when you've spent some time up here. And there was me not that many years ago sunbathing topless down in Rye this time of year.'

'Topless?' Watson reddened.

'Ha. Thought that would get your attention.' Fletcher laughed. Their work relationship had developed into good-natured ribbing. 'Okay, so I exaggerated. I was wearing a bikini. But I used to love visiting Camber Sands. I really miss it. I remember, as a kid, going for donkey rides.'

'Poor donkeys.'

Fletcher gave Watson a good-natured slap on her arm. 'Oy, I'm not that heavy.' But even so, Fletcher felt uncomfortable with the comment. She was acutely aware she hadn't lost the extra weight she'd carried when she was pregnant.

She fished the piece of paper with the address on it out of her pocket. 'This is it.' She knocked on the door. The sound of footsteps greeted them and Fletcher could hear a deep male voice coming from behind the door which was swept open by a lad of about eighteen. He had a chiselled face and fine floppy brown hair. Fletcher thought he looked like a first world war poet. 'Rach, how many times are you going to forget your key in one term? Oh,' he said, frowning on seeing the police officers. 'Sorry. I thought you were our housemate, Rachel.'

Fletcher brought out her ID, noting the English accent. No local dialect. Well-to-do. Public school educated, she thought. Not surprising in a place like Castletown. Watson followed suit with her ID. 'Can we come in, please,' said Fletcher. 'I slipped a note through the letterbox. Did you get it?' As the boy shut the door Fletcher noticed a pile of unopened post and flyers behind it. She wondered if they were still taking their washing back to mum.

'Sorry, no.' The boy reddened, then ushered them through the narrow hall into a small living area. A dark-haired girl and a boy were sitting on the couch. The girl was on the boy's knee. She leapt off and sat next to him when she saw they had visitors. Fletcher noted how she hurriedly readjusted her top.

'Is everything okay?' said the boy on the couch. Fletcher thought she could detect an American accent. The university was known to have its fair share of American and Canadian students. She looked at his freckled skin and mop of curly reddish-brown hair. *Cute,* she thought. If she had been at least fifteen years younger and still a student she wouldn't have minded being on the couch with him. Not sure she'd be sitting on his knee though. She wasn't the type.

'Can you tell me who lives here?' asked Watson.

The boy on the couch jumped up. 'I'm Davey Munroe, this is Annie McLeod, my girlfriend, although she doesn't live here.'

'I'm Will Smith,' said the floppy-haired boy who had opened the front door to them, 'and our other housemates are Ruth Skipsey and Rachel Abbie. They're both out at the moment. Oh, and Sarah Torr is in her bedroom.'

'Do you know where Rachel is?' asked Fletcher. As she spoke, a young woman entered the room. Sarah Torr, she supposed. She noticed the girl's hair was as dark as a raven's wing and she had an expressive, round-shaped face.

'She should be back by now,' said the girl who had previously had her arms wrapped round the cute, red-headed boy.

'She's gone to get a library book,' said the boy, Will, who had opened the door to them. 'I think Ruth's also at the library.'

Fletcher tensed. Again, that connection with the library. Likely both students had been walking back from the library when they'd been attacked. She fished in her handbag for her black notebook and a pen. 'What does she study?' Once more, she was thinking of the David Hume book in the dead student's bag, wondered if that had been the library book she'd been after.

'Logic and Metaphysics,' said Will.

'That's a branch of philosophy, isn't it?' said Fletcher. It sounded to her like they had their person.

'Yes, that's right,' said Davey Munroe. 'Rach and me – we're in the same department. So is Sarah Torr.'

'Do you know what book Rachel wanted from the library?'

'A book by David Hume. *A Treatise on Human Nature,* I think she said.'

Bingo.

'Did they go to the library together? Rachel and Ruth?'

Will looked confused. 'No, separately. Ruth left first but she had her parents with her. They're up for a visit.'

A Treatise on Human Nature. *The book that had been found with the body,* Fletcher thought. *But where was the girl's student ID? Would she not need that in order to take the book out of the library?* Fletcher's mind was powering ahead. Her ID was missing. Perhaps she had dropped it or left it at the library. She addressed her next question to Will. 'And would she be getting it from the central library or the departmental library, do you know?'

Will shrugged. 'S'pose departmental library but I don't know for sure.'

Two girls both attacked after leaving a library. And both blonde. Had they both used the same library? They needed to find out. From talking to Serena, they knew that she had used the central library rather than her departmental one. Coincidence, or had both girls been followed by someone who had been in the library at the same time? Had it been a random attack? Or had these particular girls been targeted? Something to mention to Carruthers.

'How old is Rachel?'

'Nineteen,' said Will.

Similar age to Serena Davis.

'Have you got a photograph of her, please?' said Watson.

'I've got those passport photos we had done,' said Sarah, jumping up, smoothing her dress out. 'We were just mucking about.'

'If you could fetch them that would be great,' said Watson.

Sarah left the room with a worried look on her face.

Will suddenly leapt into action. He pulled his mobile out of his back pocket. 'I'm going to ring her. I'm sure she's not far away.' The silence was broken by the eerie sound of a muffled phone ringing in another room.

'She's always leaving something behind is Rach. Keys, mobile. I've never known anyone so scatty.' Will was unusually cheerful, thought Fletcher, but he's obviously worried. Two red spots had appeared on his cheeks.

He brushed his hair out of his boyish face. 'She *is* okay, isn't she? I mean, nothing bad has happened?'

'Just routine enquiries at the moment.' Fletcher tried to sound brighter than she felt as she thought how that saying covered a multitude of sins. She exchanged a look with Watson.

'Is Rachel your girlfriend?' asked Watson.

Will nodded. He walked across to the coffee table and bent over to reach into a black rucksack. He brought out an address book.

Fletcher raised her eyebrows that a young man that age would still use an address book.

'How would Rachel normally get to the department from here?' asked Watson.

Will looked confused. 'She takes a short cut through Greyfriar's Wynd.'

'And would she use that short cut for the central library too?'

Will nodded.

Fletcher studied the students' facial expressions. Will looked like he might burst into tears. Of course, they would know about the previous attack on Serena Davis. It had been all over the news. Fletcher thought about the location of the first attack: Marshall Place. Serena Davis had been attacked less than ten minutes' walk away from Rachel Abbie. But Castletown wasn't a big place; everything being compact within its medieval walls. Most places were within walking distance until you got to the more recently built sprawling outskirts.

Will hesitated, then delved further into the rucksack, bringing out a pen and a spiral notebook. He tore a page out.

'What's going on? Why can't you tell us what's happened to Rach?' asked Davey.

Fletcher felt for these kids. Part of her wanted to say more, especially to Will, the boyfriend, but until there had been a formal ID of the body by next of kin her hands were tied. She thought back to the two male students who had found the body. They had been asked to keep the information of their discovery to themselves for the sake of the family, who had yet to be notified, but Fletcher was all too aware of how news like this had a way of getting out.

They needed, as a matter of urgency, to trace Rachel Abbie's father. However, if the local police couldn't get hold of him, and as unlikely as it sounded, if there literally were no other next of kin, it may well be that they would have to ask one of her housemates to ID the poor girl's body.

Being her boyfriend, Will would be the most likely candidate, but it wouldn't be Fletcher's decision to make. And it would be a tough call. Outside of family it would usually be the person closest to the deceased, but of course it was an emotional ordeal for anyone, and not everyone was willing to do it. If Will didn't want to do it they would have to turn to the girl's supervisor… Mairi Beattie. But hopefully it wouldn't come to that. Fletcher's mind turned to the forthcoming post-mortem. She wondered what the cause of death would uncover. On the face of it, it looked like strangulation, but sometimes PMs yielded surprising results.

Still smarting at how uncharacteristically undiplomatic she'd been at the hospital with Serena Davis she chose her words with care. 'We're trying to get in touch with Rachel's family at the moment. Does anyone know if they're currently away?'

Will leafed through his address book until he found what he wanted and then wrote something down and handed it to Fletcher.

'Here's her father's address and their home phone number. Her mother died a few years ago.'

Of course, he wouldn't know that someone from the local constabulary had already been round to the address. He may not know where Rachel's father currently was but it was certainly worth asking. Fletcher glanced at the sheet but then her eyes widened. It wasn't the same address as the one she'd been given from the secretary of the philosophy department. That had been an address in Nidderdale, North Yorkshire. This was an address in Ashington, Northumberland.

Fletcher frowned, confused. 'Has Rachel changed home address recently?' It was all she could think of at the moment. And that would make sense as to why the departmental address differed from the one she'd given her housemates.

Will shook his head. 'No. Why? I remember Rachel telling me they were living at her current address when her mum died in that car crash.'

Strange, thought Fletcher. 'Have any of you ever been to her father's house?' Although she addressed this to all of them, she was looking at Will.

Will ran his hands through his long, floppy hair. 'Not yet. We keep meaning to go but then something crops up and we end up having to cancel. I've met her dad when he dropped her off here at the start of the term though.'

Fletcher wasn't sure how this discrepancy had occurred but best to get the local police to send someone to this second address right away. The quicker they did that the better. Perhaps they'd have more luck with this new address. 'Have you ever heard Rachel talk of an address in Nidderdale?'

Fletcher looked round at the students as she said this. All she was greeted with were confused looks and a collective shaking of heads. The local police had spoken to the neighbours of the address in Nidderdale. Rachel's father was known to them, as was Rachel. She had been described as a quiet girl. If the Nidderdale property was where they actually lived what would they find at this other property? Or perhaps the family were wealthy enough to have two homes. It wasn't unusual. But two so close together? It didn't seem very likely.

'Does Rachel have a large family?' Fletcher addressed her question to Will.

Will shook his head. 'Not as far as I know. It's just her and her father now. Like I said, her mother died a few years ago.'

'No siblings?'

'She's an only child.'

How devastating for Rachel's father, thought Fletcher, *to lose his one child. He's still probably trying to get over his wife's death. And now this. How would he recover?* Fletcher was thinking of her own road to recovery after her miscarriage. Losing the baby had left a huge hole in her life that she just couldn't seem to fill. She couldn't imagine how Mr Abbie would pick up the pieces.

How could she ask about the whereabouts of Rachel's father without sounding alarmist? She took a deep breath, knowing she had to push on.

'Rachel didn't say what her dad is up to in the next few days, did she?'

'No,' said Will. 'Don't think so. You think something's happened to Rachel, don't you? Do you know where she is? Has she been attacked… like that other girl?' said Will. 'The one in hospital?'

'You mean Serena Davis?'

Will nodded. Ignoring the question, Fletcher said, 'Do any of you know the girl who got attacked?'

Davey was the only one of the students to answer the question. 'No,' was all he said, but it was emphatic. Fletcher noticed Will give him a sharp look. She wondered what it meant. There were mumbles and shakes of the head between the students. But she felt a new tension in the air. She wasn't convinced that they were being honest. First Serena, now Rachel's housemates. What did it mean?

Did they know Serena Davis and if so, what was the connection between the six of them? She made a mental note that at some point she would most probably have to interview Ruth Skipsey. Turning to Will she said, 'Do you normally carry your address book around with you? I'm just surprised. I thought everything was done on the phone nowadays?'

Will coloured. 'I'm into all things retro and I like the feel of a proper address book. It's my nineteenth soon and Rachel is helping me organise it. I met up with her earlier and we were going through the guest list.'

'What is she wearing today, just out of interest?' asked Watson. Fletcher noticed that Watson had remained fairly silent up till now, allowing Fletcher to take the lead.

Will shrugged. 'A denim skirt, pale blue vest top and cardigan, and she had her raincoat with her.'

The description matched the clothes of the dead girl. Fletcher suddenly felt a lump in her throat. Surely discovering her identity was all but academic now. What would Will do about celebrating his nineteenth now? It wasn't going to be much of a celebration.

The door reopened and Sarah walked back in, clutching several passport-sized photographs.

'What's happened? What have I missed?' She must have sensed the change in atmosphere, thought Fletcher, studying the photographs Sarah had given her.

'They're asking heaps of questions about Rachel but they won't tell us why.' Will rubbed his forehead.

Fletcher could hear Watson trying to calm the students down, but she was too focused on trying to work out if the animated girl in the photograph was the same young woman who was now lying dead in the mortuary, and why Rachel had given her housemates a different address to the one she had given the department.

She studied the photograph: same shoulder-length blonde hair, same oval-shaped face. It could be her. It looked like her. But they would need a positive ID to be absolutely certain. They needed to get hold of Rachel Abbie's father. Perhaps they'd find him at this second address. And she wouldn't mind looking at Rachel's bedroom. They would have to take the mobile phone. As she was forming a mental checklist of actions that needed to be taken, she wondered how Jim was getting on with the post-mortem.

Chapter seven

Jim Carruthers leant over the slim, naked body of the dead girl. He quite often used to cadge a cigarette off John Mackie before or after a PM, but the last few months he'd gone on a health kick. He'd stepped up the hillwalking and had even started running. He knew that the renewed exercise and concern about his health was due to his brother's shock heart attack. After burying his head in the sand he'd finally had his own cholesterol tested and it was on the high side. As was his blood pressure. It hadn't come as a surprise. He'd refused a cigarette, but looking at the latest murder victim he knew he'd be needing a stiff drink later that night.

He gazed sadly at the young woman who lay dead on the mortuary table. All sorts of questions flooded his mind. *Why had she been killed? Who had killed her? Would the murderer kill again?* However, first things first. They were here to establish how she had been killed. It looked like a straightforward strangulation but post-mortems sometimes threw up surprising conclusions. Swallowing down a lump in his throat he steeled himself to be professional.

'Have you got a name for her yet?' Mackie picked up the scalpel.

Carruthers dragged his attention back to the PM. 'We think she's a student by the name of Rachel Abbie but we still need someone to formally identify her.'

'So, it's still Jane Doe then,' said Mackie. 'She appears to be in good health. Nice healthy weight. Okay, let's open her up, laddie.'

Carruthers wrinkled his nose at the smell of decaying flesh. He forced himself to watch as Mackie made an incision from sternum to pubic bone.

Hearing Mackie sigh, Carruthers glanced at the older man. He thought he could see tears in the pathologist's eyes but imagined he must be being fanciful.

'Another waste of a young life, eh, Jim?'

'Indeed,' said Carruthers, hating being present at yet another PM but knowing he needed to be here for his own peace of mind. It was the least he could do for the victims, and if the PM threw up anything surprising or out of the ordinary that could help the police in their enquiries, then he wanted to be in on it. He thought back to a previous case of a couple of elderly men found dead in a Fife nature reserve. He had been present when Mackie had found a ball of cloth stuffed to the back of the dead men's throats. Inserted after death. He looked down at the peaceful body of the young woman they believed to be Rachel Abbie and hoped they weren't going to be in for any nasty surprises.

* * *

Fletcher switched the light on in Rachel's bedroom. She'd managed to get Watson to distract Rachel's housemates while she'd urgently made a second call to the control room at Bilston to get a local police officer sent to the address in Ashington.

She looked around her. Rachel Abbie's bedroom was that of a typical teenager. A poster of rapper, Stormzy, hung on her wall, attached with Blu-Tack. Piles of clothes lay on the back of a wooden chair and philosophy text books were scattered on the carpet. Fletcher spotted a copy of Adam Smith. Underneath was a copy of Ayn Rand's *Atlas Shrugged*. She picked it up and looked at it thoughtfully. Wasn't this the same book that had been lying next to the coffee cup in the hospital room of Serena Davis? She frowned and flicked through it, noting that the author had been an American philosopher. There was an old-fashioned photograph of her on the back of the book. Fletcher took in the strong, almost masculine face and intense stare. There was something she found disquieting about the photo but she couldn't put her finger on it. She looked over at Watson.

'Gayle, do you know anything about this author?'

Watson stopped going through the student's sock drawer and looked up. 'No. Why?'

'There was a copy of this book in Serena Davis's hospital room.'

'Bit of a coincidence but then again… ' She looked over at the cover. 'If Ayn Rand is as famous as Dan Brown… how many people have a copy of *The Da Vinci Code*?'

Fletcher placed the book thoughtfully on the bedside table before picking up Rachel's mobile that lay on her pillow. She tried a few buttons before waving it at Watson. 'Bugger. Password protected.' She made a mental note to ask Will if he knew Rachel's password.

'Probably like most teens she falls asleep with the mobile glued to her ear,' said Watson.

Fletcher knelt down on the floor and peered under the bed. 'Just some tissues and a hot water bottle.' She surfaced and turned to Watson. 'It used to be bloody freezing in student flats here. There was no central heating. I got chilblains.'

'Oh, I'd forgotten you went to the University of East of Scotland.'

'For my sins.' She took another look at the mobile. 'It's a different world to when I was a student. Everything's on social media. You're connected 24/7. I wouldn't want to be a teenager now,' she said, standing up. 'Don't get me wrong. I had a mobile phone and I was on Bebo. But Facebook, Twitter, WhatsApp, Instagram *and* Snapchat – whatever the hell that is. No thank you. I have enough problems with Facebook.' Occasionally, she still got the odd message from her ex – Mark. She ignored them. He'd proved himself to be a worthless shit.

'We still need to establish whether Rachel Abbie knew Serena Davis,' said Watson, as she pulled on her latex gloves.

'Serena Davis said not and Rachel's housemates didn't think so.' Fletcher lowered her voice. 'I'm not sure they're telling the truth.'

'I got the feeling they at least knew her name.' Watson glanced at Fletcher.

So, she agrees with me. Interesting, thought Fletcher. *But what, if anything, does this prove?*

'Maybe they've met her in passing. Castletown isn't that big.'

Fletcher stopped what she was doing momentarily and looked across at Watson. 'So why wouldn't they say they knew the name?'

Watson shrugged. 'I don't know. Maybe they thought it was only worth mentioning if they knew her more than in passing.'

'So much police work is trying to establish patterns and connections between people.' Once again Fletcher thought about how both girls had been to the library just before they'd been assaulted. And they were both blonde. She wondered again if that was significant.

'We also need to find out if the attacks on Serena Davis and Rachel Abbie were random or if they were pre-planned,' said Fletcher, opening a chest of drawers. She searched through the woolly jumpers. Shutting the top drawer, she opened the one below. It was stuffed full of socks. Riffling through it, her hand came across something with a sharp edge. It was a photograph. She brought it out, and with creased forehead, looked at it. It was of two middle-aged men in suits. One was handing the other a package. It was obvious from the photograph that the subjects didn't know they were being photographed. What was this doing in Rachel's sock drawer?

'Take a look at this.' She handed it to Watson.

'Looks like it's been taken with a wide-angle lens,' said Watson. 'What do you think it means?'

'No idea, but a random photograph of two men taken from a distance kept in a teenager's sock drawer? I think we need to hang on to it. It might be important.'

* * *

'She's not been tampered with sexually,' said Mackie.

'That's a blessing.' Carruthers shifted from foot to foot. He was feeling squeamish, but even as a DCI he had made himself attend the PMs. He felt it was the least he could do for the victims.

'Although she's not a virgin.' Mackie moved slowly round the body. 'As far as I can tell her attacker approached her from behind. She has bruising on her shoulder and the marks on her neck are consistent with her being strangled from the front so he must have turned her round to face him.' He frowned. 'Why did I not notice this before?'

'What is it?'

He picked up a hand. 'The tip of the index finger on the left hand has been severed.'

Carruthers looked over, horrified. Sure enough, the tip was indeed missing. A wave of nausea gripped him and he felt himself go hot, then cold. Dear Lord. He wasn't going to be sick, was he?

'Yes, it's definitely been severed.'

'Deliberately?' asked Carruthers, swallowing down bitter acid bile. He'd been to countless PMs but he'd never been sick before. But then again, he'd never faced a victim whose finger had been severed before. But it was strange. Not that long ago he'd been to the post-mortem of a man who'd been pulled from the sea. He'd had a shotgun wound in his chest. So why was he feeling so queasy about a missing part of a finger? Perhaps it was due to the suspicion he had that it had been severed deliberately. Who would do such a thing? A little voice came into his head. *A serial killer, that's who. A serial killer who has taken a trophy.* A fresh wave of nausea came on him once more.

So, there was a nasty surprise at this PM, after all. He felt gutted. *Did they have a trophy hunter on their hands?* he wondered. If they did, it was all pointing in the direction of a serial killer. His stomach lurched at the thought. In all his years as a police officer he'd never had to deal with a serial killer before and certainly not a serial killer who was a trophy hunter. He briefly wondered how the newly-appointed DCI would greet the news. The pressure to solve this case, and quickly, would be immense. She was already looking harassed. Would she crack? But the question was – did he want her to crack? After all, by rights he should have been the

DCI on this case, if his hot-headedness on a previous case hadn't got him demoted.

Mackie was examining the finger with a magnifying glass. 'Yes, I would say it was severed deliberately. It's a clean cut.'

'Before or after death?' Clearly, he was hoping it was the latter.

'There was no blood by the hand at the scene, so post mortem.'

Small mercies. Carruthers swallowed with difficulty.

Mackie paused, scalpel in hand, and looked up at Carruthers. 'The SOCOs didn't find a weapon at the scene after I left, Jim? You'd be looking for something like a butcher's boning knife. It's sharp as hell and has a slightly curved edge. You can buy them in any hardware shop.'

'No.' He thought about the SOCOs. *They would now be looking for a knife and the tip of a finger,* he thought.

He realised Mackie was still talking. He watched and listened as the old Highlander bent over the victim. How long had he been doing this job? Must be coming up to thirty-odd years.

'Healthy specimen. Of course, she was young. But she was fit. Everything is in order. We'll have to wait for the results of toxicology to come back. And I know you're chomping at the bit to know cause of death. Unless toxicology results say otherwise cause of death is manual strangulation.' Mackie looked over at Carruthers as he said, 'Whoever extinguished this wee lassie's life did it with his bare hands.'

'You definitely think it was a man?'

'Could be a woman, I suppose.' Carruthers caught Mackie looking at the lines across the throat. The man's forehead was puckered. 'But she would have to be strong. There's very few defensive marks on her body.' Once again, he picked up the hands. 'Nothing under the nails that will help us by the looks of things but we'll take more swabs.' He placed them gently down by the side of the body once again. 'If it's any consolation I think it was all over pretty quickly and, as I said, that knife is so sharp she'd most probably never have felt the cuts to her face.'

Carruthers was about to say that this was a blessing, but then he remembered the father of this young woman and how his life would soon to be changed forever. Nothing to him would be a blessing. He dropped his head and swallowed hard.

* * *

Fletcher left Strathburn Halls and went straight to the central library on King James' Way. She peered up at the building from across the road. The oldest in Scotland, it had been a library for over five hundred years. She crossed the street, narrowly avoiding a gowned student riding a bike. She tutted. *That was an accident waiting to happen.* Why on earth would a student ride a bike wearing a gown? Hadn't the police run a road safety awareness course at the university recently? That student clearly hadn't been on it. She sighed, and skipped up the worn stone steps and walked in through the enormous front doors to the information desk.

'Excuse me,' she said to the old man with the dickie bow sitting behind the desk. 'Can you help me please? I'm looking to see if a student has taken out a particular book from this library.'

He frowned at her. She noticed a half-eaten sandwich on the table. Unsmiling, he said, 'Most people usually come in here looking for books. Not looking for students who have taken out books. I'm not sure I'm going to be able to help you. Why don't you just ask the student?' He turned away from her rather rudely, picked up his sandwich and took an enormous bite out of it. Most likely supper, given the time.

Fletcher watched as a student scanned all the books she was taking out of the library, mindful it was all automated now. Another change since her university days. She flashed her warrant card at the unhelpful librarian. 'Oh, I certainly hope you can help. And you don't want to get on the wrong side of the police, do you?'

Open-mouthed, he stared at her. 'No, of course not. Always happy to help the boys and girls in blue. What did you say the student's name was?'

'I didn't.' She wished he'd shut his mouth while he was eating. She really didn't want to see the food churning around. She rummaged in her bag for the piece of paper she'd put in earlier with the details of the book found with the body. 'Can you look this book up for me and let me know if it's currently out on loan, and if so, can you tell me who took it out? The name of the book is *A Treatise of Human Nature* by–'

'David Hume,' the man finished. 'A fine piece of work. A highly prized book, in fact.' He wiped the side of his mouth with a dotted kerchief that had been in his breast pocket.

'Highly prized, as in a lot of students want to take it out?'

'Well, we have five copies in the library, although that's not what I meant. Wait a minute. Let's see what I can do.'

He tapped at the computer, hitting the return button with a flourish. 'As I thought. All five copies are out at the moment. Wait a second. Let's see who's taken them out.'

Fletcher, in her excitement, leant across the desk.

'If you don't mind taking your elbows off the table. It's made of mahogany and is four hundred years old.'

Almost as old as you, Fletcher wanted to say, but her mother had taught her never to be rude to strangers, so she kept her mouth shut. She wasn't normally so ageist but this man was really getting on her nerves.

'I can get a printout of the dates and names of students who have taken this book out in the last month, if you want?'

Fletcher was surprised at how helpful he was becoming. Some might say obsequious.

'As you can see everything is automated nowadays. People scan their own books here when they take them out and drop them off when they bring them back and we scan them back in.'

'Actually, I probably just need to know if any students have taken a copy of this book out within the last couple of days. That would be a good start.'

'As you wish.' The man typed on a few more keys. He switched the computer round so Fletcher could see the screen. 'The last person to take a copy of David Hume's *A Treatise of Human Nature* out of the library was a Rachel Abbie, earlier today, in fact.'

Bingo. 'That's all I needed to know. Thank you.' She turned away but then, with another question in mind, turned back to face him.

'Just one final thing – are you able to tell me the exact time the book was taken out?'

'Receipts are issued to the person who takes the book out.'

Fletcher didn't know that, but then again, she couldn't remember the last time she had been in a library. It might well have been when she was a student. She started to feel a bit guilty. With all the government cuts she should really start using her local library a bit more. 'We've got the book that was taken out but we don't have a receipt.'

'How careless.'

Fletcher didn't know if this odious man meant her or Rachel Abbie. Either way, her frustration with him was growing.

'Can you tell from your computer what time it was taken out?'

He peered over the computer. Yes, it was taken out at 12:04. And it's due back on the twenty-fourth. Some are late bringing them back though. And of course, there's others who never bring them back at all. Oh, before you go.' He disappeared from view for a moment, then came back holding a student card. 'I knew that name was familiar. She must have dropped her student ID badge while she was here. Another student handed it in. Here it is.'

Fletcher took Rachel Abbie's student ID from him and studied it. She turned it round so the photograph was facing the librarian. She looked down at him. 'Do you remember seeing this girl?'

He took a look at the picture in the photo but shook his head. 'The book was logged out at 12:04pm. I go on my break at 12. I must have just missed her.'

'Who would have been on duty? Are they still in the building?'

The librarian nodded. 'Wee Mary McPhee. Lovely Irish girl. One second.' He picked up a phone. 'Mary, can you come to the desk for a minute? There's a police officer would like to speak to you.'

A young woman with bleached blonde hair walked up to the front desk. She looked hardly older than Rachel Abbie. Perhaps she was a student herself trying to pay off some of her debt. Fletcher repeated the question she'd asked the other librarian and showed her Rachel Abbie's student ID card. The young woman took it and studied it before she shook her head. 'No sorry. I don't remember her. We had a bit of a rush on at lunchtime and, as Bill has probably told you, a lot of library work is now automated.'

Fletcher felt her heart sink. They'd missed a great opportunity to find out if the student had left on her own. She turned to the man. 'Do you have CCTV in the library?'

'No, 'fraid not.'

She sighed, dropped the student ID and her warrant card back in her bag while searching for her mobile, thanked him and left the building. At least the mystery of the missing ID badge had been cleared up. It was only later that she thought what a strange comment he'd made about some students never bringing their books back.

* * *

Fletcher had not been long back at the station before her mobile rang. She picked it up, wondering how the PM had gone. The photograph they had retrieved from Rachel Abbie's room had been logged and processed. Further examination of Rachel's room hadn't revealed anything else of significance. Just an ordinary student's room and, when shown, her housemates hadn't known either of the two men in the photograph.

Fletcher frowned. Unfortunately for them, not only had Rachel's mobile been password protected, but nobody else had the password. Not even Will. Fletcher was starting to wonder if Rachel Abbie was a secretive person. *Or is this normal in this age group?* Her mind went back to the anomaly with the addresses the young woman had given. What did that mean?

She answered her mobile. It was Carruthers. 'Boss?' She smiled her thanks as Gayle Watson put a cup of much-needed coffee on her desk. She couldn't remember the last time she'd eaten. She realised she was feeling very empty.

His disembodied voice came over the mobile. 'I've just left the PM. Are you back at the station, Andie?'

Fletcher sat upright. She felt a bubble of excitement. Perhaps they had some news that would further the investigation. 'Yep. How did she die? Was it strangulation?'

The reception wasn't good. Carruthers' voice kept cutting out. In an open-plan office Fletcher had to really concentrate hard to hear him and understand what he was saying.

'Yeah, listen Andie, this is to go no further…' His voice cut out for a moment. '…index finger had been severed…' The line dropped again. '…deliberately. I'm just about to phone Sandra and give her an update. Do you know if she's still in the building?'

What had he just said? She asked him to repeat it.

'The tip of Rachel Abbie's index finger has been severed. Deliberately.'

She felt butterflies in her stomach as she started processing just what this might mean. Her thoughts then went to the DCI. 'I don't know, Jim. I think she may have already left.' Despite her hand wrapped round a scalding cup of coffee the DS felt herself turn cold. She swallowed hard. 'When you say severed deliberately…'

'Clean cut done by a sharp blade, post mortem.'

Fletcher felt the coldness creep all over her. She shuddered. 'Oh Jesus, that's horrible. Do we have a trophy hunter on our hands?'

'I don't know. The finger wasn't found at the scene so it does look as if it's been taken.' Carruthers spoke urgently into the mobile. 'We need to try to keep this out of the papers.. If the press get hold of it, we might end up with a full-scale panic on our hands.'

'They won't hear anything from me,' said Fletcher. 'If we *are* dealing with a trophy hunter that makes it more likely we have a serial killer on our hands, doesn't it, which also means it's likely there'll be more attacks—'

'Let's not jump ahead of ourselves. What did you find out from the students at her halls?'

'Jim, there is one thing I need to tell you. Rachel gave a different home address to her housemates from the one she gave to the department. The address she gave to her boyfriend, a lad called Will Smith, is an address in Ashington in Northumberland. I've got someone checking it out. The thing is, she's not moved house recently, so I'm a bit stumped. I'm hoping we'll hear more when the local police get back in touch.'

'Keep me posted.' He said something else but it was lost as the mobile cut out once more.

'Will do. I've also been to the central library on King James' Way. Rachel Abbie did take out a copy of Hume's *A Treatise of Human Nature* earlier today at precisely four minutes past twelve, so we now know both girls had been to the same library on the day they were attacked, but the wee Irish girl, Mary McPhee, who was on reception at the time, doesn't remember seeing her.'

'Good job, right, get yourself away home soon and get an early night. I think Sandra wants to schedule a meeting for 8:30am tomorrow. I need you at your best.'

As soon as Fletcher had finished the call her mobile rang again. It was the control room at Bilston.

'We sent someone local to the address you gave us in Ashington.'

'Go on.' Fletcher tried to keep the excitement out of her voice.

'That's just it. It doesn't exist. It's a depot.'

Puzzled Fletcher finished the call, rang Carruthers to fill him in and then leant forward, steepling her hands against her face. The coffee Watson had brought her was all but forgotten.

Chapter eight

Wednesday

're we talking about a psychopathic serial killer?' asked the young, spiky-haired DC Helen Lennox, who had been drafted in to help with the investigation. It was 8.30am. DCI Sandra McTavish had yet to make an appearance. She had called Carruthers earlier to say she'd been held up and had given him permission to start the brief without her.

'We've only got two victims,' said Carruthers, standing by the incident board. 'It's too early to call the perpetrator a serial killer.' The young DC blushed. 'If we do have a psychopathic serial killer on our hands,' Carruthers continued, 'then let's hope to God we can catch them before they strike again.'

'And are we sure they *will* strike again?' asked Willie Brown.

'That's the big question, isn't it, Willie. The problem is we have no way of knowing. But I think at the moment we have to assume they will. And let's face it, whether they do or not we need them caught.' Carruthers turned from the packed room of CID back to the whiteboard. 'Let's build up a picture of what we already know.'

'First, we have eighteen-year-old student Serena Davis slashed across the face. She survived an attempted strangulation and is currently recovering in hospital. She was attacked on Marshall Place.'

He then pointed at the latest photograph that had been pinned to the board. 'Five days later we have our second victim attacked on Greyfriar's Wynd. We believe the victim is nineteen-year-old Rachel Abbie but until such time as we can get a positive ID we will refer to her as Jane Doe. She wasn't as lucky as Serena Davis.

She didn't survive the attack. The PM shows the girl died from manual strangulation, pending toxicology results.' He turned to Dougie Harris. 'Dougie, you were pulling the files on similar attacks in Scotland? Do you have anything for us?'

The middle-aged detective sergeant shook his head. 'If we're looking at serial killers of teenage girls there's nothing recent, boss. Robert Black and Peter Tobin are two names that spring to mind. Tobin's now a frail old man in Saughton Prison, too scared to come out of his cell apparently, and Robert Black died in prison in Northern Ireland in 2016. Emma Caldwell's murder still remains unsolved, mind.' Harris was talking about the murder of the 26-year-old Glaswegian who had sadly gone off the rails, slipping into prostitution after the death of her sister.

'Hmm. Keep digging.' But even as he said this Carruthers thought that the two recent attacks were most probably the actions of someone completely under the police radar whose recent activities in all likelihood had only just been triggered. But that was nothing more than a hunch.

'Do we know if Rachel Abbie's father's been located?' Watson straightened her tie as she asked the question. This no-nonsense lesbian had a penchant for wearing men's suits and she carried them off beautifully, Carruthers had to admit. He often wondered how she and old-style cop Dougie Harris managed to rub along so well. *Nothing as queer as folk,* he thought. If he'd voiced this to Watson she would have laughed her head off. She loved puns.

Fletcher turned to answer Watson's question when her mobile rang. 'Sorry, I need to take this.'

Carruthers nodded his permission and Fletcher stood up and made her way to the door. 'It's Bilston on the phone,' she mouthed as she exited. As she shut the door behind her Carruthers heard her say into the mobile, 'This had better be good. I'm in the middle of a team brief.'

Turning back to the expectant officers Carruthers said, 'No, Rachel Abbie's father has not been found yet but perhaps Andie will have some news for us when she returns.' He looked round the room before glancing at his watch, wondering when Sandra McTavish would arrive and if, in her continued absence, he should start assigning jobs. 'We need to step up our investigation.'

Just as he said that Andrea Fletcher re-entered the room and spoke to the assembled mass as she took her seat, smoothing her skirt as she sat. 'That was the control room. They've located Rachel Abbie's father. He's on his way up.'

He nodded his thanks to Fletcher. 'Thank goodness. That's good news. Means we don't have to ask one of her poor housemates. The station's taken a call from Will Smith first thing this morning. Rachel didn't return home last night. In my mind it's only a matter of time before we're formally able to ID our Jane Doe as Rachel Abbie. I'm afraid that's not all. What else we do know of the latest assault from the PM is that part of the girl's right index finger has been deliberately cut off. After her death.'

There was a sharp intake of breath. 'And that bit of information is not to leave this room. Are we agreed?' There was a collective nodding of heads. 'And definitely not to get into the hands of the press. We don't want to cause a panic.'

Helen Lennox cleared her throat before speaking. 'Do we tell Rachel's father? About the severed finger? I mean, if it is his daughter lying there on the slab?'

Carruthers turned to the spiky-haired officer. He wondered how she would fit into their close-knit team.

'We're going to have to. He has a right to know and these things sometimes have a habit of getting leaked to the press. Much better coming from us. But don't worry, you won't be assigned that job.'

Lennox, having turned pink, nodded, looking relieved, and returned to scribbling in her notebook. No sooner had Carruthers finished speaking than the door opened and the newest member of the station walked in unbuttoning her coat.

'I got held up,' announced DCI McTavish. 'I'm here now, though.' She addressed her comment to Carruthers. He tried very hard to maintain a neutral expression but knew he was frowning. He couldn't help it. In all his time as DCI he'd never been late for a brief this important. He took a deep breath and tried to relax his facial muscles. Out of the corner of his eye he watched Sandra McTavish plonk her briefcase down on the floor, whip her coat off, place it on the back of one of the vacant chairs. She was wearing a charcoal grey knee-length dress. Her flesh-coloured tights were wrinkled. She must have seen Carruthers stare at them as she bent her head forward and pulled them up.

'In terms of similarities between these women,' he carried on, 'both were young, both blondes, both most likely students. These crimes are nothing short of heinous and we need to catch the perpetrator.'

'Are we sure it's one person and not two?' asked Brown, smoothing down his comb-over with his right hand. He addressed his comments to Carruthers. 'Could the second not be a copycat? After all, only the second victim had her index finger severed.'

'Yes, but Serena Davis's attacker didn't get the chance to finish the job, did they?' Fletcher piped up.

'It's a fair question,' said Carruthers, his brows knitting together as he now watched McTavish, still standing, searching her briefcase for her phone which she brought out and looked at. She fiddled with it and put it back in her bag. Carruthers hoped she'd put it on silent. He didn't want any more interruptions.

'Mackie is pretty confident–,' he began, only to be cut off by McTavish who strode to the front of the room.

'Mackie's confident the two attacks have the hallmarks of the same person.' McTavish gave Carruthers a sharp look, meaning she'd now arrived, she would take over and he needed to take a back seat and let her get on with the job she was paid to do. Awkwardly, he returned to his chair.

'And of course,' she continued, 'we know from Mackie part of the index finger was severed post mortem. What we've got to work out is whether these were two random attacks or whether these particular girls were targeted. At first glance there don't seem to be any similarities between the two except that they are both blonde female students.'

'Well, you've got three similarities there already,' said Brown, smirking.

McTavish kept quiet, clearly deciding to ignore Brown. For all that she had taken his job, Carruthers was beginning to see that she was getting the measure of her staff early on.

'And both having just been to the library when they got attacked,' said Fletcher. 'And talking about books, both girls had a copy of Ayn Rand's *Atlas Shrugged* in their possession.'

'That's five then,' said Brown.

Helen Lennox lifted her hand to ask a question. 'Does the perpetrator wait for these women to leave the library and then follow them, do you think? Perhaps it's a member of the library staff or a fellow student.'

Both Carruthers and McTavish spoke at once. 'It's a possibility.'

Lennox still had her hand in the air when she spoke. 'Perhaps it's worth checking out the library again?'

Fletcher spoke up. 'I've already been to the library. The librarian that I spoke to wasn't on duty when Rachel Abbie took the book out, and his colleague,' she looked at her notes, 'a Mary McPhee, doesn't remember seeing Rachel.'

Carruthers bit his lip and allowed McTavish to answer Lennox's question. He had to remind himself who was the senior investigating officer here. And it wasn't him.

'I agree.' She turned to Carruthers. 'Jim, can you go through the details of the two victims for us.'

Carruthers nodded and turned to Fletcher. 'Andie, I believe you've got their details.'

Fletcher flipped back a couple of pages in her black notebook and began to read. 'First victim is eighteen-year-old Serena Davis. She's five-four, blonde-haired and studying history of art. Jane Doe is five-two and blonde. If she does turn out to be the missing student, Rachel Abbie, then Rachel was nineteen and studying philosophy.'

'What time is Rachel Abbie's father due to arrive in Castletown, Jim?'

It was Fletcher who answered McTavish. 'Within a couple of hours, ma'am.'

'Good. We need to confirm the ID of the victim as quickly as possible.'

Carruthers knew as soon as the formal ID had been made, the painstaking process of piecing together the girl's last movements would start.

McTavish looked around the room. 'Who's accompanying the man to the mortuary?'

Carruthers noticed his new boss had her eyes on her mobile again. He opened his mouth but didn't get a chance to speak.

'I want you here at the station, Jim. Get Andrea to go. It's a job for a DS.'

Carruthers looked at the new DCI. He was still sizing his replacement up. He cast a critical eye over her. Sandra McTavish was looking immaculate as ever. Charcoal grey clearly suited her. Her black hair was up in a smart chignon. The previously wrinkled tights were the only giveaway that she had arrived in haste. He was aware she was still speaking.

'From a press point of view this has to be handled extremely delicately. I want very little of the actual detail given to the press for obvious reasons. Gayle, are you happy to still be our press liaison?'

Watson smiled. Press liaison was quite clearly a job she relished. 'Happy and on it, ma'am.'

Carruthers thought privately that Gayle Watson was the perfect press liaison. Like Fletcher she had a calm efficiency about her but the few years she had on Fletcher could be used to good advantage. Carruthers knew she was also excellent at fielding questions.

'I want you to contact the press and set up a meeting,' continued McTavish. 'But wait until you get a formal ID on the dead girl first. Family needs to be notified. Correct procedures to be followed.'

Clearly a stickler for the rules this one, thought Carruthers. *Superintendent Bingham would approve. Probably why she had been assigned to their station. Or maybe Bingham had just got lucky.* Thinking about McTavish and her tidy desk he decided she was clearly everything that he wasn't. But then he was always on time for team briefs, he reminded himself, before he became too despondent.

McTavish looked straight at Carruthers before asking her next question. 'Is there any doubt at all that she's not your student, Rachel Abbie?'

Carruthers shook his head before he answered the DCI's question. 'There's no doubt in my mind. And the ID should take place within the next hour.'

McTavish nodded her approval. 'Very good.'

But it isn't very good, thought Carruthers. *It is very bad. Very bad indeed.* He had an ominous feeling in the pit of his stomach. And his gut was hardly ever wrong. Who was this killer targeting and why? And the most important question of all – if it was a serial killer – who would be next?

Chapter nine

Aweeping Mr Abbie was shepherded out of the mortuary by a sombre-looking Fletcher. The slim, dark-haired man had done the buttons of his striped shirt up wrong in his haze of shock and grief. For some reason this vulnerability made Fletcher want to cry.

The middle-aged man brought out a tissue from his coat pocket and noisily blew his nose into it. Fletcher wanted to give the man a hug, but protocol dictated that she remain professional.

Mackie had covered most of the young woman's body with a sheet after the post-mortem and they had done what they could to cover up the slash on the face to make things as bearable as possible for the grieving father.

Fletcher lightly touched the man's arm. 'I'm so sorry, Mr Abbie. I promise you we will find the person who did this terrible thing to your daughter.' She wasn't about to tell him at this stage about the severed finger. Not just after he'd viewed his dead daughter. It was too raw. God, no. He was going through enough. And they needed to try to keep it out of the papers too. A murderer was bad enough. But a mutilator too? She shuddered, wondering about the mindset of someone who would do this. Why did serial killers take mementos? To extend the fantasy supposedly. She couldn't even begin to understand them.

Fletcher knew from her reading that serial killers, for whom the killing often had a sexual element, liked to collect either body parts or clothes in order to relive the sexual fantasy. Fletcher looked up at Mr Abbie who was holding on to a lamp post. Thankfully his daughter hadn't been sexually violated. But then again there were different types of serial killer. Fletcher hoped it really wasn't a serial killer they were dealing with and that somehow, they had got it wrong.

They stood by Fletcher's green Beetle. Fletcher looked earnestly at Mr Abbie. 'I know this is really difficult but I do need to ask you a few questions.'

He dabbed at his eyes. 'If it helps to bring her killer to justice then ask me what you need to.'

Fletcher put a comforting arm round his back. 'Shall we drive back to your hotel? It might be a bit more comfortable to talk there. I'm going to ask a colleague, DS Gayle Watson, to join us.'

'As you wish.'

After Fletcher had made the call to Watson both she and Mr Abbie sat silently in the car, each lost in their own thoughts, until Fletcher broke the silence. 'Do you know why your daughter told her housemates that your home was an address in Ashington, Northumberland?'

Mr Abbie looked confused. 'No, we have no connection to Ashington at all. Why would she do that?'

Fletcher pushed on. 'Rachel told her housemates that out of term time she lived with you in Ashington yet the philosophy department have your Nidderdale address listed. You can't shed any light on this at all?'

'No. The only thing I can think of is that perhaps Rachel was embarrassed.'

'Embarrassed? How do you mean?'

'Look, we live in a nice place. I know Castletown's not short of a bob or two and some of the students certainly won't be, but perhaps she didn't want to tell her fellow students where she lived. I know Ruth Skipsey's family doesn't have much money, for example.'

Fletcher pondered this. Was it possible? Well, anything was possible. How likely was it that was the reason she'd given an address in a less affluent place? She honestly didn't know, but then youngsters of that age, often away from home for the first time, would sometimes go to great lengths to fit in. She wondered if

Rachel Abbie was one such person. She tried a different tack. 'Was Rachel happy here at the University of East of Scotland?'

'Yes, I think so. I mean, she'd met Will. They seemed inseparable.'

'You'd met him?'

'Oh yes, a couple of times when I visited Rachel. Nice boy. I don't really know her other housemates though. And to be honest I don't really know Will that well. I was hoping to get to know him better. Now I'll never get the chance.'

Fletcher observed the man's downcast eyes and sad expression. All of a sudden the man started to sob. Fletcher felt wretched for him.

She gave him a few moments to compose himself.

'I'm so sorry.' He sniffed.

'Please don't apologise. I can't imagine what you're going through. Was it serious? The relationship with Will?' Fletcher thought back to her own student days. She'd had a couple of flings but certainly had never met anyone she had wanted to settle down with. Nineteen was far too young in her view.

Mr Abbie heaved a great sigh. 'For Will certainly. For Rachel, I think so. The first couple of months she had a wobble about him. Wasn't sure how she felt about dating him, if youngsters still use that expression, but she seemed to get over that. I don't know how much you know but we lost Rachel's mother four years ago.'

'Yes, I did know. I'm so sorry. Was there anything bothering Rachel?' *Or anyone,* Fletcher wanted to add.

'She was struggling a bit with the course but then philosophy's not meant to be easy is it? To be honest I wasn't sure it was the best course for her.'

'Oh, why was that?'

'Rachel tends… tended to overanalyse everything. Philosophy is all about critical thinking, isn't it? I'm just not sure it's the best course for someone who already overthinks things.'

Fletcher could see the logic in that. She thought fleetingly of Carruthers having been married to a philosophy lecturer.

Wondered if any of the overthinking had rubbed off on him. She didn't think so. 'And were you and Rachel close?'

'When she was young she would tell us everything. After we lost her mum so suddenly we were close, for a while. Since she started at university, not so much. We don't…didn't spend so much time together. She used to come to church with me, well, until her mother died, but then she didn't want to go any more. I suppose you could say she lost her faith. I don't blame her, of course. And at university,' he shrugged, 'she had a new set of friends. They're not into the church. Quite the opposite in fact.'

Fletcher looked worried. 'You mean devil-worshipping?'

'Oh no, no, nothing like that. But you know what it's like when you study philosophy. For her recently it's now all about rationalism, which I guess is to be expected. And I guess she was finding it hard to marry rationalism with Christianity. She was exploring different options. And, if I'm honest, she was growing up. Wasn't a kid any more. Didn't need me as much, which is how it should be. But she was a kind-hearted person. Would do anything for anyone, but I told her to be careful.'

'Why?'

'She was a very open girl. People can take advantage.'

Fletcher wondered if someone had taken advantage of Rachel. 'Would she open up to you if she had any problems?'

Mr Abbie took his time to answer the question. 'I'm pretty sure there was something troubling her, but she wouldn't confide in me.'

'Any idea at all what it was?'

'No. I'm sorry.'

'You don't know whether it was something to do with her studies or perhaps a falling out with one of her friends?' Fletcher tried to be delicate in her probing but it was difficult.

Mr Abbie shook his head. 'You might try asking Will. I think she'd have been more inclined to confide in him. At least I told her to talk to him about what was worrying her if she wouldn't talk to me.'

Fletcher scribbled in her black police notebook. She looked up at Mr Abbie. 'Do you know if she did? Talk to him, I mean.'

'I've no idea.'

Fletcher dived into her handbag and brought out a copy of the photograph she had found in Rachel's bedroom. She showed Mr Abbie.

'This was found in your daughter's bedroom. Do you have any idea who either of the two men in the picture are?'

Mr Abbie studied it, frowning. 'Er, I do know these two men. And this photo was taken outside our house. They're, er, business acquaintances. Did my daughter take this photo?'

'We don't know, Mr Abbie, but as I said, it was found in her bedroom.'

Mr Abbie turned away, still holding the copy. 'It's ironic really. I was trying to get Rachel to confide in me about her problems but she was better at talking to me about mine.'

Fletcher looked at his red-rimmed eyes. 'What do you mean?'

He coughed. It was a rather embarrassed cough. 'It's silly, but I've had some anonymous phone calls recently.'

Fletcher's ears pricked up. 'And you told Rachel about them?'

Mr Abbie nodded. 'She wanted me to report them to the police. Since her mother died, she's the sensible one.'

'So, who are the men in the photograph?'

'I'd rather not say.'

'I'm sorry for asking awkward questions you'd rather not answer but they may be important.' Fletcher was starting to build up a picture of Mr Abbie and his daughter. She suspected that since his wife's death Rachel's father had leant on his daughter for emotional support, perhaps a little too much.

Fletcher forced her mind back to the conversation and picked up the threads once more. 'But you didn't report it to the police, these anonymous calls?'

'No, well what could I say? That I'm getting nuisance calls? You hear about the police being called out for hoaxes all the time.

I know about your limited resources. They don't need another time-waster phoning in about a nuisance whistler.'

'Sorry? What did you say?'

Mr Abbie looked at Fletcher. 'Well, that's just it. They didn't say anything. They just whistled.'

Fletcher's stomach did a somersault. It was just a whistle and yet… 'What sort of whistle? Can you describe it?'

'Not really. Just a whistle. Completely tuneless. I can't describe it. And then they hung up.'

Mr Abbie had just described the whistle in the same way as Serena Davis had described the whistle she'd heard. Tuneless. It had to mean something. It just had to. Fletcher felt her hairs prickle on the back of her neck. Serena Davis had heard strange tuneless whistling just before she was attacked. Rachel Abbie's father had received anonymous phone calls from a tuneless whistler. It was a possible connection between the cases of Serena Davis and Rachel Abbie.

This was the first important, really important, breakthrough they'd had, and it had come quite early on in the case. Fletcher felt a huge wave of excitement wash over her. Not only might it further the investigation but the fact she had been the one to find out something so vital wouldn't do her career any harm at all.

She was already searching in her black handbag for her mobile. 'Mr Abbie, would you mind if I made a quick call to the station before we get going to the hotel?'

Chapter ten

Carruthers tapped on Sandra McTavish's door.

'Come.'

As Carruthers entered his former office McTavish hastily pushed her mobile back into her leather handbag. Carruthers got the impression it hadn't been a work-related call. The DCI was looking harassed. As well she might. Carruthers noticed that the DCI was missing her tights. Perhaps she'd got a ladder.

Her eyes followed his gaze. She frowned before looking back up at him. 'What is it, Jim?'

'Thought you'd want to know as soon as possible. Andie's just told me that Rachel Abbie's father has been receiving anonymous calls which he hasn't reported to the police.'

McTavish was wearing reading glasses that were on the tip of her nose as she looked up at her DI. He wondered why she hadn't bought varifocals.

She pushed the glasses further up the bridge of her nose. 'You think these anonymous calls may be relevant to the case?' McTavish glanced down at her mobile in her bag.

What is it about this woman and mobile phones? Carruthers didn't feel he had her full attention. He bristled and held himself a bit straighter. 'It may be. Mr Abbie has reported that the person on the other end of the phone was whistling before they hung up. Tuneless whistling.'

Sandra McTavish carefully laid her pen down on her desk. 'Tuneless whistling? Didn't you tell me that—'

'Yes, Serena Davis also reported hearing tuneless whistling just before she got attacked.' Carruthers didn't mean to interrupt his new boss but he couldn't help it. It was a bad habit of his, especially with those more senior. He usually did it when he was impatient to get a point across. He remembered all the times he'd interrupted Superintendent Bingham and how irritated the man had been with him.

McTavish pursed her lips together and took in a deep breath. 'May mean nothing, of course, but you did right to tell me. And I definitely think it's worth following up. Oh, and I want you to organise background checks on all Rachel Abbie's housemates. Anything you can dig up on them, like you did for Serena Davis's housemates. I want it done with more rigour this time, Jim.'

Carruthers flushed crimson. He'd tasked Fletcher with that job and she'd been overseeing Dougie Harris. Unfortunately, he'd not passed on his findings to the team before his wife had been admitted to hospital with a medical emergency. Carruthers assumed this is what McTavish was referring to. Although there'd been a delay getting the information back in the end there had been nothing in their backgrounds to warrant concern. And they'd all had alibis for when the young student had been slashed.

He ignored his boss's comment and pressed on. 'There's something else. Mr Abbie said he thought that something had been troubling his daughter. He had no idea what it might be though. She didn't want to talk to him about it but he told her if she didn't want to talk to him then at least she should talk to Will, her boyfriend. I think that's a line worth pursuing.'

'Yes, I agree, but I still want you to do the background checks on the students.' McTavish's mobile started ringing in her bag. She frowned once more, glanced at her bag and shifted as if about to reach for her phone. But instead she clasped her hands together and ignored it.

She looked back at Carruthers before continuing. 'Most attacks are carried out by people who the assailant knows so it's perfectly normal to look into the private lives of the victim. I also want you to dig up anything you can find on Rachel's father. His background, business affairs; any extramarital relations he may have had. It's not savoury but it needs to be done. If you want to task Fletcher with that it's fine by me. She's a competent police officer. Anything at all. Okay?'

There was a short rap at the door. Superintendent Bingham stood on the threshold, hand gripping the door frame.

'Oh,' Bingham stopped short, hovering. He looked at Carruthers then back at McTavish. 'I didn't realise you had company, Sandra.' He looked at his newest DCI. 'Have you got those reports I've asked for? On my desk by close of play, Friday. Can you manage that?'

McTavish was quiet but she had started to twist her wedding ring on her finger. Carruthers wondered if this was a nervous habit.

Bingham then stared at Carruthers before glancing back at McTavish. 'And if you can't manage it you need to tell me. I'm not totally heartless. I realise you're in the middle of a murder investigation so do what you can.' He then stared at Carruthers with a disapproving look, before turning back to the new DCI. 'But no stalling tactics. They don't sit well with me.' Bingham left the office, shutting the door behind him as he went.

An annoyed McTavish glanced at a red-faced Carruthers. The unexpected look they exchanged was conspiratorial. McTavish almost had a ghost of a smile on her face until her mobile started to ring again. Then she just went back to looking harassed. The moment of newly found intimacy had passed.

'You've got a lot of work on,' said Carruthers. 'I'll leave you to it.'

McTavish was busy retrieving her mobile from her bag when Carruthers shut the door behind him. He had already been forgotten.

* * *

Carruthers stood by his desk in the open-plan office. He looked around him. The place was a hive of activity. Helen Lennox was cradling her phone while scribbling notes. Several DCs were taking calls. Even Brown was immersed in a file. Carruthers picked up his phone and called Fletcher.

'Andie, are you still with Mr Abbie? Orders from McTavish. Take him back to his hotel and stay with him for a bit. Find out all you can about him and his daughter. See if you can pick up on what their relationship was really like; how he got on with his wife before her death, what line of work he is in – that kind of thing. And see if you can get any more information on those anonymous calls of his.'

'Okay. No worries, Jim. Gayle's going to meet me at the hotel. Mr Abbie has decided to stay in Castletown for a few days.'

* * *

'Like I said, I'm sorry to have to ask these questions now, Mr Abbie.' Fletcher looked at the silently weeping father who had just lost his only daughter. 'But they're important.' She glanced at Gayle Watson, who nodded for Fletcher to take the lead.

Mr Abbie was sitting on the one chair in his poky hotel room the other side of Castletown and the two police officers remained standing. The curtains were drawn, keeping the light out. Fletcher was reminded of the old-fashioned custom of drawing the curtains to announce a death in the family. She had an urge to open a window if for no other reason than it was stuffy and airless, but thought better of it. It was inappropriate. She noticed that Mr Abbie had a copy of the Bible on his bedside table. She wondered if it was his own. She wasn't at all religious but she could see how it might give comfort to the grieving father.

Watson turned to face Mr Abbie. 'Can you tell us a bit about your daughter, Mr Abbie. What was she like? You said her mother had died in a car accident?'

'Yes, when Rachel was fifteen.'

Fletcher spoke encouragingly. 'That must have been hard.'

Mr Abbie nodded. 'Yes, it was. You don't get over something like that. Terrible shock. The suddenness of it. The next few years were very hard. It's not easy for a teenage girl growing up without her mother. I had to be both father and mother to her *and* hold down a job. However, we got through it. No other choice. If you don't cope you go under.'

Fletcher looked at the prematurely-lined face of a man who she put in his late forties, who had not only lost his wife but also his daughter. She hoped he would find the support he needed to get through this latest terrible ordeal. She wondered if his faith was strong. It would need to be. He had already borne more than most people his age. How could she ask the sort of questions Carruthers wanted her to ask? How could she find out about the state of their marriage at this delicate time? She just decided there was no easy way. All she could do was throw herself in. For once she was actually glad Gayle Watson was with her. She found the efficient and quietly-spoken woman a reassuring influence. Thanking her lucky stars she didn't have the insensitive Dougie Harris to deal with, she pushed on.

Fletcher made her voice gentle when she asked her next question. 'Was it a good marriage?'

Mr Abbie looked surprised. 'Yes, very good. She was my soulmate. We met young. When we were still at school, actually.'

'You were together a long time then.' She chose her words carefully. 'Sometimes when people have been together that long things can get a bit stale. You were never tempted by an affair?'

Mr Abbie suddenly stood up, looking affronted. 'God, why would you even ask?'

Fletcher had received the response she expected. 'Please sit down. I'm sorry if these questions appear insensitive. I'm afraid it's routine to look into the backgrounds of those affected in this sort of investigation.'

The man drew a long breath and expelled it slowly. Then he shakily sat back down in the chair. 'Yes, I suppose it is. Go on then. Ask the questions you need to ask. However, in answer to your question, no I never was. I was still in love with my wife when she died. In fact,' he said sadly, 'I still haven't been able to look at anyone else.'

Fletcher pondered what he'd just said. She had no reason to disbelieve him. He seemed like an honest man to her. She couldn't imagine a love like that. She hoped one day she might experience it.

She tried a different approach. 'What line of business are you in?' She remembered the comment from the Yorkshire police that he and his daughter lived in a mansion. Either he had some inherited wealth or he was in an extremely well-paid job. Perhaps both.

'I'm a surgeon.'

Fletcher wasn't sure what a surgeon earned but guessed it would be a hell of a lot more than a detective sergeant.

She frowned. Something Mr Abbie had said was bothering her, but it was like a shadow and she couldn't work out what it was. She struggled hard to remember. *Wait,* she thought. *Hadn't he said the two men in the photograph were business acquaintances?* That was a strange choice of expression for a man who had just told her he was a surgeon. What sort of business acquaintances would a surgeon have? She opened her mouth to ask him some further questions, but before she could speak Watson had jumped in with a question of her own.

'So presumably you have no financial worries?' asked Watson.

Mr Abbie looked rueful. He scratched his forehead just above his eye. It appeared a nervous gesture. 'I didn't until I lost my wife. I'm afraid I didn't cope well. I started gambling.'

'Are you in debt?' asked Fletcher, wondering whether that was the reason he was currently staying in such an awful hotel room. Or maybe that was all he could find at short notice. Castletown was popular with tourists all year round. Fletcher could imagine it might be a struggle to find decent accommodation if not booked well in advance.

Mr Abbie looked at Fletcher. 'Look, why are we talking about my financial situation when you have a murderer on the loose?'

'I'm sorry, Mr Abbie. We're just trying to look at things from every angle. I do need to ask you though. The two men in the photo that was found in your daughter's bedroom. Who are they?'

Mr Abbie's shoulders hunched. 'I might as well tell you. You'd find out anyway. Moneylenders. Sorry, I should have said straightaway but I was too embarrassed.'

'Are you having problems meeting the repayments? Have you been threatened?'

'Well, I wouldn't say threatened exactly.'

'Does your daughter own a camera with a long-angle lens?' ventured Watson.

Mr Abbie nodded, looking confused for a moment. 'Yes, she's a keen photographer.'

Why would Rachel Abbie have a photograph of the men who were lending her father money, thought Fletcher. *Unless…* There hadn't been a camera found in her bedroom so presumably it was back at the family home. 'Do you think your daughter was trying to conduct her own investigation into who was sending you those menacing phone calls and that's why she took these pictures?'

Mr Abbie weighed up the question. 'It's possible. When she was young she wanted to be a police officer.'

'We'll need all the contact details you've got for these moneylenders. I'm sure I don't need to tell you just how dangerous some of these people can be,' said Watson.

Moneylenders? More like loan sharks, thought Fletcher.

Fletcher swallowed a huge lump the size of a golf ball. It was time to tell Mr Abbie about the severed finger. They couldn't keep it a secret forever and Mr Abbie had a right to know the details of his daughter's death.

She took a deep breath. 'Mr Abbie?'

He looked up at her. 'You have something to tell me about my daughter's death?'

Fletcher steeled herself. 'Yes, we do. It's not very pleasant, I'm afraid.'

'Not very pleasant? Surely the worst has happened already? There's really nothing you can tell me at this stage that could make me feel any worse than I already do—'

The younger cop bit her lip. Mr Abbie misconstrued the sign. 'Oh my God, you are not trying to tell me she was… interfered with sexually, are you?'

Fletcher shook her head rigorously. 'No, no, no, nothing like that.'

She needed to tell him quickly now his mind was going into overdrive. Watson broke in. 'Like DS Fletcher just said it's nothing like that. But it's still very unpleasant, I'm afraid. After your daughter died, the person who we think killed Rachel then went and severed her finger.'

'Severed her finger? You mean deliberately?'

Fletcher nodded.

Mr Abbie buried his head in his hands for a few moments. At last he was able to make eye contact with the officers again. 'Did you find it? The finger?'

Fletcher shook her head. 'No, we haven't. It seems… it seems the killer may have taken the finger as some sort of trophy.'

The look on his face was sheer horror. 'So, someone somewhere has my daughter's finger.'

'It's likely.' Fletcher noticed Watson spoke gently. Once more she was reassured by her presence.

He looked at both officers in turn. 'Is this common with these sorts of deaths?'

'It is with…' Fletcher stopped herself saying the words, 'serial killers.' It had been on the tip of her tongue. After all, they didn't know what they were dealing with yet. 'It can happen,' she said instead. 'But it's not common.'

'And it was definitely done after Rachel died. Not while she was alive?'

'Definitely after she was killed.' Fletcher was reassured that, at least in this, she could give the girl's father peace of mind.

Gayle Watson, the press liaison, once again took over. 'We want to keep it out of the papers.'

Mr Abbie nodded.

'It's not in the public interest to share this information. And the police do strive to be sensitive to the bereaved. I would urge you not to tell anyone at this stage, Mr Abbie.'

Mr Abbie suddenly looked up, a thought occurring to him. 'Does Will know about Rachel? About her being murdered, I mean? God, he'll be devastated. Does he know?'

Fletcher looked at Mr Abbie. She knew that for the family of a murder victim the grief would never end. As a police officer she saw the very best and worst of human nature. She liked this man. In the middle of his own grief he still had the capacity to worry about someone else.

'No,' she said. 'We'll send someone round to tell him and the rest of Rachel's housemates.'

'Would you mind if I was the one to tell them? I've met them all and I know how upset they'll be.'

Fletcher thought about his request. Perhaps he needed to be the one to tell them. Maybe he needed to do things to keep himself busy. And if he could find any solace in spending time with Rachel's boyfriend and friends... but officially, it had to come from the police and she needed to be there herself to see the reaction on the faces of Rachel's housemates.

She shook her head. 'I'm sorry, Mr Abbie, I'm afraid it does need to be the police who break the news of your daughter's death.' She would have to ask each of them if they had an alibi in order to rule them out of their enquiries. As she knew only too well most murders were committed by someone close to the victim. The possibility of the murderer being a stranger or worse, a serial killer, was very rare.

Mr Abbie nodded. 'Yes, of course. I understand.'

'But we have no problem with you speaking with them afterwards if it will give you some comfort.' She thought of the press release that would be going out later that evening. She would need to get round to the student accommodation and speak to Rachel's housemates before then.

'What societies or clubs had Rachel joined?' This from Watson.

'There was quite a list. Women's Rugby Club was the latest. She was a great one for trying out new things. Really was starting to come into her own.'

Fletcher was trying to picture the petite, slim young woman playing rugby and couldn't, but then again, she'd never watched women's rugby. 'Can you make a list of the societies or clubs Rachel was in, Mr Abbie?'

'I'm not sure I'd know all of them. You'd be better off asking Will.'

'Mr Abbie,' said Watson, 'you told my colleague here that you'd been receiving anonymous phone calls and that although the person on the line hadn't spoken, you'd heard somebody whistling?'

'That's right.'

'This needs to be kept strictly out of the press but you'll also be aware that another young female student has been attacked within the last week?'

'Yes, is there a connection?'

'We're still trying to establish if there is. However, in the last couple of days a new piece of evidence has emerged, and that is that the young woman, Serena Davis, heard tuneless whistling just before she got attacked.'

'Oh my God. Surely it's the same man?'

'At the moment it's the only thing we've got to link the two cases. We just wondered if you'd ever met this other student – Serena Davis?'

Mr Abbie shook his head. 'No, I don't think she's one of my daughter's friends.' He leant forward. 'I'd like to speak with this girl, Serena Davis. Would that be possible?'

Fletcher exchanged a look with Watson. 'Oh, I don't think that's a good idea. The lassie's still pretty traumatised and, to be honest, what information could she give you that she couldn't give the police?'

Mr Abbie put his head in his hands and let out a sob. 'I just need to do something. Anything. We need to find this man and

I need to know why he attacked and killed my daughter. Maybe he'll do it to someone else's little girl. He has to be stopped.'

A few minutes later they left Mr Abbie in his hotel room. As Fletcher shut the door quietly behind the two officers, she stole a backward glance at Mr Abbie, who had got up out of the chair and was now sitting on his bed leafing through the Bible.

As they took the lift down to reception Watson glanced at her watch. 'Shit. I need to get back to the station and prepare the briefing that's going out later on TV. Can you manage without me?'

Fletcher was checking her mobile for messages. Reassured she had none, she put it back in her bag. 'Yeah, sure, I'm needing to speak with Jim's ex-wife, then I'm going to head over to break the news to Rachel Abbie's housemates and boyfriend.' She glanced at her watch.

'Shouldn't you be doing it the other way round? Speaking to Rachel's housemates first and then interviewing the ex-wife?'

Fletcher felt a surge of annoyance at what she perceived as criticism.

'Ordinarily, I'd do it the other way round, but I've got a better chance of catching Mairi Beattie now, before she leaves the university to go home, and the students later once they've headed back to their accommodation.'

Watson shrugged. 'Fair enough.'

'And I want to interview them when they're all together.' Fletcher fished her mobile out of her bag. 'I'll see if Jim wants to come with me. It'll also give me a chance to fill him in on the debt Mr Abbie's in.'

Chapter eleven

Fletcher jumped into her green Beetle and made the short trip to the philosophy department to interview Carruthers' ex-wife. Carruthers was still happy for her to go and interview Mairi Beattie on her own, but he wanted to join her when she broke the news to the students of their friend's death.

Ever practical, she was a firm believer in trying to kill two birds with one stone, especially when in the midst of a police investigation and time was of the essence. So, it was perfect that the students lived within a fifteen-minute walk of the philosophy department.

Before she got out of the car, she dragged her hairbrush through her hair and reapplied her lipstick. Then she wondered what on earth she felt she needed to do that for. It wasn't like she saw Mairi Beattie as competition. Nor did she see Jim Carruthers as partner material. And she wasn't going for a job interview. All she could conclude was that since she'd lost Lara, she'd lost her confidence among other women. Thankfully, for the most part, it was starting to come back at work, but not yet in her personal life.

She flicked away a fleck of dust from her skirt and opened the car door. A fine rain had started to fall. Fletcher turned up the collar of her coat. Just as she was about to step onto the pavement a female student walked straight into her path. She cursed and jumped out the way. The young woman looked up, startled. Fletcher almost gasped out loud. With her short cut hair, masculine face and stern expression she was the dead ringer for the woman in the photograph on the back of the book found in Rachel Abbie's room. The woman must have been aware of Fletcher staring. She gave her a brief quizzical look and muttered an apology before continuing to walk with her head down. No doubt she'd walk into a lamp post if she carried on with such little regard for everything around her. Irritated, and feeling old, Fletcher shook her head and carried on walking.

That Mairi Beattie was every bit as stylish and attractive as she had imagined was an understatement. Slim and petite, she made the now size fourteen Fletcher feel like a hippopotamus, which was ridiculous.

'Thanks for agreeing to see me.' She introduced herself to Jim's elegant ex-wife and flashed her ID card.

Mairi Beattie tucked a tendril of dark hair behind her ear. 'Please take a seat.' She looked worried. 'How can I help you?'

Fletcher met the woman's worried look after taking in the small office which was tastefully decorated in mute colours. Like the secretary, she also had a sea view. Fletcher sat down on the chair she'd been offered. How wonderful it must be to have a sea view at work, but then she decided if it was her, she'd never get any work done. She smiled at the lecturer, who looked almost as young as the students she taught.

The police officer started the conversation carefully. 'This piece of news isn't yet in the public domain and I would like to keep it that way, so please keep this as strictly confidential.'

Mairi Beattie nodded, looking even more troubled than before.

'I needed to speak with you because one of your students, Rachel Abbie, has been found dead, I'm afraid.'

Mairi put her hand to her mouth. 'Oh my God, that's absolutely awful. Was it suicide?'

'No, but that would be a reasonable assumption to make.'

The young professor nodded. 'I suppose when you think of young people dying, especially students, you often think of suicide. I'm afraid we've had a few over the years. Young people are so vulnerable, aren't they? We help them in any way we can but I never feel it's enough.'

Fletcher nodded. Being a police officer in a university town, she was all too aware that self-harm was the biggest cause of death among people in their early twenties in the UK.

'Going away to college can be a very stressful time in a young person's life,' continued Mairi. 'Can I ask what happened?'

'It can indeed.' As she said this, Fletcher remembered her own college experience, first in London, then in Scotland. She'd enjoyed getting away from the confines of rural East Sussex, although she still loved her home visits. She hadn't had any trouble adapting to student life or being away from home, but she knew this wasn't the case for every student. She brought her discussion back to why she was here. 'Unfortunately, Rachel didn't die by her own hand.'

Mairi's eyes had widened. 'You mean–'

'Somebody took her life.'

'Oh my God.' Mairi was silent for a moment, before looking at Fletcher with her almond-shaped green eyes. 'Do you think her death, murder, has anything to do with the recent attack on that other young girl, Serena Davis?'

Fletcher wasn't surprised that Mairi Beattie knew the name of the recent slashing victim. It was a small town, the victim another university student, and the attack had made headlines in the local news.

'At this stage we really don't know. We're keeping an open mind. At the moment we're trying to build up a picture of Rachel Abbie. I've yet to break the news of her death to her housemates so the utmost discretion is needed.'

Mairi bit her lower lip. 'Of course.'

Fletcher nodded. 'In fact, I'm going to see them as soon as I've finished here.'

Mairi looked up at Fletcher, compassion in her eyes. 'I don't envy you. That's not a conversation I'd like to have.' She hesitated before she asked the next question. 'Do you mind me asking how she was killed?'

'I'm afraid we're not able to release that information to the public yet.'

Mairi nodded. 'Oh yes, of course, I understand. I was the wife of a cop for long enough.' She bit her lip. Fletcher was interested in what she would say next. 'Just out of interest, are you at the same station as my ex-husband, Jim Carruthers?'

'Yes, I am. He's a close colleague.'

Mairi nodded. 'Do you mind me asking if he's working on this case?'

'Yes, but he's not the lead,' Fletcher thought of DCI McTavish as she said this, 'but he *is* working on the case.'

'Oh, I just thought… being DCI and all that.'

'He's not–' She stopped herself short. How would Carruthers feel if she spilled the news to his ex-wife that he had been demoted? Not too happy she bet. 'He's not the lead.'

Fletcher studied Mairi as she spoke. It was pretty obvious what had drawn Carruthers to this woman. She was attractive, clearly intelligent and just came across as a genuinely nice person. Being protective of Jim, Fletcher had built up a picture in her head over the last couple of years of what his ex would be like, painting her as some sort of ogre. She had to admit she'd got it completely wrong. Once again, she wondered what their relationship had been like in happier times. She imagined it would have been a good one.

She pressed on with her questions, putting any speculating about their personal lives aside. 'Mairi, what can you tell me about Rachel? I believe you were her tutor?'

'Yes, I am, was, I mean, but sadly I can tell you very little. I only saw her in class and in passing. We didn't chat socially. It was all work-related. I don't know how much use I can be, to be honest.'

'Anything at all would be useful.'

'Okay, then.' Mairi crossed one slim ankle. 'She was a good student. Conscientious, bright, hard working. A good timekeeper. She hadn't missed a tutorial.' Mairi fell silent as she tried to think.

Fletcher could see that Mairi was trying her best to help but was already struggling. She clearly had no personal knowledge of the dead girl and therefore no personal details to impart to the police officer. Fletcher was disappointed. 'Was there any branch of philosophy she enjoyed in particular?'

Mairi brightened. 'I would say ethics. I don't know if you know, but this university is unique, in that it has two different departments. Logic and metaphysics, and moral philosophy.'

Fletcher leant forward. 'Did you ever hear her become heated with anyone in class?' This question needed to be asked. It was an important one. Ethics, in particular, might be a subject that stirred passions. She knew she was clutching at straws, but with no murder weapon, no DNA and no witnesses, that's all she had to go on. She knew most people were killed by someone they knew, but surely nobody could be killed because they had fallen out in a philosophy class?

But then she remembered a case in North America where two female friends had fallen out on Facebook and one had enlisted the help of her partner and her father to have the former friend murdered. People sometimes got murdered for the most ridiculous of reasons. It was definitely worth asking.

'Well, no, can't say I did. She got on with more or less everyone in her tutorial group.'

Pushing away her disappointment, Fletcher asked, 'Can you give me the names of all those in her group, Mairi?'

Mairi nodded. 'Yes, of course.' She scrabbled about for a bit of paper and picked up a pen. 'Actually, I think the only person I ever heard her argue with was John Campbell.' Fletcher's ears pricked up. 'But then again, everyone argues with him at some point. He's just that sort of person.'

Fletcher tucked that piece of information away in her head.

Mairi leaned in closer to Fletcher. 'Now you're here, I did want to ask you something. Actually, it's about—' There was a knock at the door of the office. Mairi looked towards the door, a little flustered. 'Damn. Come in.'

A tall, dark-haired young man put his head round. Fletcher noticed his build was that of a rugby player. 'When are we having the next tutorial again?'

Mairi frowned. 'It's tomorrow. I sent an email out about this.' He mumbled an apology, and withdrew from her office and shut her door. Fletcher had the feeling the apology wasn't very heartfelt and noticed that the student had kept his eyes on Mairi just a bit longer than was necessary.

Mairi sighed. 'Talk of the devil. That was him.'

'John Campbell?'

'Yes.'

'What were you going to ask me?'

Mairi shook her head briskly. 'Oh, it doesn't matter. Nothing to worry about.'

Fletcher observed the woman closely, thinking she appeared a little uncomfortable. 'John Campbell's visit seemed to unsettle you. Are you sure everything's okay?'

'Yes, everything's fine.' Mairi forced a smile. It didn't reach her eyes. Fletcher wasn't convinced and wondered what she was holding back.

* * *

'Shit, I hate this part of the job.' Fletcher straightened her skirt as Carruthers rang the bell at Strathburn Halls.

'Nobody enjoys it. It's one of the worst parts of policing.' Carruthers' mouth was set in a tight line. Fletcher glanced up at him and his youthful face was beset with frown marks. The stress of the investigation was already beginning to take its toll. 'After we break the news to Rachel's housemates, we'll need to take a statement from each of them to find out if they all have alibis for when Serena got attacked and Rachel murdered. I want them in different rooms when they get interviewed.'

'You surely don't think any of them – I mean, I know we have to follow procedure, but you don't really think any of them attacked Serena and murdered their own housemate, do you? I wouldn't normally say this, Jim, but I've met them all, apart from Ruth Skipsey. They honestly don't seem capable.'

'I don't think anything at this moment. I'm trying to keep an open mind.'

Fletcher thought about this before ringing the doorbell again. 'I'm still struggling to believe it could be one of them, that's all.'

'Well, seeing their reactions when we give them the news could be telling. That's one of the reasons I want to be here.'

There was the sound of running feet and the front door was yanked open. Will almost fell out. 'Thank God, you're finally—' He frowned, looking at one police officer to the other. 'Oh. It's you. What do you want? Sorry, I don't mean to be rude. You'd better come in.'

Fletcher looked around her as they entered the living room. Sarah was stirring a big pot of spaghetti with a dark-haired girl at her side. Fletcher guessed that must be Ruth Skipsey but she'd need to establish that.

'We're sorry to barge in like this,' began Fletcher. She looked over at the dark-haired girl she hadn't met before.

'I don't think we've been introduced. I'm Ruth Skipsey.' The girl smiled shyly at Fletcher.

Fletcher remained unsmiling but tried to soften her features. 'DS Andrea Fletcher, and this is DI Jim Carruthers.'

Davey was drinking from a bottle of beer. He placed it on the table and looked up expectantly at the officers.

Will, having gone red, raked through his long fringe. 'Sorry, didn't mean to be rude just now. Thought you were Rachel. Do you have any news of her?'

'I'm glad you're all here. It's about Rachel.' Fletcher let Carruthers lead the way but she noted Will's drawn face and the shadows under his eyes. 'The news isn't good, I'm afraid. There's no easy way to say this. A body of a young woman was discovered yesterday in Greyfriar's Wynd. Rachel Abbie's dad identified it as being the body of Rachel earlier today.'

Sarah, who had been stirring the pot of spaghetti, dropped the wooden spoon and it clattered noisily to the ground. Almost immediately, Fletcher was by her side, switching the gas off and steering the young student towards a chair by the table. The last thing they needed was an accident in the kitchen. Will let out a cry and seemed to fold in on himself, clutching his stomach, looking for all the world as if he'd been shot. As for Davey, he'd gone a shade paler, and as far as Fletcher could see was blinking back tears. All the students had elicited the sort of response you'd expect when they'd just been given the worst news imaginable. Surely none of them had had anything to do with their housemate's murder?

As Fletcher knew only too well though, as unlikely as it was, they had to keep an open mind. Somebody out there was responsible.

Will rounded on Fletcher, fists clenched. 'That's why you were asking all those questions about Rach. You already knew she was dead.' Shock had already turned to anger. He raised his arm, and for a terrible moment Fletcher wondered if Will was about to strike her, but Carruthers pulled him back and the student collapsed into the older police officer's arms. Fletcher watched as the former DCI held the young man close for a moment while he cried. After a few moments, he pulled away from Carruthers, wiping the tears out of his eyes with the cuffs of his shirt. Between sobs he said, 'Why didn't you tell us last time you were here? You let us go on believing she might still come home. You already knew. How could you? How *could* you?'

Fletcher realised Will was in shock. She made her voice as gentle as possible. She really felt his pain. 'I'm sorry. A body of a young woman had been discovered, but we didn't, at that stage, know it was Rachel. And with any death, especially in suspicious circumstances, there is always a procedure to be followed.'

'Do you know who killed her?' Davey had found his voice. 'Was she attacked in the same way as Serena?'

'Is it the same person?'

'Did she suffer?'

'Are we in danger?'

All the questions came at once. Fletcher expected a barrage of questions from the students once they found their voices. She only wished she had answers for them.

It was at the most painstaking, and if she was honest, frustrating part of the investigation. So far, they had too few leads to go on. They didn't even know if the perpetrator would attack again, thought Fletcher glumly. And if he did, who would be next, and why? Was it random or were people being targeted? They still didn't even know that. Fletcher wanted to give the students answers, she really did, but at the moment she had none to give and with each student as a potential suspect until ruled out, the police officers would have to keep their answers vague. Fletcher just hoped the CCTV that she would be going through later that evening would yield something useful.

Sarah Torr started crying in earnest. Will, Davey and Ruth rushed over to her side and the four of them stood, arms wrapped round each other, in a miserable huddle. Fletcher did notice, however, that Sarah winced when Davey put his arm round her. *What's going on there?* she wondered.

* * *

Several hours later back at the station, Fletcher was trawling through CCTV with Helen Lennox. Every so often her mind would return to her meeting with Mairi Beattie. She had been so curious to meet Carruthers' ex and fascinated that Mairi had asked her if Carruthers was working on the case. *Perhaps she's just as nervous about seeing Jim as Jim is about seeing her.* Her stomach rumbled. Both women ignored it. Fletcher forced her mind back to what they were doing. None of them would get home anything but late that evening. Fletcher had even forgotten to eat any lunch but she'd grabbed a Snickers bar from the canteen and that would have to do for now. This was a time-consuming job but a vital one. Unfortunately, it hadn't revealed anything useful.

'Shit,' said Lennox, raking her hands through her spiky hair. She reminded Fletcher of Carruthers when she did that, except his hair wasn't as spiky and there was a lot more grey in it. 'An hour of this and no' a bean. My back is killing me,' she grumbled. 'And I'm dying to get home, get a nice hot bath and something to eat.'

'You and me both. Keep going,' Fletcher instructed. 'CCTV has to pick up our victim soon, unless she took another way from the library that we don't know about. I'm surprised: we know the exact time she took that library book out but yet she hasn't appeared.'

'Maybe she took it out and then last minute decided to look for more books?' Lennox got up and stretched her back. 'I'm going to get myself a coffee. Do you want one?'

Fletcher also stretched and rubbed her neck. 'Or maybe she stayed and did some work in the library before she left. Probably a more likely scenario. Milk, no sugar please.' She didn't really want to have a coffee, but she was feeling tired and decided she needed a caffeine hit.

Settled with their coffees, another hour passed. 'Stop the fast-forwarding. There she is.' The cry from Helen Lennox was triumphant, back pain all but forgotten. Fletcher sat bolt upright too and watched the cameras pick out the slim, blonde-haired student – the recognisable sight, albeit grainy, of the last known movements of Rachel Abbie. The two women narrowed their eyes, Fletcher watching Rachel like a bird of prey about to pounce on an unsuspecting mouse.

'She's walking on her own,' announced Lennox. Fletcher nodded, not wanting to speak at such a crucial moment. Her eyes were fixed on the figure. She watched the young student leave the library and walk up King James's Way towards Bell Street. Then she was out of view. At that point nobody else was in the footage. A few moments later a couple of male students passed, in conversation with each other.

'Rewind it. Let's watch it again. Maybe there's something we've missed,' said Fletcher. They watched it again. And again. And a third time.

Lennox sat back, her flat voice betraying her disappointment. 'There's nothing.'

'Keep watching,' urged Fletcher. 'The camera might pick her up later.' The women watched in virtual silence. Then a few minutes later they spotted her at the bottom of Bell Street crossing the road towards Greyfriar's Gardens. 'There she is. She's not far from Greyfriar's Wynd.'

Fletcher turned to Lennox, hand holding her now empty coffee cup. She shook her head. 'There's no CCTV on Greyfriar's Wynd, though. There's a fair amount in Castletown but I can't see anything suspicious. No footage of either attack. And there's no CCTV on either street where the two girls got attacked. But we do want to find those two students who were in the frame seconds after our victim.' Fletcher sat thoughtfully for a moment. 'It was two male students who found the body, but not the same two people who were in these images. Those two men were slim built and tall. These two are shorter and burlier. What they're wearing is different too. One of the men in this footage is wearing a hoodie and the other two were wearing parkas.' Fletcher stood up. 'I think it'll be a good idea to have a word with Carruthers about seeing if we can organise a reconstruction of Rachel's last moments. Perhaps it will prompt someone to remember something.'

'The attacks both occurred away from CCTV.' The disappointment in Lennox's voice was obvious. She turned to Fletcher. They were both thinking the same thing. 'It's looking more likely the attacker chose his or her place of attack with a great deal of care.'

Fletcher drained the cold dregs down her throat as she spoke as calmly as she could. 'Which means that chances are the attacks were premeditated rather than random.'

'Aye, it's looking that way.'

Fletcher walked towards the door. 'I'd better fill Jim in.'

She found him back at his desk. She shook her head as he looked up. 'Nothing,' she said. 'Just gone through CCTV. We've picked up Rachel Abbie's movements but not the attack. Not a bean. Either a lucky coincidence for the murderer or he or she has specifically chosen the places that have no CCTV to do their killing.'

Carruthers leafed through the statements that had been taken from the students. He shook his head. 'I've got the students' alibis here, Andie, for when Rachel got attacked. Davey Munroe was over visiting a friend, an Annie McLeod.'

'I met her when I first visited them.' She visualised the dark-haired girl sitting on Davey's lap.

Carruthers carried on speaking. 'Sarah Torr and Will Smith were in tutorials and Ruth Skipsey was with her parents who are up in Castletown for a visit. All the alibis check out.'

'Well, you didn't really think it was one of the students we met, did you?'

Brown approached the desk and gave Fletcher a buff file. She nodded her thanks before taking it.

'Make it a damn sight easier if it was rather than the alternative.'

She looked up from the file. 'Some random, you mean, that's not in any way known to the victim?'

'That's more the serial killer scenario, isn't it? Okay, so the alibis work out. How are you getting on with checking out the backgrounds of Rachel Abbie's housemates?'

Fletcher double-checked her notebook. 'We're getting there. There were four students to check. Done all of them except for Davey Munroe and Sarah Torr. We haven't come across anything of interest yet. Wait a minute. Let me just check what's in the file Willie's given me.'

She ripped open the file and started reading. 'It's the information I asked for on Sarah Torr.' She skim-read. 'All looks pretty normal to me.' She shut the file. 'Can we organise a reconstruction, Jim?

There were two lads who were picked up on CCTV moments after Rachel Abbie was spotted. We need to find them.'

'Leave it with me. I'll ask McTavish.'

* * *

Carruthers let himself into his cottage in Anstruther with his fish supper. By rights he should be eating something healthier, but it was late and he was too exhausted to start cooking. The plaintive crying of Rachel Abbie's friends was still ringing in his ears. Dumping his supper on the coffee table in the living room, he walked into the kitchen and pulling open the cupboard door, selected a bottle of Old Speckled Hen. He loved the ale's rich, malty taste and fruity aroma. It was one of his favourite beers.

He noticed the winking of the answer machine. He sighed. Absentmindedly, he played the message. It was his brother. Carruthers was aware he was only half listening to what Alan was saying. Something about asking to stay with him for a few days. It barely registered as he glanced at his watch, his head full of the investigation.

He sat in his favourite shabby, brown leather chair and settled himself in front of the TV, having long since forgotten his brother's call. He debated putting the wood-burning stove on but in the end decided against it, instead switching on the evening news as he tucked into his fish and chips. When he saw the news item he'd been waiting for, he sat upright, his Speckled Hen fizzing over the side of the bottle as he placed it on the table.

'Is it true the attacker has struck again? Do we know who the victim is?' asked one reporter.

'Does Castletown have a serial killer who mutilates women?' Carruthers recognised this sharp-faced female reporter who worked for a tabloid newspaper. *Shit. Does she know about the missing finger? No – calm down. Of course she doesn't. She's talking about the fact they've been slashed.*

'Why haven't you caught this deranged psychopath?'

'What are the police doing to stop him?'

Carruthers watched Gayle Watson, calm and collected, reading the prepared police statement. She ignored the flashes of light from the bulbs of the cameras that lit up the room.

'At approximately 3:40pm yesterday afternoon the body of a young woman was discovered in Greyfriar's Wynd, Castletown. Her family have been informed. Cause of death was by strangulation. It's too early to speculate as to whether her attack is linked to the earlier attack on Serena Davis. The police are currently following several lines of enquiry. We ask the public to remain calm but vigilant and at the moment we would recommend that if you are female you make sure you don't walk on your own. I'd like to confirm that we're not saying we are looking for a serial attacker of women but the advice we are giving is just precautionary in the circumstances. If anyone has any information, they should call the number I'm about to give out. We are particularly keen to talk to two young men who were seen in the vicinity just before the attack.' Gayle Watson described the two men and then read out the number of the hotline from her prepared speech.

'Serena Davis was also an attempted strangulation. How do you know this is not the work of a possible serial killer?' shouted one reporter.

Watson made eye contact with several of the reporters before continuing to speak. 'There will be a further update tomorrow. In the meantime, can I just ask that everyone remain calm. And can I repeat that if anyone has any information, however insignificant it may seem to you, or concerns about anybody acting suspiciously, can I ask them to call us. I'll just repeat that number.' Watson gave out the number once more, thanked the press for their time and walked out the room, followed by a number of journalists still shouting their questions over each other.

She handled that well, thought Carruthers. The only sign that Watson had been under any stress at all was the telltale sign of a pink flush spreading up her neck. It was not an easy task to handle the press, especially the tabloid press, under these circumstances.

Carruthers idly wondered how his new boss, DCI Sandra McTavish, was bearing up.

Carruthers put his mouth to the neck of the bottle and drank from it. Despite not having eaten much that day he was losing his appetite. He picked at the fish and chips, pushing the food around on his plate.

The news focused on another story. Something about two brothers who were missing out walking in the Cairngorms. Once again, his mind was back on his brother. Carruthers looked at his watch. Too tired to call him back now to find out what he actually meant about staying with him, he watched the rest of the news and weather, stripped off, had a quick shower then got into bed. He looked at the copy of Ian Fleming's *From Russia with Love* that lay forlornly on the bed. He was too tired to even read his favourite author.

He lay on his back, naked, staring at the ceiling with the white sheet scrunched over half his torso. He thought of the tuneless whistling. Was this the connection they needed that linked the two cases? Having spoken to Fletcher it was now looking as if they had a potential serial attacker who carefully targeted their victims rather than picking them at random. That showed a degree of premeditation that caused a knot in Carruthers' stomach. Carruthers' gut instinct was telling him, like Fletcher's, that the two cases were linked. And it was possible that the killer knew his victims.

Chapter twelve

'The hotline has taken several calls. They need to be chased up,' said McTavish. 'The normal share of nutjobs. Three callers all claiming to be the murderer and a fourth claiming these attacks are the work of the Devil. Clearly a religious oddball but I still want her interviewed.'

Carruthers wiped the sleep out of his gritty eyes. He hadn't slept well the night before. Tossing and turning, he'd been awake till the early hours. When he hadn't been thinking of the case, he'd been fretting about why his brother had been calling him. His brother never called him and what was this about wanting to stay a few days? What was wrong with his own pad?

Impatiently, he pushed thoughts of his brother out of his mind. Returning the call was just going to have to wait. He then felt immediately guilty. How many times had he said that to himself particularly when his mother had rung him? His family had to understand though, that being a police officer was not a normal job and being in CID carried with it a huge weight of responsibility.

Thinking of phones, Carruthers was thankful that so far Sandra McTavish's mobile had been quiet. They needed to keep the momentum going. He'd really love to know what was going on in her personal life though. He dragged his mind back to the cases. Hopefully the previous night's TV interview would produce some fresh leads.

'Okay, people, come on,' urged McTavish. 'What have we got?'

Andie Fletcher was first to answer. 'It appears Mr Abbie is in financial difficulties which he'd kept hidden from Rachel. At least he was honest enough to admit he has a gambling problem. He's clearly found it difficult to cope after his wife died.'

'Do you think those calls he's been receiving have been from loan sharks?' said Carruthers.

'I wouldn't be surprised. We all know how these people operate.'

McTavish nodded. 'Might be worth putting a tap on his phone with his permission and finding out who these people are.'

Fletcher nodded, writing into her notebook.

'Okay, I want to know where Mr Abbie has been borrowing money,' said McTavish. 'If it is loan sharks as I said, we want to know.'

Watson, who had also been taking notes, put her pen down. 'I've been thinking about this. I actually think we might be wasting valuable time. It's highly likely the attacks on both women have been carried out by the same person. Why are we wasting time looking at Mr Abbie's finances when there's no connection between the Abbies and Serena Davis?'

'I agree we're clutching at straws at the moment but what else do we have to go on?'

Carruthers was listening to his new DCI carefully. He had his head tilted at an angle.

'But to be honest we've already found one link between the two cases – that of the whistling. Unless it's just a massive coincidence, but when have we believed in coincidences? I've been thinking it over and I do think there might be something significant in the whistling. We need to find out what it is.'

McTavish turned to Fletcher and Watson. 'I want you to start looking into the family of the other victim – Serena Davis. See what you can find out, however small.'

Gayle Watson nodded.

'Have we found anything out about what was worrying Rachel Abbie before her death?'

Fletcher shook her head. 'I went back and reinterviewed her housemates. Nobody knew what had been worrying her, but Will agreed that she hadn't been herself for a few weeks, so her dad was right. Something was troubling her.'

'Keep digging,' McTavish said. 'Somebody must know something. Just to say we've got Bingham's permission to organise a reconstruction. I want that to go ahead as quickly as possible before the trail goes cold.' She looked across at Carruthers. 'Can you oversee that?'

'Yes, I'll get it organised immediately.'

'Good.'

At that moment the door to the incident room opened and balding Willie Brown popped his head round.

McTavish looked up. 'What is it, Willie?'

'You're no' going to like this. That was the hospital on the phone. Mr Abbie has turned up and is making a bit of a scene outside Serena Davis's room.'

Fletcher turned to Carruthers. 'Shit, I forgot to tell you, Jim. He wanted to speak with Serena Davis himself. Thinks we're not doing enough to help catch the perpetrator. I told him to keep away.'

Willie Brown continued speaking. 'He's been detained by security staff, but he was caught trying to push his way into the bedroom of Serena Davis. Apparently, the wee lassie's freaked oot.'

Carruthers ran his hand over his bristles. 'Oh Jesus.'

McTavish made eye contact with Carruthers. 'Okay Jim, get someone sent to the hospital, will you. The last thing we need is the father of a murder victim turning into a lone vigilante. I want you to try to persuade him to go back to Yorkshire and leave the policing to us.'

'You cannae blame him,' said Helen Lennox. 'He just wants answers.'

Don't we all, thought Carruthers.

'We've got a young woman currently recovering from a horrific ordeal in hospital, clearly very frightened. I want a guard on her door until this man's caught.'

He was surprised Clare Stott hadn't chucked the man out. Perhaps she wasn't currently in the hospital. Probably too busy liaising with whatever newspaper she worked for.

Fletcher raised her hand. 'Will the budget–'

'You leave the budget to me,' said McTavish. Carruthers wondered if it was because she had a daughter herself only a few years younger. He also wondered if she would end up butting heads with Bingham the way he had been since he had arrived at the station. This he would pay money to see. And as loath as he was to say it, Sandra McTavish would have his full support.

* * *

Fletcher laid a hand gently on Mr Abbie's arm and tried to guide him out of the hospital. 'We understand how upset you are over your daughter's death but what did you think might be gained from terrifying Serena Davis? Don't you think she's been through enough?'

Mr Abbie pushed her hand away roughly and, turning round, started walking back in the direction of Serena Davis's room. The two hospital security staff men jumped forward and grabbed Mr Abbie none too gently. Fletcher put her hand up to stop them. 'Show some respect, will you? This man has just lost his daughter.'

Fletcher caught up with him and stood in front of him. 'I can't let you do this. You've been asked to leave the hospital. Imagine if that was your daughter lying in that bed.' As soon as the words were out she regretted them. Once again, she very gently put a comforting hand on his shoulder.

Mr Abbie's face was contorted with remorse. 'I wish it was my daughter. At least that way she'd still be alive.' He allowed Fletcher to guide him down the corridor. She briefly stopped at the nurses' station and took a handful of tissues out of the box offered by one of the staff. The look of concern on the face of the nurse said it all. The unimaginable pain that man was going through right now didn't bear thinking about. Certainly something no parent should ever have to go through. And he wasn't thinking rationally. That much was clear.

He dabbed at his eyes with the crumpled tissues. 'I don't know what I was thinking. I wasn't thinking. Not really. I just felt she had to know more.'

'How could she? The man was wearing a mask and the attack was over within seconds.'

'So my daughter died not even seeing the face of the person who killed her? She died at the hands of a coward. And that coward is still walking the streets. God knows, maybe he's following another young woman as we speak.'

Fletcher's skin crawled and she felt a sense of foreboding. Would there be another attack? And when would the police get that elusive breakthrough? They couldn't afford to wait to see if someone else got murdered. This evil person had to be stopped. She thought of something that might placate this distraught father.

'We're organising a reconstruction. They can be highly successful in jogging the memories of the general public. There've been several documented cases of how they've nailed the murderer. And we'll keep you fully informed, of course, but I don't think you can do anything useful here, Mr Abbie. We share your anger and frustration but you don't want to start hampering the police investigation.' Fletcher looked at him kindly. 'Perhaps it's time to go back home?' She hoped to God Clare Stott wouldn't suddenly appear. She didn't want a further confrontation with the woman.

Mr Abbie nodded and looked at Fletcher through red-rimmed eyes. 'I'll check out of my hotel today. Will you promise to keep me posted of any developments?'

Fletcher's features softened. 'Of course.' And as she responded, Fletcher made herself a promise that they would get justice for Rachel Abbie and Serena Davis.

* * *

Carruthers handed Fletcher a cup of coffee and a ham sandwich. He was standing by her desk. 'God, what did he think he was doing going to the hospital?'

Fletcher thanked him and took a mouthful, thinking that if she drank any more coffee she'd explode. 'He's off his head with grief. I think he already regrets going to the hospital. Christ, I'm tired. And I'm actually starting to feel a bit sick with all this coffee but I need it to keep me going.'

Carruthers pulled a face, but it wasn't entirely unsympathetic. 'We're all tired, Andie. How's Serena Davis doing?'

Fletcher sighed. 'Apparently she was hysterical. She didn't know who Mr Abbie was. As far as she was concerned, he might have been her attacker.'

'Yes, that was unfortunate. McTavish has put a uniform on the door. Apparently, she's going to square it with Bingham later.'

Fletcher raised an eyebrow. 'Good luck with that one.'

Carruthers took his mobile out from his trouser pocket and glanced at it. 'Where's Abbie now?'

'Going back to Yorkshire. I left him checking out of his room.'

Carruthers placed the mobile back in his pocket. 'Oh well, I suppose that's something. There's nothing he can do up here. So, are any of our loose ends tied up yet? We've got a fake address given by our victim and a photograph of two men.'

Fletcher shook her head. 'We still have no idea why Rachel gave a fake home address. Mr Abbie thought it might have something to do with being embarrassed at having a posh house. You know how desperate youngsters are to be accepted.' She looked up at him. 'Oh, we do know something though, but it's not good news. The swabs that were taken from underneath Serena's fingernails are back. They're not a match with anyone we've got on file.'

'Bugger.' Carruthers picked up the photograph found in Rachel Abbie's room. 'We need to find out who those two men in the photograph are.'

'We've got the name of the money lending company,' said Fletcher. 'It's GetMoneyFast. They're based in Yorkshire. It actually looks to be a legitimate company but we'll get it chased up. Perhaps it's worth showing the photo of the two men to Serena Davis? After all, it's possible there's a connection in these cases.'

'Let's get the reconstruction done first. Who did you get?'

Fletcher's face lit up. 'PC Amanda Selway. She's very enthusiastic. She's about the right height and weight. She's going to wear a wig as she's a natural brunette. And of course, she looks ridiculously young for her age.'

'She'll need to. She has to pass for a nineteen-year-old.'

Fletcher picked up her handbag and brought out her miniature make-up case. She waved it under Carruthers' nose. 'Make-up can do wondrous things.'

* * *

The young-looking Amanda Selway patted her blonde wig and adjusted her denim skirt. Her make-up was subtle and she had finished the look off with a slash of natural lipstick. 'Do I look okay?'

'For Christ's sake yer no' in a beauty pageant,' said Harris. 'Let's just get on with it. I need to get back to the hospital and check on my wife.'

'Okay, sorry sarge.'

The young officer was clearly excited but nervous. Fletcher wondered if this was the PC's first reconstruction. She looked at her watch. It was a few minutes off three o'clock. She had organised the reconstruction for three, which was the approximate time Dr Mackie thought Rachel Abbie had been killed.

Fletcher scowled at Harris before giving an encouraging smile to PC Selway. 'Oh, just ignore him. You look fine. And you're doing an important job. The victim is the focal point of any crime scene investigation. Come on. Let's get started.'

'Do ye always have to sound like you swallowed the police manual?' Harris barked. 'Friggin' graduates.'

Harris is back to his irritating self, thought Fletcher, reddening. She ignored his comment, wishing he'd just go back to being quiet again, but now wasn't the time to start a row.

Fletcher had arranged for the reconstruction to go out on the local news later that evening. She prayed that the weather would hold. It hadn't been raining the day Rachel Abbie had been killed, although the day had been dark, but in the last few minutes the sky had turned grey and it had started to spit.

As the PC set off from the central library on King James' Way Fletcher felt her heart skip a beat. With her blonde wig and short denim skirt Amanda Selway looked just like Rachel Abbie. They'd even managed to find virtually the same canvas bag in lost property.

As she passed the first CCTV camera on King James' Way where Rachel Abbie had been picked up, Fletcher glanced up at it once again, wondering whether it was just sheer good fortune for the perpetrator that there had been no CCTV at the point of murder, or whether it had been planned that way. Whoever they were they were cunning. And it occurred to her that they had a good knowledge of the geography of the town.

The young wig-wearing PC walked the length of King James' Way and then took a right onto Bell Street, walking awkwardly in her red wedge shoes. At the end of Bell Street, she crossed the road, entering Greyfriar's Gardens. When they got to the entry point of Greyfriar's Wynd where the horrific murder had taken place, Fletcher could see the girl looking over her shoulder nervously as she entered the darkened medieval alley. She was either a fine actor or she really was incredibly nervous. As the PC walked into the alley, she tripped but righted herself before she fell, her shoes clacking on the cobbled stones. Fletcher imagined that maybe PC Selway wasn't used to wearing wedge shoes.

Fletcher watched her take the three worn steps carefully. On another day she would have spent time wondering about the lives of all the people over the centuries who had lived in Castletown and who had walked down this alley, but not today. She was fully focused on the reconstruction.

They'd got a male police officer, PC Jaynoy, to play the part of the murderer, and when PC Selway was a third of the way down the alley he appeared at the top of the Wynd. A large young man, dressed all in black and wearing black gloves, he pulled the clown mask over his face at the last minute. Watching him, Fletcher felt depressed. How could the image of this man jog anybody's memories? They'd been given such a vague description by Serena Davis of her attacker. There were no distinguishing features at all to identify him to the public. And was the person who attacked Serena Davis even the same person who murdered Rachel Abbie?

She watched as the man, still walking, increased his speed and covered the ground between him and his victim. She stared in fascinated horror as PC Selway started to run unsuccessfully in her short denim skirt and red wedge sandals, now aware somebody was behind her. By the time the young police officer was two thirds down the alley PC Jaynoy was bearing down on her. Fletcher found herself holding her breath, imagining the last few moments of the terrified university student. With pounding heart, she crossed her fingers that the reconstruction would produce some solid leads.

Chapter thirteen

Mairi left the philosophy department early. She had no tutorials that afternoon and wanted to get home at a reasonable time for once. Having locked up, she started walking towards the staff car park, gripping her briefcase before pulling up short. Bugger. The car was in for its annual service and today she had to get public transport. She glanced at her watch. She could pick up a bus from across town but she would have to hurry if she didn't want to be late for the visit from her parents. She felt a few drops of rain on her arm and glancing skywards saw some ominously dark clouds. The temperature was colder than average and she wished she'd brought her winter coat. She debated stopping to put on her mackintosh, which was flung carelessly over her left arm, but decided against it. She hurried on, feeling a bit fretful. She heard the scream of police sirens across town and stiffened.

Mindful of the visit from DS Fletcher and the awful news of the death of one of her students, she shivered. Crossing the road, she turned up Cowper's Street. It was narrow, with a pub at the bottom. On the few instances she'd taken the bus instead of driving, she'd run into a couple of her students coming out of the pub. By their drunken state she'd reckoned they'd been in there all day, which would have been fine, but they'd missed her lectures to do it. She knew the pub was a regular haunt for her students and she avoided drinking in it.

Once again, she thought back to her meeting with Andrea Fletcher. She wondered what the woman's relationship was like with her ex-husband. Was it strictly professional? She had hoped that when Jim realised that she wasn't going to go back to him he'd leave her in peace and return to London or go back to Glasgow, but that hadn't happened, and it looked like he was here to stay.

She hadn't analysed how she felt about the fact they were both working in such close proximity. But perhaps it was quite useful having an ex-husband as a cop at the moment, especially if things with John Campbell escalated. There was something about him that scared her.

Her smart, new shiny shoes clacked along the pavement. The wind took a stray lock of raven black hair and swept it over her face. She flicked it away with her right hand. The rain started to get harder. She heard it plop onto the street. This time she did stop and put on her grey mac. It was as she was buttoning it up that she heard a noise behind her. The echo of footsteps, hardly discernible above the noise of the sudden heavy rain. She turned round. There was a stationary male figure in the shadows with his back to her, hat pulled so low Mairi couldn't see his face. Sizing him up, she wondered why he had stopped. Shrugging, she walked on, but for some reason her senses were on high alert.

Although she was no longer with Jim, she'd been married to a cop long enough to know when something didn't feel right. The loud piercing noise of another police siren penetrated the air and she felt herself jump. A cold shiver passed through her. Frowning, she turned round. The lone figure had disappeared. The alley was empty. She started to walk again, her movement more hurried and purposeful. Having got to the end of the street, instead of turning left to the bus stop, she wrenched the door of the pub open and went inside.

* * *

The phone on Carruthers' desk rang. Brown's voice was on the line. Carruthers pictured the overweight DC with the comb-over. 'Jim, we've just taken a phone call. Don't know how to tell you this–'

'Spit it out. What's with the suspense?' He absentmindedly picked up his empty polystyrene cup, felt its weight, and knowing it was empty, flung it into the bin.

'The caller. It was your ex-wife. The thing is she says she's being followed. I told her we'd get someone out straightaway.'

Carruthers' keen blue eyes widened. 'Who's been sent?'

'Nobody yet.'

'Why not?'

'She's asking for DS Fletcher and Andie's still doing the reconstruction. Shall I say you'll go instead? That'll be an interesting meet-up.'

Instead of getting angry, which he often did rather well, Carruthers tried to think about his ex-wife in a detached manner. Although there were times he'd like to shake or punch Willie Brown, and Dougie Harris, come to that, Carruthers had learned his lesson the hard way. In his first big case in Fife he'd punched his nemesis, Superintendent Alistair McGhee when McGhee had bated him about his ex. Utterly stupid. Carruthers had brought his demotion from DCI on himself. He could see that now. Carruthers stood up and grabbed his coat, wondering how she'd feel about seeing him again. 'Okay, where is she?'

'Inside The Pilgrims Arms, here in Castletown.'

Carruthers hung up and left his desk. As he passed Brown, who was still holding the receiver, presumably about to make another call, the older man said, 'Have you seen her since your break up, your ex-wife?' Carruthers remained silent, knowing that by the time he returned to his desk after his meet-up it would be all over the station that his ex-wife had been on the phone.

Carruthers took the short drive from the outskirts of Castletown to the centre of town. As luck would have it, he found a parking space opposite the pub, cut the engine, jumped out and strode over to The Pilgrims Arms. A couple of students were coming out and Carruthers held the door open for them. He walked into the gloom, letting his eyes adjust before searching for his wife.

He spotted Mairi sitting at a round table by herself near the window. His heart did a somersault. She looked absorbed, staring into the contents of a glass of colourless liquid. He wondered if she still drank slimline tonic. He fought to keep down all the feelings that were threatening to spill over – anger, hurt, confusion and concern. She looked good. Smart and professional. She had her slender legs crossed and her dark hair was shoulder length and loose, longer than he remembered it. How should he play this? He had no idea. There was nothing in the police manual about how to greet your ex-wife.

She saw him, looked puzzled, but recovered and then smiled as she stood up. He was too far away to see if her smile was genuine. He walked across, closing the gap between them, and for a moment it was as if they were still together and just meeting in the pub for a drink. He felt a knife tear into his heart and a loneliness wash over him. Pity it hadn't worked out with Jodie Pettigrew, John Mackie's assistant, he thought. If it had, he probably wouldn't be feeling like this.

Carruthers watched a blush appear up his ex-wife's neck. She clenched and unclenched her hands. 'I was expecting DS Fletcher.' He could see she was trying not to look flustered.

'She's just finishing up a reconstruction at the moment. You'll have to make do with me instead. Is that okay?'

She shook her head as if to chase away whatever dark thoughts she'd had. 'Sorry Jim. I appreciate you coming out. Of course it's okay.'

Good. I would hate to have had a wasted journey. And at least I'm appreciated.

Mairi pointed at her glass. 'Can I get you a sparkling water or something?'

She still remembered he drank sparkling water.

'No, it's okay, thanks. I might get a drink in a minute.'

She sat back down again. *No kiss then.* He followed suit on a chair opposite. *I'm not disappointed she's not kissed me.* As soon as the thought was in his head he pushed it away. Now was not the time to analyse his feelings for his ex.

He looked across the table at her. 'You spoke with Detective Constable Willie Brown on the phone. He says you think you were being followed? Did you see whoever it was?'

Mairi Beattie leant forward, placing both hands on the round table. Carruthers noticed that she wasn't wearing any rings on her fingers. But he was sure he could still see the indentation of where her wedding band had been. Damn. He was struggling to remain professional.

She took a quick sip of her drink and placed it on the coaster in front of her before looking up at Carruthers. 'From a distance, but he had his back to me and was wearing a hat. There's not much I can tell you to be honest. Male, dark-haired. Average height.'

'Are you sure you were being followed?' asked Carruthers.

'It was a feeling I had. More than a feeling. An intuition. I've been the wife of a cop for long enough.'

Carruthers chased the momentary pain away that he felt when she said that. It felt like an arrow going into his heart. His mouth felt dry and scratchy. It must be nerves. He could do with a soft drink after all but didn't want to break the discussion at this point. He swallowed uncomfortably before continuing. 'What did you hear as you were walking?'

'What do you mean?'

'I just wondered if you heard him say anything? Did he try to talk to you?' He remembered what Serena Davis had said. 'Did you hear him whistling?'

'No, I don't think so.' She frowned.

God, even when she was frowning she was lovely. Carruthers cursed silently.

'Your DS Andrea Fletcher came to see me at work. I know about Rachel Abbie's murder. Rachel was one of my students, Jim. What's going on? Did the same person who attacked Serena Davis kill one of my students?'

'At this stage we really don't know. We're trying to keep too many details, the precious few we have that is, from reaching the papers, so anything that I tell you must remain in strictest confidence.' He frowned, thinking briefly about Clare Stott. If she had any sense she would know to keep silent about certain things. Then again, he remembered how hysterical she had been.

He was surprised she was a journalist. He certainly wouldn't have her pegged as one. A stroke of bad luck, that was. He sighed.

Mairi looked up at him, nodding.

'I'm really sorry she was one of your students. Bad enough when there's been a murder but when you know the person…' His voice trailed off. There were tears glistening in his ex-wife's eyes. Damn. She looked like she was going to burst into tears. How would he cope with that?

Her eyes were huge. 'Did she suffer?'

Carruthers thought of the girl's severed finger. Thankfully that had been done post mortem and his ex-wife didn't need to know about that. 'It would have been over very quickly.'

'Shit. I can't believe it.' She bit her lip. Taking a deep breath she once again blinked back tears. Carruthers could see Mairi was trying very hard to compose herself in front of him. *She always did have a caring heart,* he thought. Then a small voice came into his head. *Just didn't care enough for you.* He pushed that last thought out of his mind as quickly as it had entered. This was not the time to be feeling sentimental. Or sorry for himself.

Carruthers leant in. 'How well did you know her – Rachel Abbie?'

Mairi scratched her head. 'As I told DS Fletcher, she was bright, intelligent. Got her work in on time. What more can I tell you? She was one of my students but I didn't socialise with her after work.' Mairi frowned. 'I told DS Fletcher all this. Jim, do we have a serial killer?'

Everyone naturally wants to know if Castletown has its first serial killer, thought Carruthers. He looked at his ex-wife and wondered why she'd really rung the police station. Irrespective of the attacks she wasn't the sort to get spooked.

'Did the man who attacked those girls whistle?'

His ex-wife wasn't stupid and she'd know there was a reason he had asked her if she'd heard whistling.

'Serena Davis, the first girl to get attacked, hasn't been able to give us very much, I'm afraid, in terms of physical description.

I think she's still in shock, although when we last visited her she'd remembered something new. She remembered hearing her assailant whistle just before she got attacked. I must emphasise, please keep this information to yourself. It's not in the public domain yet.' He stared at Mairi. How long had it been since he'd seen her? Three years? *Why did you leave me?* he wanted to shout. *Why were you so cruel that you had to change your number?* He wanted to hate her. He couldn't even have a normal conversation with her without sounding like a stuffed shirt. But he looked at her lovely, oval-shaped face, clear complexion and green eyes and knew that a bit of him still loved her. A big bit.

'You asked me if I had heard whistling?' she prompted.

He forced his mind back to what she was saying.

'Look, the thing is Jim, this isn't the first time I've felt as if I was being followed.'

Carruthers sat up straight. 'How many times?'

She shrugged. 'Two or three. A couple of times when I've left the department and once when I was shopping in Castletown.'

'So it's only when you've been in Castletown you've felt this? Not in Cupar?'

'I'm not in Cupar any more. I've moved to Ceres.'

'Ceres?'

'I'm now in that little cottage we used to like on School Hill. Do you remember it? I was lucky it came on the market.'

Carruthers was taken aback. But then he thought about it. Of course, she'd moved out of her parents. Moving in with them would only ever have been temporary. *To get away from me.* He thought of Ceres – the pretty little village nestling in a glen in Fife a couple of miles south east of Cupar. He wondered if she lived alone.

For some reason Carruthers had the urge to reach out and hold her hand. If for no other reason than to comfort her. He fought the urge and won. He kept his hands resolutely on his lap under the table.

His ex-wife leant into him. 'Do you think it's the same person doing this?'

Carruthers thought of the whistling. 'It may be. We can't be sure yet but we want all women to take extra care until the perpetrator's caught. Try to take the car to work, or if you have to walk anywhere, try not to walk on your own. Also–'

A mobile started to ring in Mairi's bag. She looked at Carruthers apologetically. She dipped into her handbag, looked at the screen and smiled. The noise of the mobile stopped Carruthers in his tracks. He wondered once more if Mairi had a man in her life. An insane shot of jealousy went straight through him. He remembered it had been his jealously that had killed their relationship in the first place. *Of course, she's got a man in her life. She's beautiful. And clever. And caring. And she'd ripped his heart to shreds.* He must stop thinking like this. He met her eyes as she put her phone away.

'Sorry about that,' she said. 'What were you going to say?'

He wasn't going to ask. It really was none of his business any more. Let her have a boyfriend. In fact, let her have several if that's what she wanted. Carruthers tried to harden his heart but it wasn't working.

He took a deep breath. 'I was just going to say that it might be an idea to vary your daily routine. If you always take one route into work make sure the next day you take a different route.' As he said this, he thought about what the latest victim's housemate had said of her when she had been told the body had been found on Greyfriar's Wynd, "that's the short cut Rach always takes." He should also tell the students at Strathburn Halls to vary their routines. He didn't want to worry them unnecessarily, but being less predictable in their routines couldn't hurt.

'Jim, can I just say something to you?'

His thoughts dragged back to the present. Carruthers looked at Mairi and was slightly alarmed to see the searching look on her face. He had no idea what was coming next.

She was staring straight into his eyes with an intensity that burned. 'I'm sorry. I know I hurt you when I left you. And I'm also sorry for changing my phone number and for cutting you off completely.'

Carruthers could feel himself colouring but worked hard – very hard – at making his expression unreadable. *Bet you're not sorry for changing your name back though,* he thought. 'Why did you?'

She shrugged. 'It wasn't easy… leaving you. I wasn't happy. You know that. I still loved you but I had to leave. I needed a fresh start.'

Mairi was still staring at him. Carruthers felt a tightening of his heart and tried to hide the pain in his eyes. He remained silent. Finally, he said, 'It's all water under the bridge now.'

If only. No, he thought, *strangely if I think about it, it still hurts.* And then another thought came into his head. *She loved me even when she left me.*

He looked at her intensely. 'And did you get it? A fresh start?' Their eyes locked.

'In a manner of speaking.' Mairi was the first to look away. She stared at her drink.

What the hell did that mean? Was she with someone new or wasn't she? And why did he even care? But he knew the answer to that one. *How many years is it going to take before I'm over her?* He was starting to regret agreeing to meet up. He should have sent someone else.

'I'm glad I've had this opportunity to see you, Jim. I've felt I owed you an apology. But there is something else. Something I haven't told you.' She leaned in closer to him, crossing one slim leg over the other.

He tried not to look at her ankles.

'I have a student in one of my seminar groups. Male. John Campbell. DS Fletcher met him briefly. He knocked on the door when I was talking to her in my office. There's something about him. I'm concerned about him. I want you to check his background out.'

'Why?' He stifled a yawn. It had been a long day. 'We can't run background checks on just anyone. There has to be a good reason.'

'There is a good reason.' Carruthers watched as his ex-wife spoke. 'He's been bothering me.'

'I'm not sure that's enough.'

'He's in the same tutorial group as Rachel Abbie. It might mean nothing but I have the feeling he'd been bothering her, too.'

Carruthers stood up. 'Before you carry on, I'm just going to get myself a drink. I've got a bit of a tickle in my throat.' He looked over at Mairi's near empty glass. 'Get you another?'

She smiled. 'That would be lovely. Slimline tonic please.'

* * *

Carruthers came back from the bar with a glass of sparkling water for himself and a slimline tonic for Mairi. He took a thirst-quenching gulp. 'Can you be more specific? When you say bothering her?'

'Well, as I said, I don't socialise with them, the students. I mean it's not professional. I'm their lecturer. But there were a couple of occasions when they came into my tutorial groups and Campbell was trying to talk to Rachel and she just cut him dead. It's nothing specific, really. More of a feeling I got, but well, I felt that there was a bit of history between them.'

'And when you say history? You mean sexual?'

'Oh no, nothing like that. Just that Rachel seeing Campbell as a bit of a nuisance wasn't anything new. I overheard her one time telling him to stop texting her. I just got the feeling that perhaps Campbell liked Rachel in a way she didn't like him and that he was coming on a bit strong. I felt there was just a bit of friction between them. But obviously what happened outside my classroom I couldn't comment on.'

'Did you tell DS Fletcher all this?'

Mairi reddened. 'No, I didn't. To be honest, I don't know why I didn't. I might have mentioned that I was concerned about him, but I think I was so shocked when she told me about Rachel's murder that everything that I should have said went out of my head. That's one of the reasons I asked to see her today. To tell her what I've just told you.'

'And when you say you got the feeling he came on a bit strong with Rachel, and her feelings for him weren't the same, is that what happened to you then?'

Mairi hesitated and Carruthers could see she was mulling over how much to tell him. 'Oh no. He's actually threatened me. It was pretty unpleasant.'

'When you say threatened, what exactly do you mean?' Carruthers brought out his little black notebook from his back pocket, flipped it open and searched for a pen in one of his pockets.

* * *

Several hours later Carruthers let himself into his cottage. He was tired and hungry. He'd ended up spending another forty-five minutes with Mairi in the pub, and then had walked her to the bus stop and waited with her until she'd got the bus, before going back to the station. It had felt strange spending time with his ex-wife.

He searched his cupboards and brought out some pasta. He didn't feel like cooking but the Anstruther Fish Bar had already shut and he really shouldn't eat a carry-out two nights in a row. As he was cooking the pasta his phone rang. He picked it up.

It was his brother, Alan. 'Jim, did you get my message?'

He stirred the pasta while cradling the phone under his chin. 'Yes, I did. Sorry, haven't had a chance to ring you back. Work is hectic.'

'Is it okay then? Can I stay?'

Carruthers had to think on his feet. He wracked his brains. He couldn't remember his brother giving him a date. 'Sorry, when is this? When do you want to stay?' Turning the gas down, he left the pasta and walked over to the calendar on the wall. Taking it off the wall he realised he had it on the wrong month. He flipped it over with his free hand. Perhaps his brother wanted to mend some bridges, although by rights it should have been him who made the first move. The guilt returned. He supposed he could spare a few days the following month before he went on holiday. He hoped they would have cracked the case by then.

'Well, to be honest, as soon as possible. Tomorrow?'

Carruthers nearly dropped the calendar. And the phone. 'Why? What's wrong with your own place?'

'I just need to get away for a few days and clear my head. Shouldn't need to be with you longer than a week—'

He replaced the calendar back on the wall. It was time to put his foot down. 'Look, it's really not convenient right now. We're in the middle of a murder investigation and not just a murder investigation, there's been—'

'That's so typical of you, Jim. You haven't changed a bit. You're never willing to put yourself out for anybody else, especially when it's a member of your own family. Mum said you'd be happy to have me stay for a few days.'

Carruthers experienced a quick burst of anger. 'That's not fair. And in ordinary circumstances of course I would be happy to have you stay.' That wasn't strictly true but he wasn't about to say as much. 'But unfortunately, these aren't ordinary circumstances. You may have heard the news. There's been two female students attacked in Castletown.'

There was a pause before his brother spoke. 'Can't say I have.'

Carruthers bristled at his brother's obvious disinterest. Carruthers didn't know whether to believe his brother or not. It would have made headline news around the UK and, let's face it, his brother was only living in Glasgow. It wasn't like he was living in the back of beyond. But then again, when had he ever shown any interest in what Carruthers was doing?

Thinking of far-away destinations, he wondered if they were any closer to contacting Serena Davis's parents. He hoped so. And not just for her sake. If it meant that awful Clare Stott could go home, he'd be a happy man. His mind wandered back to his brother. He wondered if Alan was being churlish. He hoped not.

'So, I can't stay?'

'Look, it's not a good time. I'm working long hours and I'm up to my eyes. And you still haven't told me why you want to. You have a perfectly good home in Glasgow.' Now Carruthers knew he sounded peevish but he was getting frustrated. He glanced at his watch and the pasta was now overcooked. All he wanted to do was finish the call, get something to eat and go to bed.

'So that's a no then?'

Carruthers switched the gas off. 'Look, Alan, give me one good reason why you want to stay. But unless you're prepared to tell me what the reason is at such short notice then yes, it's a "no".'

There was a silence on the other end of the phone.

After a few moments Carruthers couldn't bear the silence a moment longer. Feeling guilty, he asked the question, 'Are you going to tell me what's going on? How's your health? Are the stents working okay? No breathlessness?'

'What do you care? Were you there for me or Mum when we needed you? Like fuck you were. Anyway, you know what?'

'What?' Carruthers couldn't believe the bitterness in his brother's voice and knew he wasn't going to like the rest of the sentence.

'You know it should have happened to you. Not me.'

'What should?'

'The heart attack.' Then the line went dead.

Chapter fourteen

Friday: 9am

'Jim, that student you wanted me to investigate, John Campbell–' Fletcher placed a cup of black coffee in front of Carruthers. She took one look at him. 'Jesus. You look awful. What's up?'

He nodded his thanks. 'Nothing.' He didn't want to tell her about the phone conversation with his brother or the details of the meeting with his ex-wife. Fletcher was always telling him that he should have better contact with his family. Sometimes she acted like his older sister rather than his younger and more junior colleague. It was hard to believe that she was all of ten years younger.

'Did you find anything out about Campbell?' As he asked the question Carruthers pushed all thoughts of his ex-wife and his brother out of his head. It hadn't helped that he'd dreamt about her last night. She'd been shagging his brother of all people and his brother had gone and had a heart attack during coitus. God, dreams were weird. He had woken up in a cold sweat. Thank God it was just a dream.

But when he thought of what his brother had said to him, he flinched. Why was it siblings always knew how to press your buttons? It was almost as if his brother could see into his mind. The same question had gone through Carruthers' head numerous times. Why hadn't it been him that had had the heart attack? Perhaps Alan was right. Perhaps it should have been.

The problem was that when his brother had had his unexpected heart attack Carruthers had felt guilty. Why should the fitter brother have a heart attack? It didn't make sense. There was only a couple of years between them. It hadn't helped that the operation wasn't fully successful. The first lot of stents hadn't worked so in the end his brother had had to have a bypass. But the worst of it was the realisation that his brother blamed him. Blamed and resented him. And that feeling of guilt had stayed with Carruthers. He dragged his mind away from his brother and made a concerted effort to focus on John Campbell.

Fletcher clicked her fingers in front of him. 'Jim. Earth to Jim. God, you're miles away. Sure you're okay?'

'Yes, sorry. What did you want to say?'

'It's about Campbell. He's got form. For assault. Apparently, he broke the collarbone of a fellow student at a previous university. The female student got hospitalised.'

Carruthers' ears pricked up.

'Seems they were both students at the University of East Anglia when the assault occurred,' Fletcher continued. 'Looks like it happened two years ago. Campbell dropped out of his course and left Norwich soon after. But the interesting thing is that the student later withdrew her complaint.'

'Let me see.' Carruthers reached out an open hand and took the printout Fletcher offered him. He ran a troubled eye over it before looking up at Fletcher. 'I wonder if there's a link? Our victims were slashed and throttled, though. The MO isn't the same.'

'I still think he's a person of interest, particularly in light of what Mairi told me about him. And he's in the same tutorial group as Rachel Abbie. We need to talk to him.'

Fletcher nodded. 'I agree. But there's something else. You know how I've been doing some background checks on the housemates who live with Rachel Abbie?'

'Yeah, have you done the last two?'

'Yes. Nothing on Sarah Torr at all to be concerned about. But Davey Munroe is another prospect altogether.'

'Okay, that sounds promising. What have you got?'

'Davey Munroe lives in Canada. His parents moved over when he was ten years old. I thought I could detect a North American accent. The thing is... I've found out both his parents are dead.'

'That's very young to have lost both.'

'Yes, it is, but the interesting thing is that neither died due to natural causes. It appears Davey's mother was known to the police as a domestic abuse victim. Davey and his mother spent some time in a refuge for abused women. She'd left her husband, Davey's father, by then. It appears six months later he may have caught up with her and given her a beating. She died from it.'

'May have?'

'Nothing was proved so he didn't stand trial for it.'

'I see.' Carruthers stroked his stubble. 'You said he'd lost both his parents. How did his father die?'

'Six months later his father's body was found at the foot of the stairs where he lived with his son.'

'Same son?'

'Yep. Looks like Davey was an only child. Father and son were living back together.'

'What age was Davey then?'

'Fifteen.'

'Still a minor, then? What do we think about the fall?'

'Looks like he tripped on the top of the stairs. Suffered a fractured skull. Apparently, the carpet was pretty loose. Davey's dad was going to fix it but he'd never got round to it.'

'So it could have been an accident.' Something struck Carruthers. 'It's very unusual that he was back living with his dad in those circumstances, isn't it?'

Fletcher nodded. 'I'd say so. And it could have been an accident but seems a bit of a coincidence, doesn't it?'

'Okay. Keep digging. And Andie, good work.'

Fletcher's face lit up.

'Have you seen Dougie?'

Fletcher pulled a face. 'No. Did you know his wife is back in hospital?'

'When did this happen?'

'I'm not sure. It was Willie who told me.'

'Shit. What else did Willie say?'

'Dougie is spending every spare hour at her bedside.'

It was hard to believe the tough, no-nonsense throwback to the seventies cop was such a devoted and loyal husband. It just showed you should never judge by appearances, or even behaviour, come to that. Carruthers had to grudgingly admit that there was clearly more to Dougie Harris than met the eye.

'Jim?'

Carruthers looked down at Fletcher.

'You don't have to answer this, but I just wondered how you felt seeing your ex-wife again?'

As fond as he was of Andie, if she had one big failing it was that she was too nosey by half. He stood up. It was the best way to break the conversation and he could do with getting himself a drink of water. 'You're right. I don't have to answer that, and to be honest I don't really want to talk about it. Not at the moment anyway.'

Fletcher pulled a face. 'Fair enough. Just out of interest, how are you finding our new DCI?'

Carruthers thought about it for a moment. 'I haven't made my mind up yet. It's hard to be objective when she's doing the job I should still have.'

'Can't be easy.'

'It isn't. But then again, I only have myself to blame. I can see that now.'

'Jim, can you spare me for an hour?'

'What for?'

Fletcher lowered her head. 'I've needed to bring forward my counselling session. Alison Gray can fit me in but only at 3pm today.'

'Are you okay?'

Fletcher nodded but remained unsmiling. Carruthers wasn't convinced.

'You know I support you one hundred per cent, Andie. It's difficult to give you time off in the middle of a murder investigation but I know you wouldn't ask for it if you didn't need it.'

'It's just for an hour.'

'Go for it. I'll clear it with McTavish. And if you want to talk, I'm here for you. Any time.'

* * *

Fletcher fidgeted in her chair. She finally made eye contact with Alison Gray.

The counsellor smiled before she spoke. 'So why do you think you're suffering from depression again?'

Fletcher was sitting perched on the edge of her seat. She felt like bolting. It had taken nerve to make the appointment. 'That's why I've come to you. So you can tell me. It just seems to have come out of the blue.'

A mobile rang, the noise coming from Alison Gray's handbag. The ringtone was of a baby gurgling with laughter. Fletcher looked at Alison who had gone red and at least had the decency to look embarrassed. 'Sorry,' she said. 'Thought it was on silent. That's my granddaughter.'

Fletcher swallowed the lump in her throat. Tears pricked her eyes. Even this nondescript plain-looking counsellor had bloody children. Or at least one child. And grandkids. Life just wasn't fair.

Alison took a long, hard look at Fletcher. 'You're thinking how unfair life is that I have kids and grandkids, aren't you?'

Christ, thought Fletcher. *This woman is a mind reader.* She then felt guilty at the unkind thoughts that had been going through her head.

Alison gave Fletcher an encouraging smile. 'Tell me how you've been feeling.'

'I'm okay, unless it's a really sunny, warm day. I used to love the sun and heat. But now–'

'Yes?'

'Now I hate it.'

'Can you explain why?'

'Well, it brings the families out. The kids. And happy parents. I can't stand it. It feels like it's being thrown in my face. It reminds me of the family life I'm never going to have. I know I'm being over-sensitive but that doesn't seem to help. I just want to run away and hide.'

'But you don't?'

'No, I don't. I've got a job to do.'

'And I know how important your work is to you.'

'Yes, it's the only place I feel I can really make a difference. When I'm at work I feel as if I belong.'

'And the rest of the time?'

Fletcher shrugged. 'Sometimes I'm okay.' She felt tears prick her eyes once more. She had never seen herself as an overly emotional person before, but now? Everything had changed since she had had her miscarriage.

'And at other times?' Alison reached over and pulled a tissue out of the box and handed it to Fletcher.

Fletcher dabbed the corners of her eyes. 'Other times I'm not. I was wondering if I'm suffering from spring depression. I googled it and it exists.'

'Yes, it does exist, although it's not so well known about. Perhaps you should go back to your GP? Get a proper diagnosis?'

Fletcher shrugged.

'It's going to take time to get over the shock and pain of what happened.'

Fletcher folded her hands in her lap. 'You going to tell me time is a healer?'

Alison smiled. 'It's true. Time is a healer. It'll never go away. Not totally. But the pain will lessen. You're still young.'

'Meaning I can still have a family?'

'If you want to.'

'That's the problem though, Alison. I can't. I can't have a family. I'm never going to be a mum. When I had my miscarriage, the medics told me they were really surprised I'd managed to carry as long as I did. I've been told I'm very unlikely to be able to carry to full term. You're the first person I've told. I haven't been able to face talking about it. Not even my parents know. I just have to be strong and deal with it.'

Alison's face tilted towards her; a sad look in her eyes. 'Are there any friends you can confide in about how you're feeling?'

Were there? When she'd joined the police force she'd lost touch with a lot of her friends, and since she'd been in CID, well, when was there time to socialise? Fletcher thought about the close working relationship she had with Carruthers but somehow, she didn't want to confide in him. At least not yet. Briefly her thoughts turned to her boss. And in that moment, she understood why he didn't want to open up about how he felt about seeing his ex-wife again. Some things were just too raw. Too painful. In that instant she realised something about her boss. He still loved his ex-wife.

Chapter fifteen

'We've finally managed to unlock Rachel Abbie's phone.' Fletcher walked over to Carruthers' desk. 'The good news is that she wasn't great at deleting messages or texts. There are scores of them. No details yet but we've got Speccie Tecchie on the case,' she said, referring to their resident IT expert, John Forrest.

'That's great news, Andie. I've got a feeling that what's found on her phone could be important to the case.'

'Let's hope so.'

'You seem a bit brighter. Did it help going to the counsellor?'

'Do you know, I think it did. I think it's something to do with talking to someone who doesn't know you and won't judge. It's like, well, a weight off your chest.' She smiled.

'You can always talk to me, you know,' said Carruthers. He felt a moment of sadness that he could offer a heart-to-heart to Fletcher so much more easily than to his own brother.

Carruthers stood up and grabbed his jacket. Fletcher looked up at him questioningly.

'I'm heading across town. I think it's high time I had a chat with John Campbell.'

'Ooh, do you want me to come with you?'

'No, no,' Carruthers answered hurriedly. The last thing he wanted was an audience when he talked to Campbell about his ex-wife.

'Okay, well in that case I'll stick around here. I'm interested to see what Forrest uncovers. I'll ring you if we find anything.'

* * *

Carruthers stood waiting for John Campbell outside the philosophy department, breathing in the salty sea air. As he waited, he looked at the gothic building with its two blue doors. It took him back to the early days of courting Mairi. Hanging around outside her department like a lovesick puppy. He thought of the girlfriend of the dead squaddie he had met on a previous case. Siobhan Mathews had also studied philosophy. She had reminded him of his wife. He wondered where she was now.

Suddenly the doors of the department opened and a knot of students burst out chattering. Carruthers spotted John Campbell immediately. Tall, dark-haired, broad-shouldered.

'Mr Campbell?' Carruthers started to walk towards the group. The students had separated, going in different directions, leaving Campbell alone looking at his iPhone.

The student looked up, frowning. 'Yes?'

'I'd like a word. Please.' Carruthers brought out his police ID badge and flashed it in front of the startled student's face.

'What's this about?'

Carruthers sized Campbell up, noting his unreachable blue eyes and thin mouth. He knew the lad had form but could he see him as The Student Strangler, as the papers had called the murderer? He wasn't so sure.

'I need to have a bit of a talk with you.' Carruthers gestured for Campbell to follow him to a bench across the road from the philosophy department. It was the same bench that Carruthers used to sit on to wait for Mairi to finish her lecturing.

'We've received a complaint from a member of the public to say you've been harassing her.'

Campbell turned beet red but said nothing.

He knows what I'm talking about, thought Carruthers, *and he knows he's in the wrong.*

'Who?' said Campbell, sitting on the bench and splaying his legs.

'Have you been harassing more than one woman?'

'I haven't been harassing anyone. Who's the complaint come from?'

'My–' God, he'd nearly said ex-wife. Carruthers corrected himself in his momentary error. 'My information is that you've been pestering one of your professors – Mairi Beattie.' He almost stumbled over the surname. He was so used to thinking of her as Carruthers.

'No.'

Carruthers looked at Campbell's face. The expression on it was unreadable.

'In fact, she says that you've threatened her.'

'That's not true.'

'Perhaps you'd like to tell me what's been going on.'

Silence.

'Can I ask you where you were between one-thirty and three-thirty Tuesday afternoon and between ten and twelve last Friday?'

'You talking about those women who got attacked? You're not going to pin that on me just because–'

'Because you've got prior form you mean, or because you've threatened your philosophy lecturer?' finished Carruthers. 'I've seen your record, John. I know you assaulted a female student at the University of East Anglia. You broke her collarbone.'

'That's not how it happened. We were horsing around. You make it sound like I'm some sort of nutter.'

'And you're not, of course. She made a complaint?'

'Which she later withdrew.'

'So, you're sticking to your story of it being a bit of horseplay that got out of hand. I've never broken someone's collarbone in a bit of horseplay. If she made a complaint against you then she didn't see it as a bit of fun.'

A moment of doubt entered Carruthers' head but he didn't voice it. It *was* possible that a bit of horseplay *could* result in a broken collarbone. His mind went back to an incident that had occurred on the football pitch when he was at school. A player had broken the collarbone of a teammate while celebrating his friend's goal. However, if it had really been the case of just a bit of horseplay, why would the female student in question report it? No, the simple truth of the matter was Carruthers just didn't believe Campbell, although he would like to get to the bottom of why the young woman had withdrawn her complaint. For that there was one obvious answer.

'Like I said, she withdrew her complaint.'

'Threaten her, did you?'

Carruthers observed Campbell as he got out a packet of Marlboro from his jacket pocket. The student took a lighter out of his jeans pocket and lit the cigarette. The only sign that he was rattled was that he was sucking on the cigarette in short bursts.

'Let's start with your philosophy lecturer, Mairi Beattie,' said Carruthers. He winced as he said her maiden name. 'Why would she accuse you of threatening her?'

The boy went red. Still staring at his shoes, he said, 'So the complaint came from her.'

'You've got a crush on her.'

Why on earth does this twerp think he has a chance with Mairi? She is totally out of his league. And he is, well, still a boy, really.

Not for the first time Carruthers wondered whether Mairi was seeing someone. Had she dated since she'd left him? She must have done. It had been over three years. Carruthers felt a stab of jealousy somewhere in the region of his heart. Not good. Not for the first time he found himself wishing she'd never got in touch with the police.

'It's more than a crush.'

God, he's got it bad, thought Carruthers. 'So, when she turned you down you got angry?'

The student whipped his head up, swivelled round and stared Carruthers straight in the eye. 'She didn't turn me down. She said yes.'

Carruthers was incredulous. 'So, you're telling me you've been having a relationship with Mairi Beattie?'

'Yes, and she's spoken about you, you know. I know you used to be married to her.' It was Carruthers' turn to redden. The wee scrote could have found that information out from anywhere, but still, it was worth mentally noting that he'd gone to the trouble of finding out about Mairi's exes. John Campbell had a nasty smile on his face. 'She said she couldn't wait for the divorce to come through and to get her maiden name back.'

The wee prick. He's enjoying this. *Why the hell would my ex-wife be interested in a waste of space like you?* thought Carruthers. But a little warning voice in his head asked him how the student knew so much about his ex-wife.

'You don't believe me, do you?' He moved closer to Carruthers. The detective could smell his smoker's breath. 'I've got proof.'

'What proof?'

'That I've been having a relationship with your ex-wife. I've seen the birthmark she's got on her left buttock. Now how would I know that unless I had seen her naked?'

Carruthers thought of the last time he'd seen the birthmark. It was a long time ago now. He looked at Campbell through narrowed eyes. He knew the boy was lying. He had to be. There was no way Mairi would have an affair with one of her students, least of all a nasty piece of work like John Campbell. The boy was clearly a fantasist. There must be some other explanation of how he knew of her intimate birthmark.

'Do you know Rachel Abbie?'

Campbell looked confused. 'Not personally, no. I mean, I know her in passing. We're in the same department and the same tutorial group but we're not friends.'

'If you're in the same tutorial group you obviously know her a bit more than just in passing.'

The student shrugged.

'Have you ever met up socially?'

Campbell shook his head. 'No.'

Carruthers stood up. 'I'll be in touch. And John?' Campbell looked up. Carruthers leaned in to him and hissed, 'Leave my ex-wife alone.'

'Or what?'

Carruthers didn't dignify that with an answer. Instead, he looked skywards as the rain came on.

* * *

Fletcher looked up as Carruthers marched into the office and stood by the side of her desk. 'What are you doing at the moment, Andie? Any joy on Rachel Abbie's mobile phone front?'

'Still waiting for John Forrest to get back to me. I'm currently trying to find out if there's a link between the two girls. I can't yet find anything that connects them though. Rachel was studying philosophy and Serena history of art. We've started to interview friends of the girls but it doesn't look like they did know each other.'

He leant over her desk. 'Do something for me? Get hold of the mobile number of that wee scrote from the philosophy department, John Campbell, and check it against the numbers on Rachel Abbie's phone.'

'What's got you so riled? Bad interview?'

How Fletcher would love to know what John Campbell had been insinuating about his ex-wife. But there was no way in hell he was going to tell her. What would she make of Campbell knowing about Mairi's birthmark? And he still didn't understand how the boy could know about it. It's not like his ex-wife would tell him. He could just see it now. 'Okay, so today we are going to talk about the pre-Socratic philosophers and by the way, I have a birthmark on my left buttock.'

The point was though, how the hell *did* he know about it? All sorts of thoughts were racing through his head. None of them good. In the end he concluded that the most likely scenario was that somehow Campbell had seen his ex-wife naked in the shower.

And unless he was in there with her, which frankly was laughable, then he had been stalking her and knew where she lived.

He looked Fletcher square in the eyes before answering. 'I don't trust Campbell.'

* * *

Mairi let herself into her flat in Ceres, thinking about her meeting with Jim. She hesitated at the door then locked it behind her. She put her back against the doorframe and expelled a long, deep breath. When she closed her eyes, she could still see Jim's face. He looked the same. Well, no, that wasn't quite true. Same blue eyes, same shaped face. Perhaps he'd put on a little bit of weight. His hair was slightly greyer and he had a few more wrinkles, but he suited them. She had to admit he had been looking good. She'd worked hard at putting her relationship with Jim behind her, had even started dating other men, but she'd never managed to totally get him out of her head.

She walked to the living room window, looked out and, seeing nothing but her neighbour, Malcolm, working in his garden, pulled the net curtain tightly shut. She took the stairs to her bedroom but just as she was about to dump her shoulder bag on her bed, she pulled up short. There on her pillow was a single, long-stemmed red rose. Her breath caught in her throat. Somebody had been in her bedroom.

Rooted to the spot, she looked around her. Nothing else looked out of place and yet, what was that? A cigarette butt had been stubbed out on a glazed ceramic dish she kept for her earrings on her bedside table. She sniffed the air suspiciously. Yes, there was a faint smell of cigarette smoke which she hadn't noticed when she'd first set foot in the room. She strained to hear any noise but the only sound, other than birdsong, was Malcolm's voice as he talked to his wife. Mairi ran down the stairs to the back door but it was still locked securely. Had she left a window open? Is that how the intruder had got in? She went in and out of all the rooms but when she walked into the bathroom, she found the window ajar. She didn't remember leaving it open but she must have done.

She cursed under her breath and ran down the stairs to the front door which she unlocked and opened. She popped her head round.

'Malcolm?' she called.

Malcolm Duggan, who was leaning over his flowerbed, straightened up and turned round, smiling. Seeing her face, he frowned. 'What's wrong, hen?'

'I think someone's been in my house. Have you seen anyone hanging around?'

Malcolm leaned heavily on his hoe and shook his head. 'No, I havenae. Have you been broken into?'

'I think they may have got in through the bathroom window. Looks like I might have left it open when I left the house this morning. But they don't seem to have taken anything. Someone's definitely been in though.' She kept quiet about the long-stemmed rose. It just seemed too weird to mention.

Malcolm laid the hoe down and hobbled over. 'Do you want me to come and look round the house for you or call the police?'

Did she? And did she really want the police involved? Who could have been in the house? Could it be John Campbell? It didn't really seem his style leaving roses on pillows.

'No Malcolm, thanks, but that won't be necessary. I'll phone the police myself.'

'If you're sure, hen, but I'd be happy to help.'

'No, thank you all the same.' Mairi turned away from him and hurried inside to make the call.

Chapter sixteen

Saturday

Carruthers checked his watch. Mairi was late. He started to strum his fingers on the table in impatience. He only had an hour before he needed to be heading back to the station.

Had he made a mistake by agreeing to meet up? He'd offered to go round to her house last night, but she'd insisted she was okay, so they had agreed to meet the following morning. In all actuality it wasn't his place as a member of CID to attend a break-in, but then again, he wanted to talk to her about John Campbell and the boy's accusations, and it was more than likely she felt the break-in was connected to her recent claims of being followed.

He checked his watch again just as there was a rush of cold air. The front door of the pub opened and in walked his ex-wife. She had insisted on meeting here rather than at her home. Carruthers didn't want to start analysing why. She had been adamant. It would, of course, make more sense to meet at her home but if that's what she wanted… She came hurrying over to his table, dumping her briefcase on the floor by his feet. He recognised it straightaway. It was the expensive slim, black briefcase he'd given her for her thirty-eighth birthday.

'Thank you for meeting me, Jim.'

'What have the police said?' He looked at her flushed face and the anxiety in her eyes. His own heart started to race. He'd heard somewhere that stress was contagious and he could well believe it. He could always read Mairi like a book, well, until towards the end of their relationship, and taking one look at her now he knew she was genuinely troubled.

'Well, I have been broken into. Perhaps not so much broken into but someone's definitely been in my house. I think they must have got in through the bathroom window. I'm sure I locked it when I left the house but when I got back and examined the window it was ajar.'

'Did they make a mess? Take anything?'

'No, that's just it. I wouldn't have known anyone had been in the house except when I walked into the bedroom. Whoever it was left a red rose on my pillow. To be honest, it's freaked me out.'

Carruthers leant forward. Mairi's hand was resting on the table. He forced himself not to cover her hand with his. Once more, he kept his hands resolutely down by his side.

'Do you think it was your student, John Campbell?'

'I don't know, Jim. I really don't know. At first I didn't think it was his style but now—'

'What's changed?'

'I've been thinking about it. I don't get the impression he's a romantic. I wouldn't have thought leaving a rose was his style but—'

Carruthers called to mind the little he knew about John Campbell. It was enough. 'Perhaps not a romantic, but I could imagine he's the sort of guy who would be happy to mess with your head.'

'Yes, I think he's probably quite a manipulative person.'

Carruthers' eyes locked onto Mairi's. 'He's been a bit more than manipulative. Your John Campbell is a nasty piece of work. Keep away from him.'

'What do you mean? It's a bit hard to keep away from him when I'm his tutor. And don't call him *my* John Campbell.'

'Sorry. Look, you might as well know I've met him.'

Mairi's mouth dropped open and she looked aghast. 'When?'

'I waited outside the department for him and we had a talk.'

Incredulity turned to fury as she unleashed her temper on him. 'Oh, for God's sake. Why did you do that? You've just gone and made things ten times worse.'

'I warned him to stay away from you outside class.' He studied Mairi closely. It was obvious she was furious.

'Well if he's the one who's been in my house then it's not worked, has it? And anyway, since when do I need you to fight my battles for me?'

Now it was Carruthers' turn to feel angry. Angry and hurt. 'Well you clearly do, otherwise why did you ask to see me? I could have sent Fletcher or Watson to interview you.'

Carruthers could see two spots of colour on his ex-wife's cheeks. Perhaps his talk with Campbell hadn't been such a good idea after all. But then again, if he hadn't had the chat, he'd never have known the boy was a fantasist. 'I think you should know what John Campbell is saying about you–'

'Well, go on. You can't leave the conversation like that. Spit it out. What *has* he been saying?'

'He's claiming you've been sleeping together.' Now it was Carruthers' turn to go red. 'He knows about the beauty spot on your left buttock. How would he know about that?' As he said this he watched his ex-wife's reactions carefully.

She was clearly speechless. Apart from the two red spots of colour on her cheeks there was a vein pulsing in her neck.

'Is there any truth in it? You haven't slept with him, have you?'

She picked up her briefcase and stood up. There was a glint of tears in her eyes. 'For God's sake, I can't believe you're even asking me this. I would have thought you'd know me well enough to know I would never sleep with a student. Especially him. And if I say I haven't then I haven't. But then again, you never did trust me, did you?'

Carruthers winced at the barbed comment. It pained him to be forced to think back to that dreadful time when he'd virtually accused Mairi of having an affair with Superintendent Alistair McGhee. Soon after that she'd left him, telling him that she could no longer live with his jealousy. He hadn't even realised he'd been the jealous type, but he could see it now – see the fact that the marriage breakdown had been his fault. 'I'm sorry, Mairi. Don't go. We need to talk about Campbell. I'm afraid there's more.'

Reluctantly, she sat back down again. 'I'm sorry, Jim. I didn't mean to bring up the past like that. It wasn't fair of me. What else has Campbell been saying? He's lying by the way.' She looked away from him as she hurriedly wiped the back of her hand over her eyes.

'I know he is.' This time Carruthers covered her small, cold hand with his larger one. He squeezed it before she withdrew it. He was left with his hand rather awkwardly extended on the table.

'It's not about you. It's about him. Mairi, did you know that before he became a student at the University of the East of Scotland he was at UEA?'

'No. Why did he leave?'

Carruthers paused.

'I'm not going to like the answer to this, am I?'

'Truthfully? No. I did some digging on him. He was asked to leave. He'd assaulted a fellow student.'

'Female?'

'I'm afraid so.'

She covered her mouth with her hand. 'Oh my God. How bad?'

'He broke her collarbone. She later withdrew the charge of assault. He's clearly violent, but in all honesty, I don't think he's behind Rachel Abbie's murder. It's not the same MO, is it?'

'I suppose not.' Mairi looked miserable.

'However, I'm going to find something that gives me a chance to bring him in for questioning. Is there anything at all I can use to strengthen my case?'

She dipped her head down. 'There is one thing, Jim. Whoever managed to get into my house and left the rose, left something else.'

She produced a plastic food bag from her briefcase. It contained a cigarette butt. 'He was stupid enough to smoke a fag in my bedroom. I haven't touched it. Handled it wearing gloves.'

'I always said you'd make an excellent detective. John Campbell does smoke,' said Carruthers, recalling how Campbell had lit up outside the department. 'But would he be stupid enough to leave his DNA all over a cigarette butt?'

'He's cocky enough to, but stupid? I didn't have him down as stupid.'

Carruthers wondered what the time was. He glanced at his watch. His life seemed to be governed by its two hands at the moment. He stood up. 'Mairi, I'm sorry. I've got to go. The advice I'm going to give you is to have minimal contact with Campbell. Try to ensure you're not alone when you leave the department and don't ever get into a situation when you are alone with him. I'm going to do some more digging and I'll be in touch.' He put the plastic bag containing the cigarette butt into his trouser pocket.

Mairi stood up and, rather awkwardly, he bent his head forward and kissed her on the cheek. The warmth of her skin infused his whole body and his nerve endings quivered. As he walked out of the pub, at the very last minute, he glanced behind him. She was still looking at him.

* * *

'Helen, can you get this sent to the lab for me? And analysed as fast as possible?' Carruthers handed over the bag containing the cigarette butt to Helen Lennox that Mairi had found at her home. He was convinced the results would be a match for Campbell's DNA if only they could get a copy of it. Carruthers remembered how Campbell had idly flicked his cigarette butt onto the ground the day before. Highly likely it was still there by the bench but it had started to rain as he'd walked away. He also knew that if the charges had been dropped by the young woman who had accused Campbell of assault, even if Campbell's DNA had been taken, it would have now been destroyed. But still, you just never knew what might be on the database.

'Jim, I've got something,' said Fletcher, walking up to Carruthers' desk. 'We've managed to unlock Rachel's mobile. Looks like John Campbell had been pestering Rachel Abbie. There are about thirty phone calls from his mobile number and only one call from her to him. What's the betting she called him to tell him to leave her alone? And there are literally scores of text messages from him. I'm asking for a printout of them all as Forrest told me the messages become increasingly desperate and threatening. Have we got enough to bring him in?'

Carruthers felt like punching the air. 'We better do this by the book. I'll speak to Sandra. Reckon we've got enough to bring him to the station but I want to be the one to conduct the interview. What I don't understand is why none of Rachel's housemates said anything?'

'Perhaps they didn't know.'

'Why wouldn't they, though? Surely she'd have told Will? And if he knew about it, he would have told us. It doesn't make sense.'

'I can't answer that but you're right. It's a bit of a mystery.'

'I think we need to talk to Will again. But we also need to formally interview John Campbell.'

Fletcher smiled. 'Knew you'd say that.'

'When we do get him in for interview, I want you to take Gayle and go to his student accommodation. Interview the other students who live with him. Find out what he's like and what his housemates think of him. Have a dig about if you can. I'm going to put in for a search warrant. I want you to search his room. And do it thoroughly.'

Fletcher put on a face of mock outrage. 'Do I ever search a room any other way? You think he's done it?'

'At the moment he's our best bet. He's got previous for assault on a female student; he not only knew one of the victims, but had been sending her threatening messages, and on top of that he's been pestering one of his philosophy lecturers.'

'Oh, is this Mairi you're talking about? That would explain why she was so jumpy when I was interviewing her. It's interesting that she told you but she didn't want to tell me. I'd tread carefully there if I were you.'

Carruthers ignored that comment. 'Apparently, she meant to say something to you but I think she was in too much of a shock at Rachel Abbie's murder. I would really like to get hold of Campbell's mobile and see if he's been sending Serena Davis any messages.'

'Easiest thing is if we ask Serena.'

Carruthers nodded. 'Well, let's talk to Campbell first. He's lied to us about how well he knew Rachel Abbie. I want him in for interview.'

* * *

Carruthers pulled up outside John Campbell's residence. A young man was just coming out of the front door. As luck would have it, it was Campbell himself. Carruthers got out of the car smartly, locked it with a beep of his car key and strode over to the student.

'Christ, what is it now? This is tantamount to police harassment.'

Carruthers ignored that. 'I'd like to ask you if you're willing to provide a DNA sample?'

Campbell stopped short. 'Why would you want that?'

'We want to be able to rule you out of our investigation.'

'I don't have to give you one, do I?'

'No. But it would look much better for you if you complied with our request and did it voluntarily. Castletown's not a huge place and we'll be taking everyone's in due course. Then you won't have an option. Much better if you cooperate with us now.' Carruthers waited with bated breath, interested to see how Campbell would respond.

'No.'

'You're refusing?'

'I am.'

'Well, in that case I'm going to invite you down to the station for questioning.'

Campbell started walking away. 'You've got to be joking.'

'Let's just say you've become a person of interest.' Carruthers matched his stride to that of the younger man. 'You've got previous form for violence against women; you're currently harassing your philosophy lecturer and the IT department have just managed to unlock the mobile of Rachel Abbie and what do you think they've found? Dozens of threatening texts from you. That, in my books, makes you our number one suspect.'

* * *

Carruthers was standing opposite DCI Sandra McTavish in his old office. Since he'd last set foot in it, she'd brought in a couple of enormous potted plants which were either side of the window. *When had she had the time to do that,* he wondered?

'I've put Campbell in interview room one, Sandra. Thought he could sweat for a bit.'

'I certainly agree that we have enough to bring him in and question him, but I don't want you to conduct the interview, Jim. I'll do it myself. He's been asked if he wants a solicitor present and he's declined. I'm curious as to the reason why.'

Carruthers opened his mouth, but before he had a chance to say anything his new boss silenced him with a hand. Her voice was gentler, quieter, but it's what she said that cut deep. 'You have a conflict of interest, Jim.'

Was that a *pitying* look she gave him? God, he hoped not. For all that he was a police officer he'd never been great at reading women.

'I understand this John Campbell has threatened your ex-wife, Mairi Beattie. That, in my books, makes it a conflict of interest.'

How the hell does she know about that? Who would have told her? Certainly not Fletcher or Watson. Surely Dougie Harris was too caught up worrying about his ill wife. It had to be that weasel Willie Brown. He remembered the way the man had been smirking when he'd told Carruthers he'd had the DI's ex-wife on the phone.

He looked at the pursed lips of McTavish and this time had no problem reading her body language. And she was right. It *had* become personal. He was itching to have a go at Campbell and wipe the smirk off his face. He tried a different tack. 'I've dispatched Fletcher to Campbell's residence. The search warrant got fast-tracked.'

'Good. Bingham will be pleased to see you've gone through the right channels.'

Carruthers wondered how much Superintendent Bingham had told McTavish about his previous unorthodox methods. Whatever he had said, McTavish should surely know he wasn't unprofessional enough to jeopardise any case that they might be able to build against Campbell. He bit his lip. He looked up to see McTavish watching him.

She was looking him straight in the eye. 'You don't think he did it, though. Do you?'

Carruthers let out a sigh and shook his head. 'Well, I have no doubt he's threatened both Mairi and Rachel. We have his texts on Rachel's phone to prove it. He's clearly got previous form for violence towards women. I also think he's a fantasist.' As he said that he thought of Campbell's claim that he had slept with his ex-wife.

McTavish's voice was insistent. 'But you don't think he's a murderer.'

He expelled a quick breath and raised his eyebrows. 'I can't see it. Look, I know you think I'm too close to the case, but Mairi is my ex-wife and there's been no contact for several years. I would really like to be the one to conduct the interview.'

'I'm sorry Jim, I can't allow you to do that. Anyway,' she twisted her wedding ring around her finger, 'I'd quite like to have a crack at him myself. I think being interviewed by a woman will bring a different dynamic to it, especially if he has an issue with "the fairer sex". If he has a problem with women, as I suspect he might, he may just give himself away.'

Carruthers didn't like it but he could see the logic in his DCI's thinking. She stood up, grabbed a file and her mobile and walked towards the office door. He followed her out of the office, shutting the door behind him. She threw her next comment over her shoulder at him as she walked towards the interview room, Carruthers hot on her heels. 'If it helps, you can listen in to the interview.'

Oh, I intend to, thought Carruthers. *I want to watch Campbell's every move.*

Chapter seventeen

'Do you know why you're at the station, Mr Campbell?' Carruthers watched intently through the glass as DCI Sandra McTavish started her interview.

Campbell sat back on his chair, hands behind his head. 'No idea.'

First lie, thought Carruthers, disgusted.

Campbell's chin jutted out in an arrogant fashion. 'Am I being arrested?'

McTavish crossed her legs. 'No. You're not being arrested. You are merely helping us with our enquiries.'

The student looked McTavish up and down. 'Nice legs.'

Frowning, McTavish uncrossed her legs and placed them under the chair. She sat bolt upright.

Carruthers watched, fascinated. Just how would she conduct this interview?

She shuffled her notes. 'Now–'

Carruthers saw Campbell smile. *What did he have to smile about?*

'I want to make a complaint.'

'What?'

'Against Inspector Jim Carruthers.'

'What on earth for?'

'Harassment. And I want it on file.'

Carruthers, clenching his fists, turned away from the glass. 'Fuck,' adding under his breath, 'little prick.'

If McTavish was blindsided by Campbell, she didn't show it.

'All in good time, John. Your complaint will go through the proper channels. And if Inspector Carruthers has been hassling you then I can assure you it will be dealt with properly through the Police Ombudsman. First, let's talk about the reason you're in the interview room.' She dug into her handbag and brought out a black mobile phone, which she slid across the table towards him.

Campbell shrugged. Carruthers watched him through the glass. It was pretty obvious Campbell was one of these guys that liked to be in control, even of a police interview. He wondered how the student would behave if he lost all semblance of control.

McTavish's voice took on a steely quality. 'That's Rachel Abbie's mobile. I want to know why there are over fifty nuisance texts from you on it.'

Silence.

'I understand you've also been threatening Mairi Beattie?'

Staring straight into McTavish's eyes unflinchingly, Campbell said, 'We're having a relationship.'

'That's not what she says.'

'Well, she wouldn't, would she? I mean, you're not supposed to sleep with your students. Won't she get struck off or something?'

Carruthers swore under his breath again. He could sense the power struggle going on in the interview room. He felt the tension building. *Gallant to the last.* In one fell swoop Campbell had got both Carruthers and his ex-wife into trouble. The interview hadn't started well. All Carruthers could hope for was that Campbell would slip up and lose his cool. He wanted to know why the boy was being so cocky. And why had he refused a solicitor? Most suspects brought in for interview were nervous, defensive even. Not John Campbell though. Something didn't add up.

McTavish leant forward, maintaining eye contact with Campbell, her face unsmiling. 'Where were you between one-thirty and three-thirty Tuesday afternoon?'

'Why you asking? This the time Rachel Abbie got killed?'

'Murdered. Yes. Are you going to answer the question or are you going to answer every question with another question? If so, this is going to be a long and tedious interview.'

'I don't have classes between one-thirty and three-thirty on a Tuesday so I guess I was at home studying.'

'You guess? Can anyone vouch for you?'

Campbell shook his head. 'I don't think anyone was at home. Frances, my housemate, came back at about four. We had a cup of tea together then I went out to rugby practice at five.'

Carruthers put his hand against the glass. Mackie had said that Rachel Abbie had been killed within the hour and her body had been found at three-forty. Campbell could have killed her and been home for four o'clock. All he could think of was that John Campbell had no alibi.

* * *

Fletcher pulled up in the car park of Campbell's residence. Unusually for Castletown it was a new build.

They both got out of Fletcher's green Beetle and shut the car doors. She caught Watson looking up at the building. The older woman whistled. 'You really telling me this is student accommodation? Obviously high end.'

Fletcher laughed. 'Looks more like a modern stately home, doesn't it?'

'Right, number 82,' said Watson. She yawned. 'I hope we catch this maniac fast. It's wrecking my social life.'

Fletcher wondered about Gayle Watson's private life. She was even more reluctant to discuss it than Carruthers was to discuss his. Fletcher wondered if Watson had a partner in her life.

'Have you got a partner, Gayle?' Before she knew it, the words were out.

Watson turned to Fletcher, frowning. 'I have, yes. Why?'

'Oh, I just wondered, that's all. It's just you don't say very much about them.' Fletcher worked hard to keep her language gender neutral.

'I like to keep my work and personal life separate.'

'That's understandable. Look at the gossip doing the rounds about Jim at the moment. His ex-wife's back on the scene.'

'I had heard.'

'Can't be bloody easy. Apparently, Sandra won't let him conduct the interview with Campbell. She's citing a conflict of interest. He's fizzing.'

'Well, there *is* a conflict of interest. C'mon. Let's get on with this. We don't know how long he'll be at the station for.'

Disappointed she still hadn't found anything out about her colleague's private life, Fletcher followed Gayle up to the building and watched her press the bell.

A studious-looking teenager opened the door, her blonde hair in plaits. 'Can I help you?'

'Do you have a housemate called John Campbell?'

The girl nodded. 'Yes, what's this about?'

The police officers took out their ID cards and showed the student. 'We need to come in and conduct a search of his room,' said Gayle.

The young woman looked at them both in turn. She didn't look too happy. 'He won't like that. He doesn't let anyone go into his room. He keeps it locked.'

'Where does your landlord live?' Fletcher knew he or she would most likely keep a spare set of keys.

'Glasgow.'

Not such a viable idea to get them to open the door. They couldn't afford to wait while the landlord came through from Glasgow. How interesting, thought Fletcher, that John Campbell never let anyone inside his room. *What has he got to hide?* 'Can we come in please?'

'Yes, of course. My name's Frances, by the way.' She showed them down a long hall which had doors on each side. She stopped outside one. It was the only door that was closed.

'This John Campbell's room?'

The girl nodded.

'You've never been in his room?'

'God no.' The girl looked appalled at the mere thought.

'Does he have a girlfriend?'

The girl looked a bit cagey. 'I don't know.'

Watson raised an eyebrow. 'You don't know if he has a girlfriend?'

'Well, he's very private is John. He won't be happy with us discussing his business. I think he has a girlfriend but none of us have met her.'

'What do you know about her?' Watson looked frustrated as she asked the question.

'She's older than him.'

Fletcher jumped in with her own question. 'How many students live here?'

'Just three of us. Me, John and Aaron.' The girl glanced at her watch. 'Is this going to take long, only I have to go out?'

'It'll take as long as it takes,' said Watson smartly.

Her colleague certainly didn't mince her words, thought Fletcher, as she asked her next question. 'Okay, we'll need to talk to both you and Aaron. Is he here at the moment?'

'Studying in his room. What's John done?'

Watson glanced at her watch. 'Nothing as far as we know. This is just a routine police enquiry but we don't have time to waste.'

The girl frowned. 'It doesn't sound like a routine police enquiry – breaking into someone's bedroom. Aren't you supposed to have a warrant or something?'

'This you mean?' said Watson, flashing it under her nose, as they turned the door handle. As expected, the room was locked. 'I don't think it will be too difficult to get in.' She stepped back and then gave it a hefty shove. The wood splintered as Frances gasped. They were in.

* * *

'Right, we've had enough beating about the bush, John. We have irrefutable evidence on the mobile of Rachel Abbie that you have been harassing her.'

Carruthers thought about this as the new DCI spoke. It occurred to him that not one of her housemates had told the police about the harassment. Why not? Surely, she would have said something to them.

Campbell brought out a packet of Marlboro and laid it on the table.

'Can I smoke?'

McTavish bristled. 'You know as well as I do smoking is forbidden inside a place of work.'

'I bet that really rankles, doesn't it? Bet you'd like nothing better than to let me light up in your police station. I bet you're just dying to say yes.' Campbell waved the cigarette right under the DCI's nose. 'After all, you'd have my DNA all over that cigarette butt.'

'What good would that serve?' Carruthers could see McTavish was still maintaining her cool but he knew she was inwardly seething.

'By the way, are you on your period?'

'What?'

'I can smell it.'

Campbell sat back in his chair, laughing. Carruthers felt the colour rise to his face. He balled his fists together. He glanced at McTavish. She looked like she wanted to explode. He couldn't blame her. He wanted to slap the ned for that comment. That's all he was. A jumped-up ned. And in that instant the realisation hit him. His new boss had done the right thing by insisting on conducting the interview herself. He was far too emotionally involved not to lose his cool.

He thought back to the first case he'd conducted in Fife. Welsh terrorists operating in Scotland. Who would have thought...? And the terror expert they'd had to bring up from England, fellow Glaswegian, McGhee, came back into his head. His nemesis. Only after their punch-up in the station McGhee had then saved his life by taking a bullet meant for Carruthers.

'Like I said, you'd love me to light up. You'd love to analyse the DNA found on this cigarette after I walk out the station. And I will be walking out of the station, by the way. We both know you won't be able to hold me.'

'You were going to tell me why we would so badly want your DNA, John.'

The young man put the cigarette back into its packet. 'Well then you'd be able to match the DNA found on this cigarette to the DNA you've found on the fag in Mairi's home in Ceres.'

He gave Sandra McTavish an insolent look as he sat back in his chair with his arms above his head. Carruthers went cold. Here was someone who was playing a dangerous game. Campbell had just admitted to being in Mairi Beattie's house. But just how dangerous was he and what sort of game was he playing, and why?

'You've just admitted to being in the home of your lecturer, Mairi Beattie?'

'Of course I've been in her home. I'm having a relationship with her.'

'Are you a fantasist, John?'

For the first time since the interview started John Campbell appeared to lose his cool. He leant forward so quickly his chair legs clattered. 'Now that's not very nice. Why are you calling me a fantasist? Do you think it impossible that I could be shagging my lecturer?'

McTavish narrowed her eyes and looked at Campbell squarely in the face. Although she maintained a dignified silence the look on her face said it all.

* * *

The first thing that hit Fletcher after they'd broken into John Campbell's bedroom was the smell. She wrinkled her nose in disgust. It was a mixture of sweat, smelly trainers and mouldy food. She snapped the light on. His overflowing bin and empty food packets told their own story. But it was when Fletcher looked at the walls of his bedroom that her heart nearly missed a beat.

There was an enormous montage of photographs on the wall. Every spare inch was covered with pictures of Mairi Beattie and, more importantly, Rachel Abbie. What became immediately apparent was that none of the photos had been taken with the knowledge of the subject. The women had simply not known they were being photographed. Fletcher shook her head. She found this sort of thing seriously disturbing.

They wandered round Campbell's room looking at each individual picture. 'There are no photographs of Serena Davis,' said Watson.

Fletcher took a closer look at a picture of Mairi Beattie. 'No. That's a shame. We still don't have anything to link Campbell to her yet.'

'Perhaps not, but we definitely have a lot to link him to Rachel Abbie. And not just text messages. Look at all this. It's like a shrine in here.' Fletcher had moved away from the earlier photograph she'd been looking at of Mairi and waved her hand round the room. There must have been fifty photographs of Rachel Abbie. Her eyes then alighted on an ashtray on Campbell's bedside table. There were several cigarette butts in the tray. 'Bingo,' she said. She whipped out an evidence bag, donned a pair of latex gloves that she produced from her pocket, and dropped a couple of cigarette butts in the bag.

'Now hopefully we might be able to find out if the DNA on this butt matches the cigarette butt he left at Mairi Beattie's house. And if it does, then it will prove he's been in her house without her permission.'

'But it won't though, will it? My understanding is that he's claiming they're sleeping together. It's her word against his. And there's no evidence a crime's been committed. Leaving a rose on someone's pillow isn't a crime. If it was, thousands of lovesick people would be locked up.'

Fletcher shrugged. 'Oh well, at least we'll have his DNA on file if nothing else.' Fletcher left Campbell's study desk and went back to the wall. There's lovesick, then there's this. God, look at all these photographs. They are seriously creepy. I think we need to get Jim down to see this room. Bloody hell, I wonder how he's going to feel when he's sees that one?'

She was pointing to a photograph of a nude Mairi Beattie stepping out of the shower. The photo had been taken with a long lens. It was a side profile and once again it had clearly been taken without the knowledge of the subject. Unaccountably, Fletcher felt a twinge of insecurity coursing through her. This woman was at least ten years older than her and had a better body. *Look at that flat stomach and toned thighs. She must work out at a gym.* Fletcher placed a hand on her saggy gut. She still hadn't found her mojo. As she scrutinised the other photos she decided that she really must get back into her exercise.

She couldn't stop herself exclaiming out loud. 'Oh, my God. Has this man got a buttock fetish or something?' There were several photos of women's buttocks.

Gayle came over. 'They're all photographs of the same woman. If you look closely you can see a birthmark on the left buttock.'

'Jesus, so that's how he knew she has a birthmark on her backside. What a sicko. Well, this will be the end of his university course, I should imagine. And Beattie certainly won't want to tutor him after news of this gets out. If nothing else, he's clearly a serial stalker of women. We can get him for that. And he's a fantasist.'

'Being a fantasist isn't a crime,' commented Watson.

'No, but stalking is, and I reckon in light of all this it won't be too hard to get permission to get his DNA analysed.'

'True, but the big question is, is he also a murderer? There's a hell of a gap between being a stalker and being a murderer.' The stockier woman took a couple of books out of Campbell's bookshelf, leafed through them and then put them back.

'Oh, I don't know. Stalking behaviour has been identified in a high percentage of these types of murder.'

'I wonder how they're going down at the station with the interview?'

Fletcher gestured to his wall. 'I reckon this is enough to hold him. At least overnight. There's a few charges that could already be brought against him.' She fished out her mobile. 'I'm going to phone the station and tell them what we've discovered.'

'Hang on. What's this?' Watson selected another book and showed Fletcher.

It was a copy of *Atlas Shrugged* by Ayn Rand. 'Didn't you find a copy of this book in Rachel Abbie's bedroom?'

Fletcher walked over and took the book from Watson. She was still holding her mobile. 'And also in the hospital room of Serena Davis. So, what's the significance of this book?'

* * *

Carruthers knocked on the door and then put his head round. He knew interrupting the interview at this stage wouldn't be popular but this wasn't something that could wait.

'Sandra, can I have a word with you please?'

McTavish frowned as she looked up. 'What is it Jim? Can't this wait?'

Carruthers looked at Campbell before returning his gaze to McTavish. 'No, I'm afraid it can't. I think you need to hear what we've found.'

'Very well'. She stood up, her chair grating on the floor behind her. She followed Carruthers out of the interview room, leaving John Campbell staring after them. In a matter of seconds he had lost much of his cockiness. For the first time in the interview he looked nervous.

As soon as he had shut the door after the DCI, Carruthers spoke in a low voice. 'I've just had a call from Fletcher. She and Watson are in John Campbell's bedroom at his halls.'

'And? Is this going to be a guessing game, Jim? We're against the clock here.' Carruthers looked into her eyes. They were beseeching him to give her something she could use in the interview.

'Fletcher says his bedroom walls are covered with naked photographs of both Rachel Abbie and Mairi Beattie. He's clearly been stalking them both. The only other thing they've discovered is a copy of the same book that was in both the rooms of Serena Davis and Rachel Abbie.'

'Just remind me what the book was again?'

'*Atlas Shrugged* by Ayn Rand.'

'Hmm. Well, sounds like we've got grounds to keep him in overnight at least with the discovery of the photos.' She opened the door to the interview room and leant into Carruthers as she spoke. 'I'll just finish the interview then we'll stick him in a cell.'

They both looked at Campbell, whose left knee was now pumping up and down as if he was on drugs. Carruthers knew in his case it was more likely to be nerves.

McTavish glanced at her watch. 'I've got somewhere to be later tonight for a couple of hours which is bloody awkward, but I can't get out of it. However, I'll be on the mobile if you need me. I want Watson and Fletcher to go over that room with a fine-tooth comb.'

Carruthers nodded solemnly. McTavish didn't need to remind him. They were looking for a severed finger.

Sandra McTavish retook her seat opposite John Campbell. She smiled at him. The dynamics of the interview had completely changed. She now had the upper hand and they both knew it.

'If you don't charge me, you're going to have to let me go, you know.'

'Plenty of time for that, John, and you won't be going anywhere anytime soon. I've had a warrant to search your room in halls.'

Carruthers watched carefully through the glass as Campbell exploded. He stood up so abruptly his chair crashed over. 'You had no right to go into my bedroom and go through my things. My stuff's private. I don't let anyone into my room. I want my father present at the interview and I want a solicitor.'

'Sit down. We had every right. You are clearly a danger to women. You're not just a fantasist, are you? You're also a stalker. You have quite a photograph collection in your room. The officers present wondered if you were going to open a gallery. Why are you taking pictures of Mairi Beattie and Rachel Abbie?'

'It's not against the law.'

'Stalking is though. Sit down.'

Campbell remained standing.

'I said sit down.' There was a steely edge to McTavish's voice Carruthers hadn't heard before. Reluctantly, Campbell righted his chair and sat back down on it. His agitation was clear for all to see.

McTavish picked up her notes and shuffled them. 'Let's talk about Rachel Abbie. We've got evidence you harassed her. You bombarded her with text messages. You've been following her around taking her photograph. What we want to know is when did your thoughts turn to murder? Was it after she turned your advances down?'

Campbell turned white. It was finally dawning on him that he was in serious trouble. 'She didn't turn my advances down. I've slept with her.'

Disgusted, Sandra McTavish turned away. 'My God, you really are a fantasist.'

'It's true. We had a fling not long after she got together with Will. She said she was confused. Didn't know what she wanted. In the end she chose him.'

Carruthers watched this exchange through the glass. For once, he got the impression Campbell was telling the truth.

'And you couldn't cope with that, could you? Is that why you killed her?'

'I've already told you I didn't kill her.'

'Well, the fact she threw you over for Will now gives you motive for murder. Wouldn't be the first time a lovesick boy had killed his ex.'

Campbell shook his head. 'I don't see her as my ex. Like I said, we had a fling. It wasn't serious.'

'Perhaps not for her.'

'I didn't kill her.' Campbell stretched his legs out under the desk and folded his arms. 'I want my father. And a solicitor.'

McTavish stood up. 'It's getting late. We'll carry on with the interview tomorrow.' She turned to the uniform present, who was quietly standing in the corner. 'Take him to the cells.'

The student jumped to his feet. 'You're not seriously going to stick me in a cell overnight?'

McTavish remained unsmiling. 'That's exactly what I'm going to do.' She walked out of the interview room, and as she passed Carruthers, she whispered, 'Cell's the best place for him. I need to get going. It's late. Go home, Jim and I'll see you tomorrow at eight.'

* * *

Carol Nichols watched the tall boy she'd had a crush on all term from her vantage point of a high stool at the bar in the Earl of Fife pub. He was standing talking to a couple of his male friends.

Right, that's it, she thought. *Enough Dutch courage.* She looked away from him to put her glass of vodka lime soda down on the bar. Really, she didn't want to take her eyes off him, he was so hot – but she could just imagine trying to put her glass casually on the bar but actually dropping it so it smashed all over the floor. Definitely not the cool look. And it smacked of that tragic episode in *Only Fools and Horses.*

You don't want to be pissed when you talk to him, she thought. The bartender said something to her. Over the noise of the bar Carol didn't hear him. Perhaps he was asking her if she wanted another drink. She waved her vodka lime soda at him as if to say, look, I still have half the glass left. But when she had put the tall glass back down, and turned round, she couldn't believe her eyes. The two friends had disappeared to be replaced by a redhead sitting on Toby's knee. What a tart! She'd missed her opportunity.

Disappointment welled up in her. She grabbed her glass and walked over to her own friends. 'Have you seen that?' she hissed. 'I'm too late. That American girl is throwing herself at him. She's practically wrapped round him like a boa constrictor.'

Her housemate Hazel tried to put a consoling arm round her while trying not to spill her Jägerbomb. 'Look, come back and join us instead.' Carol shrugged the arm off.

'I have to say you did look a bit desperate sitting on that bar stool all on your own. And it was pretty obvious you fancy him. His friends were laughing at you.'

Carol was starting to feel dizzy and a bit sick as the drink took effect. 'I had to pick my moment. Couldn't concentrate being around you lot. Anyway, don't want to join you. Want to go home. And they weren't laughing at me.' She plonked her drink down on the table.

Hazel tried to grasp her arm but she prised it away and started walking off.

'Don't walk on your own. Wait for us. I've nearly finished my drink. I'll come with you.'

But Carol didn't listen and was out the door before Hazel took her next swig.

It was a clear, cool night, the air smelling of salt and the sea. Carol walked unsteadily through Castletown's dark streets. As she took the coastal path by the now quiet children's play area she could hear the sound of the sea lashing against the rocks. It sounded like the noise a seashell makes when lifted to the ear. She heard the noise of running behind her and a shout which made her stop in her tracks. The hair on the back of her neck stood up. She froze.

'Carol, wait up. You know I was going to walk you back. Why didn't you wait for me?' Carol swivelled round to see drippy Stu standing holding his sides. He looked up at her. 'I thought we had an arrangement? I don't want you to walk anywhere on your own late at night until they catch the lunatic who attacked those students.'

Carol tapped at her watch after looking at the time. 'Stu, it's only 9pm and it's very sweet of you, but I don't need you to walk me home. I'm perfectly capable of getting there by myself,' she said through clenched teeth before hiccuping. *God,* thought Carol, *if only Toby hadn't gone off with that bimbo redhead.* Carol had had her eyes on Toby for ages. She'd spent a good part of the night trying to shake off Stu so she could stand on her own, planning her move – only to turn round and see Toby with the bimbo sitting on his lap.

She threw a furious look at Stu. 'Look, will you just piss off. I don't want you walking me back to my room. I thought I'd already made myself perfectly clear.'

'Christ, well if you feel like that. I know you've got the hots for Toby. It's all over the department. He's not good enough for you. And he treats women like shit.' He bowed his head in defeat, Carol caught the glint of tears. 'What do they say? The good guy always comes last. Well, I'm not hanging around to be insulted.' He almost spat the last words at her. 'Get yourself home. And just so we're clear I'm not helping you with that fucking term paper.'

Carol watched Stu go, both shocked at his swearing and wondering why she had never noticed he was such a diva before.

Letting out a sigh, she walked on. Bugger. She'd been relying on Stu to help her with her latest paper. She really didn't have a scooby. She heard a muffled noise some way away and increased her pace. For the first time she felt misgivings about walking after dark on her own. Why hadn't she listened to the police advice?

She had just walked past the moored boats and empty lobster pots when she heard loud footfall just behind her. She then heard a scuffling noise. *Christ, she hadn't got rid of Stu, after all. What was it going to take?*

'For Christ's sake, Stu, can't you take a bloody hint?' As she swung round an arm shot out and she felt herself being grabbed round the neck. She screamed.

Chapter eighteen

A weary Carruthers approached his cottage. Christ, he was tired. He had the start of a headache and every time he thought about the case it just got worse. When were they going to finally get a breakthrough? The only positive note was that John Campbell was now banged up until tomorrow morning, which was when his interview would continue. This time with a solicitor present. But Carruthers still wasn't sure the perpetrator of these violent crimes was the philosophy student, despite the man's stalking behaviour and history of violence towards women. But then if it wasn't him – who was it?

As Carruthers reached in his pocket to get his house keys, he saw a shadowy figure slink out of the darkness towards him from the side of his house. It was unexpected and Carruthers was immediately on guard.

'Who's there?' The figure came into view. Dark-haired, gaunt-faced. It was his brother, Alan. 'Jesus, you scared me half to death. What were you doing skulking round the back of my house?'

'Hoping to find you'd left a window or door unlocked. I'm getting cold.'

'I'd make a pretty poor detective if I'd left my own back door unlocked, wouldn't I? Why didn't you just ring me?' Irritated, Carruthers opened the door to his property.

'What's the point? You don't return my calls.'

Carruthers looked warily at Alan. 'You'd better come in.'

Instead of following him into the cottage his brother slipped back round the side of his house again. Where was he going this time?

'I'll just get my holdall,' Alan called out. Within seconds he was back with an enormous bag.

Carruthers eyed it suspiciously. Dear God. Why the hell would his brother need an enormous holdall? Exactly how long was he planning to stay for? The size of the holdall suggested at least a week.

Alan stepped into Carruthers' home and plonked the bag down in the hall.

When Carruthers had shut the door behind him, he switched the hall light on, and turned to face his older brother. How long had it been? Months. Carruthers was shocked at how old his brother looked. He'd lost so much weight and it had aged him. Gone was the robust former rugby player he had grown up with. In front of him stood a shadow of the man he once knew. Carruthers swallowed a lump in his throat.

'I know what you're thinking. I look like shit. Have you got any lager? I could murder a drink.'

How could Carruthers lie and say his brother looked well when he didn't?

Still facing his brother, Carruthers said, 'I wasn't thinking that. What I was thinking was how could you just turn up on my doorstep like this, with no notice, especially after the way you ended the last phone call?' Before he had a chance to answer, Carruthers had covered the distance between them and enveloped Alan in a clumsy hug.

In silence, Carruthers then walked into the kitchen. The older brother followed him. They stood awkwardly for a moment. Carruthers opened the cupboard and brought out a couple of real ales. Before his heart attack Alan had been teetotal, but he'd heard from their mum that the once fit older brother had started to drink, and heavily at that. Carruthers knew better than to tell Alan it probably wasn't a sensible lifestyle choice, given his triple heart bypass, but he kept quiet and said instead, 'I don't have any lager, I'm afraid.'

'You never did like the stuff.' His brother looked at the Iron Maiden beer Carruthers had given him. He pulled a face. 'That's okay. I'll still drink this.'

Carruthers felt a moment of irritation. It was one of his favourites. He led the way back to the living area and took a seat in his old comfy armchair. His brother sat on the sofa. He opened his own bottle of Hobgoblin before passing the opener to his brother.

Carruthers looked at Alan as he took his first swig. He still didn't know why he'd turned up needing a bed in the first place, but he was determined to find out before they got stuck into the beer. Just as he took his second swig his phone rang. He picked up. 'Jim.' His ears pricked up. It was the voice of Sandra McTavish. What would she be doing phoning him this late? There was a lot of background noise. He could hear music and the low babble of voices. *Where was she?*

'Sorry to phone you at this hour.' Her voice was rushed, breathless. 'You're needed back here in Castletown. Another girl's been murdered.'

Carruthers shot to his feet, his beer jolted, and foamy liquid spilled down the sides of the bottle and all over the front of his jeans. It looked like he had pissed himself. 'Fuck,' he muttered. He'd have to change. Couldn't leave the house smelling of booze, and trousers stained to boot.

'What's up?' he heard his brother ask.

He ignored him, focusing instead on the voice on the phone. He heard a tinkling laugh in the background and then McTavish's voice came back on the line. 'Can you drive or do you need someone to come and get you?'

He looked at the bottle of Hobgoblin. He hadn't taken more than a couple of swigs. 'I'm fine to drive. I'm on my way.'

'Right, I'll text you the locus and I'll meet you there.'

He cut the call, turning to his brother, 'Look, I need to go out.'

His brother grasped his arm. 'But I just got here. I need to talk to you. Can they not get someone else?'

'I'm sorry. It's an emergency.' As he ran up his stairs to change his jeans he shouted, 'There's some food in the cupboard if you're hungry. I wouldn't wait up.' Hesitating half way up the stairs, he turned round and shouted, 'And we will have that talk, Alan, we just can't have it right now.'

Carruthers changed his jeans, grabbed his jacket, wallet and keys, shut the door and sprinted to his car. A squally wind was beginning to gust. Another girl dead? Surely this was now confirmation, if they had needed it, that Castletown had its first ever serial killer. He had no time to think about why Alan had pitched up on his doorstep. Whatever his brother wanted it was going to have to wait. *Another dead girl.*

He drove the six miles from the fishing village of Anstruther to the ancient university town. He phoned Sandra on the hands-free for the locale as he hadn't received a text. Her voice seemed strangely high-pitched. Perhaps it was the shock of another murder. They didn't know how many victims there would be. They didn't know how the killer targeted their victims. Or even what his motivation was. There was no certainty about any of this except for one fact: the killer of this victim couldn't possibly be John Campbell. He was locked up in a cell at the police station.

Having parked up, he dashed to the scene. The first person he bumped into was Liu, the police photographer. The Chinaman was still doing up his flies. He had obviously left his post for a sly piss. Normally one to indulge in a bit of black humour at the scene of a suspicious death, he was strangely quiet. 'Where's the DCI?' Carruthers asked, as Liu picked up his camera.

'Over here, Jim.' Out of the undergrowth stepped Sandra McTavish. She was wearing a short cream jacket over a knee-length red evening dress. The wind was tugging at the hem. She smoothed the floaty dress back down with a hand while pulling off her clip-on pearl earrings with the other. 'I was at a dinner party with Mike. I've only just arrived.' Delving into her jacket pocket, she brought out a white handkerchief and began to wipe off the red lipstick.

'Where's the body?' asked Carruthers, taking in his boss's uncharacteristically pale face. He noticed a sheen of sweat on her brow.

She gestured with her hand. 'Over there. We're all professional, but I had better warn you, it's not pleasant.'

Carruthers walked through the undergrowth towards the unnatural glow of light provided by the SOCOs. The branches of nearby trees swayed with the wind.

'No further until you get these on,' said one of the SOCOs. Carruthers thought her name was Karen. She handed Carruthers the paper footwear, the latex gloves and boiler suit. Carruthers put them on with practised ease and followed her. He could sense Sandra McTavish struggling to get into hers behind him.

He saw the legs of the victim before anything else. Her feet were bare, revealing slim ankles. 'Where are the shoes?'

'Haven't been found yet.' The gravelly voice was of Dr Mackie, who was kneeling beside the victim. Carruthers was betting the old pathologist would be desperate for a smoke.

'What have we got?' asked Carruthers.

Mackie kept his head down. 'A real mess. That's what we've got.' As he looked up, he said, 'He's made a real mess of this one.'

Alarmed at Mackie's uncharacteristic muttering Carruthers was craning his neck to get a look from behind Mackie's frame. 'What do you mean?'

'He's used a blade to cut her throat.'

Carruthers swallowed hard as he felt his heart lurch in his mouth. It had seemed that their perpetrator had graduated from strangulation to using a knife, this time to kill. As Mackie rose up to the balls of his feet with difficulty, the round face and shoulder-length dark hair of the victim were exposed. Blood covered the girl's top. Carruthers gasped out loud. He recognised her.

'The perpetrator's severed the carotid artery. Nearly severed her windpipe too.'

So, if it was the same killer, he'd graduated from throttling his victim to almost severing the windpipe with a sharp instrument. The neck and throat was a mass of still glistening, congealing blood. Carruthers was glad he'd had no time for his supper. The thought occurred to him, that however seasoned he was, there was a chance he would have brought it back up again.

The MO's different, thought Carruthers once again. *What can this mean?*

A horrible thought came into Carruthers' head. 'Have you seen her—'

A grim-faced Mackie nodded. 'I know what you're about to ask. The index finger's been severed. Looks like we've got a trophy seeker on our hands, Jim.'

Carruthers swallowed hard, feeling his heart hammering in his chest. He wiped the sweat from his hands onto his jeans. 'Is there any ID on her?' He didn't need to ask the question. The last time he'd seen her she'd been standing in a huddle with the rest of her housemates.

A SOCO nodded in Carruthers' direction. 'Her student card says Sarah Torr.'

He didn't need to be told. Sarah Torr. Rachel Abbie's housemate. And another dead philosophy student. Just what was going on in the philosophy department?

'How long has she been dead?' asked Carruthers.

Mackie scratched his head. 'Not long. I'd say she's been killed within the hour.' He turned to Carruthers. 'You're looking for someone tall, Jim. At least five-ten, five-eleven to be able to apply the force. Looks like he's severed the jugular and the carotid before getting to the windpipe. Most likely, he was standing behind the victim when he did it.'

Carruthers turned to the female SOCO who had given him the paper overalls. 'Who found the body?'

One of the younger SOCOs answered. Carruthers vaguely recognised her as well. 'An elderly couple walking their dog. They've given their statements already.'

Carruthers stood facing McTavish. A look of deep concern was in the eyes of the DCI who had her arms folded. She shivered. Carruthers couldn't tell if it was with the cold or adrenaline. And when she spoke it was obvious that the same thought had crossed both their minds. 'It can't be John Campbell. He's still in police custody.'

'Could it be a copycat?' He didn't take his eyes off the victim as he spoke.

'Perhaps, but if it was, how would they know about the severing of the finger?' McTavish wiped away the last of her lipstick and put the soiled handkerchief back in her handbag. 'Can't think of any other way. The information must already be in the public domain. These things have a habit of getting out despite our best efforts. Someone must have leaked it.'

'Not someone from the station, surely?' Even saying it, Carruthers felt a tightening of stomach muscles.

'Let's hope not, otherwise they'll find themselves on a serious disciplinary.'

Carruthers went red. The mention of a disciplinary brought back bad memories, but now wasn't the time to think of his own previous shortcomings.

'The other option,' continued McTavish, 'is that Rachel Abbie's murderer isn't John Campbell. We have to face the fact we might have the wrong man in custody.'

McTavish retrieved her mobile from her black shoulder bag. 'Well, I want him to stay in the cells overnight. I'm not releasing him till morning. We can't get him for what's happened tonight, but he's still a person of interest for the Rachel Abbie murder, if for no other reason than the harassment we found on her phone and the fact he's clearly a stalker. And, to be honest, he doesn't have much of an alibi.' She looked at her phone, then put it away again. 'Let him stew it out at the station. Talking of the station, let's get back. There's nothing we can do here. Get on the phone and get the rest of CID in. We'll have a brief in an hour. Jim, we need to handle this extremely sensitively.'

She turned to the nearest SOCO. 'I want a finger-tip search of the area. We're looking for a sharp knife or blade of some description, the girl's shoes and a severed finger.'

One of the SOCOS exploded with laughter. 'Fingertip search when you're looking for a severed finger. Very good, that one.'

Carruthers felt a moment of irritation listening to this inappropriate banter, but he had to remind himself that humour was a coping mechanism for a lot of people in this line of work. He remembered their very own Dr Mackie once commenting on how he was looking forward to having a nice bit of roast beef for lunch when seeing the body of an elderly man who had been nibbled by animals. It had turned his stomach but then he'd never had a strong constitution.

'Just get on with it, will you,' snapped McTavish. Clearly the DCI didn't have much of a sense of humour at the scene either.

Carruthers nodded. He was already punching in Fletcher's mobile number.

'We also need someone to inform the parents of Sarah Torr and get a formal ID done.'

Carruthers nodded. When a tired-sounding Fletcher answered her phone he was aware he was barking out his instructions.

Liu had finished taking photographs and was packing his equipment away. He was still silent. Carruthers knew nothing of Liu's private life. Perhaps he had a teenage daughter of his own. He realised how little he knew about him. He didn't even know if the man was married.

'Are you okay to drive, Sandra?' Carruthers noticed his DCI was still holding her earrings, which were now clenched in her white-knuckled hand. Her face had gone even paler.

'My daughter's fifteen,' she said. 'This girl's not much older.' Now Carruthers understood why it had affected her so much. He couldn't imagine what it would be like to lose a child in such a terrible way.

His new boss looked distracted but then seemed to pull herself together. 'I've been drinking, Jim. I came by taxi. I'll need you to drive me to the station.'

'No problem.' He wondered how much she'd had. There was a glazed look in her eyes, and now her colour was back, her cheeks were ruddy. Or maybe it was just the shock. And the cold.

'I'm not drunk if that's what you are wondering. I've just had a few glasses of red,' she finished. 'Takes a hell of a lot more than that. But I wouldn't chance driving even on one. We all know the drink drive laws here in Scotland. It's just not worth it.'

Carruthers knew Superintendent Bingham kept a bottle of whisky in his office at the station. He'd often wondered if the super had ever driven himself home over the limit. Since DCI Sandra McTavish had come into the station at Castletown he'd had less to do with Bingham. He'd heard on the grapevine the man had finally split up from his wife, Irene. He hadn't felt the need to go and console him.

Chapter nineteen

There were about a dozen officers all crammed into the incident room back at the station. Tension hung heavy in the air and a feeling of uneasiness pervaded.

'Dougie's still at the hospital with his wife. He'll be here soon,' volunteered Brown.

McTavish gazed round the room as she spoke. 'Other than Dougie then we have a full complement of staff.' She sipped from a plastic cup of water. Her eyes still looked a little bit glazed. Carruthers wondered just how much she really had drunk. Even Bingham was back at work, albeit sitting at the back, letting McTavish do her job as senior investigating officer.

McTavish addressed the room. 'What we need to know is what this nutter's motivation is and how he selects the girls he chooses to attack. We also need for someone to officially ID the body, although we think the victim's Sarah Torr.'

Fletcher lifted a hand. 'I'll get onto that.'

McTavish nodded. 'Her parents have already been informed.'

'How confident are we the perpetrator's a man?' asked Brown. Carruthers glanced over at him. He could smell the cloying cigarette smoke from where he was sitting. As far as Carruthers knew Willie Brown was single. He wondered if he'd been out with friends. More likely he'd been nursing a few pints on his own down at his local over a copy of the Scottish Sun.

The door opened and in walked Dougie Harris. 'Sorry I'm late,' he mumbled. Carruthers hadn't seen much of him recently and he was shocked at how he looked. Pale of face, eyes bloodshot, stubble on the chin. But then, sitting at the hospital bedside of your very ill partner could do that.

'How's your wife, Dougie?' asked one of the DSs.

Harris just mumbled an answer. He looked as miserable as hell. *Not good then,* thought Carruthers.

'I'd like to bring a profiler in,' said McTavish. She glanced towards Bingham when she said this, who was still standing at the back of the room. She tugged at the hem of her clingy dress, which had risen above her knee. Carruthers wondered if she felt uncomfortable. He waited for Dougie Harris to start arguing with McTavish about why they should need a profiler, but the man was ominously quiet. He knew she'd struggle to get Bingham to agree to it. No doubt he'd cite the station budget.

'You know the budget won't stretch to a profiler, Sandra.' This from Bingham.

How predictable, thought Carruthers. But then, to a large extent, even Bingham's hands were tied. The recent cutbacks affecting the police had been brutal.

Carruthers watched McTavish take a deep breath and draw herself to her full height. 'I think it would be useful.'

Fletcher raised a tentative hand. 'I think there's some merit in bringing in a profiler. We've done it before.'

Harris snorted. 'Waste of time.'

However irritating it was to hear Harris say that, it was almost a relief that he was acting more like his old self. Carruthers glanced at the reddening Fletcher. She clearly didn't feel the same way. From the very first moment he had arrived at the station these two had been having a constant go at each other. Occasionally it was amusing. Most of the time it was just irritating. He hoped she would cut Harris some slack now he had an ill wife to look after.

Fletcher whipped round to face Harris, her anger rising. 'Okay, so how would you go about catching him, then?' She ignored the warning look Carruthers threw her.

Harris rubbed his nose. 'Plain clothes police officers. And we set a decoy. That was good enough for us back in the day.'

'It's bloody dangerous as well,' said McTavish. 'I'm not prepared to put any of my officers at risk.'

Bingham cleared his throat. 'The budget won't stretch to bringing in a profiler, Sandra, we've got bugger all money in the kitty.'

McTavish's cheeks grew as red as her dress. 'Profiling's controversial, I grant you, but there are occasions when it's been used very successfully in the US.'

'Let's stick to good old-fashioned police work,' said Bingham. There was a mumble of agreement from Harris.

'And when you mean good old-fashioned police work, I'm assuming you don't mean set a decoy, like Detective Sergeant Harris suggested?'

'Good lord, no. Far too dangerous.'

Fletcher sat back and crossed her arms, smiling smugly at Harris, who just snorted again.

'When I suggested profiling, I didn't mean for it to replace traditional investigative police work.' McTavish was clearly not to be outdone. Carruthers was beginning to admire her tenacity.

Bingham remained silent. He looked round the room. 'Any thoughts?'

'I think Sandra's idea is a good one,' said Carruthers. 'What about asking Dr Greg Ross?' Fletcher nodded in agreement to Carruthers' suggestion. They'd used him in one of their last high profile cases, trying to catch the killer, who had been targeting elderly men and killing them in a local nature reserve. Once again, Carruthers remembered the shocking discovery of the balls of cloth rammed to the back of the men's throats. They'd found Dr Ross pretty useful and he was bound to have something to say on the subject of why the murderer was taking severed fingers.

Carruthers looked at the DCI as he spoke. 'His rates were reasonable, if I remember rightly.'

'Well, if his rates are okay, we might just be able to find a small budget from somewhere.' Bingham clearly realised he was in a minority. 'Can I task you with giving him a call first thing tomorrow, Andrea – see if he's free to pop in?'

Fletcher nodded.

'We need to get results. And quickly. This lunatic has targeted three women in almost a week,' said Bingham.

'I don't need to be reminded of that fact,' growled McTavish. 'And he seems to be growing more and more violent. Damn. I had my money on it being Campbell.' She looked at Bingham before she spoke. 'I suppose we had better get him released, although I still want to lay charges on him for stalking and harassment, but we can't keep him locked up indefinitely.'

Bingham looked at his feet before he spoke. He gave an awkward cough. A number of officers looked round at the superintendent. 'He's already out, Sandra. I gave the order for him to be released earlier this evening.'

There was a shocked silence in the incident room. Carruthers' throat was dry as McTavish spoke. Her voice was low and angry. 'What time earlier this evening?'

'About 8pm.'

McTavish was biting her lip. 'So, he could have gone out and murdered again.' She had fury in her eyes. Carruthers couldn't imagine how she felt. Well, he could. He was feeling the same level of shock, disbelief and anger towards their superintendent for keeping them all in the dark.

Bingham puffed his chest out. As far as Carruthers could see he was going to try to brazen it out. 'We have no evidence he murdered Rachel Abbie and we had no reason to hold him overnight.'

'He was and still is our leading suspect,' snapped McTavish. 'Why did you let him go?'

Carruthers was all too aware that the DCI had been drinking earlier that evening and prayed she would be able to keep calm and not say something she might regret when sober. Suddenly, he realised he was rooting for McTavish, uniting with her in a common enemy in Bingham. He then reminded himself that there could be nothing more sobering than the awful sight of what they had witnessed that evening.

McTavish once again managed to voice Carruthers' thoughts. 'With all due respect, John Campbell has no proper alibi for the time Rachel Abbie was killed, he's clearly a stalker *and* he has previous form for assaulting women. He's definitely a person of interest and I'm more than disappointed you let him go without consulting me.'

Bingham's voice was curt. 'Sandra, we'll continue this conversation in my office later. There were extenuating circumstances that you know nothing about.'

McTavish shot back immediately. 'What extenuating circumstances, precisely?'

It was starting to dawn on Carruthers that DCI Sandra McTavish was much more similar to him than he had originally imagined. She was dogged, determined and clearly liked getting her own way. He couldn't imagine that going down well with Bingham. The superintendent now had two awkward members of staff to deal with rather than just the one. He almost found himself smiling.

The former DCI looked at McTavish and considered just how much pressure she was under. She'd be cut no slack for being new. She'd be only too aware of how badly swift results were needed. He suddenly felt sorry for her. By rights she was doing his job but it wasn't her fault he'd fucked things up. He resolved to give her his full cooperation. He shook his head. He still couldn't believe Bingham had let Campbell go without telling McTavish first. Talk about undermining her. If he had been McTavish, he would be seething. Suddenly, the new DCI's mobile rang. 'I need to take that,' she said, with forced brightness. 'Won't be a moment.'

Carruthers wondered if she was using the ringing phone as a way of calming down and taking a few moments out of a tense situation, but then he reminded himself that she had been receiving personal phone calls at the most inappropriate of times all through the investigation.

McTavish walked out of the incident room and stood in the doorway. Carruthers glanced down at his mobile. No messages. He was grateful his brother hadn't tried to call him. He suddenly realised he needed the toilet so he followed her out.

'I'm in the middle of a bloody murder investigation. You know that,' she hissed. 'No, I won't be returning to the party.' She started when she saw Carruthers, and turned her shoulder on him. 'I'll be back when I'm back. You knew I was a police officer when you married me. Well, you'll have to give them breakfast if I'm not back in time. For God's sake do I have to do *everything*?' She snapped her mobile shut. Carruthers hurried to the gents.

A few moments later, Carruthers came out the gents and round the corner of the corridor to see McTavish gathering herself together. She took in a deep breath and headed back into the room. As did Carruthers.

'As you all know the early stages of any investigation are crucial,' McTavish said. 'We have several investigations going on simultaneously. I don't need to tell you all leave is cancelled until we catch this person. With three women now having been attacked every indication is that we are dealing with a serial killer.' She looked round the room as she said this. 'I'd like to get your thoughts.'

'Are we sure the news about Rachel Abbie's severed finger wasn't leaked to the press and that rather than having a serial killer, what we actually have is a copycat killing?' said Fletcher. 'After all, the MOs aren't the same. Rachel Abbie was strangled and slashed whereas Sarah Torr had her throat cut.'

Sandra McTavish dismissed that claim almost immediately. 'I have it on good authority that the press have not got hold of the information about the severed finger. And if it's not been leaked by the press then realistically the only other option, unless leaked by the station, is that the perpetrator who murdered Rachel Abbie also murdered Sarah Torr.'

Carruthers' thoughts strayed to Clare Stott, the rude family friend of the Davis's. After all, she was a journalist. However, as far as Carruthers was aware, she didn't know about the severed finger.

The silence in the room was punctuated by the ring of another mobile. Fletcher dipped into her handbag and looked at the screen. 'I need to take this. It's Rachel Abbie's father.' McTavish nodded and Fletcher stood up and left the room.

'What's it gonna take to catch this wee bastard?' Helen Lennox was munching her way through a bag of crisps when she spoke. She wiped her mouth, screwed up the crisp packet and pocketed it. 'Sorry, didnae have time for supper.'

'Media involvement will be crucial, as will the assistance of the public,' said McTavish. 'As you all know catching a serial killer can be a long process. We all need to double our efforts. I want nothing short of one hundred per cent. But we'll also have to hope the bastard screws up and makes a mistake.'

An ashen-faced Fletcher re-entered the incident room. 'Rachel Abbie's finger has just turned up.' All eyes were on her. She shook her head in disbelief. 'It's been sent to her father in the post. He received it this morning.'

'What the fuck?'

'What sicko would do that?'

The incident room exploded in shock and anger.

Carruthers glanced at McTavish, who picked up a glass of water and took a sip. He noticed her hand was shaking slightly. She took a deep breath and her voice was steely as she spoke. 'We need to step up this investigation and catch this madman. And what I want to know is what is the connection between the father of Rachel Abbie and the murderer? There has to be one. There just has to be.'

Helen Lennox's eyes were wide. 'Does that mean Sarah Torr's finger will be sent to her dad? Is this all part of extending his fantasy?'

'I think we need to get the police psychologist in. In the meantime,' McTavish looked round the room and nodded at Bingham, 'Actions. What we need to do is gather and analyse physical evidence, look for patterns in the murders, get a profile of the killer. All this takes time but time is not on our side. As the super has pointed out, there have been three attacks in nine days, resulting in two murders. At the moment the killer is one step ahead of us.'

'What we have to ask ourselves is, are these killings spontaneous or are they planned? As I said, we'll need the help of the general public but we've also got to be very careful. We mustn't cause a panic. We will also have to deal very sensitively with the press. We need to find out Sarah Torr's exact movements before the attack, interview her friends and family. We'll also need to speak to Rachel Abbie's father again. However, the very first thing we need to do is to locate John Campbell and find out if he has an alibi.'

'They have to be planned,' said Helen Lennox. 'The killer must know the victims. How else would he know where to send Rachel Abbie's finger? He has the Abbies' home address.'

There were murmurings of agreement.

'I agree. I'm going to leave you lot to start brainstorming.' McTavish turned to Bingham. 'If you're free I'd like to have that word with you now.'

It was stuffy in the incident room and McTavish had gone from being flushed to looking unnaturally pale. Carruthers wondered if she was feeling queasy. Bingham marched to the front of the room and opened the door, followed closely by McTavish. Carruthers felt in his jacket pocket and pulled out two painkillers. He stood up and slipped them into McTavish's hand as she neared the door. She looked down at what she'd been given and just about managed a ghost of a smile in gratitude. What Carruthers would give to be a fly on the wall during her next conversation.

Chapter twenty

Sunday

Carruthers let himself into his cottage, wondering if his brother would still be awake. He thought not. It was gone 3am. He wondered how McTavish had got on talking to Bingham after the meeting. He couldn't imagine she'd get much sleep. He'd tapped on her door before he'd left the station but she hadn't been in her office. Unlikely she'd still be in Bingham's office, but you never knew. He ditched his jacket and, walking into the living room, ran his hands through his hair when he saw the mess.

His brother was asleep, fully clothed on the sofa, snoring gently. There were empty bottles of beer all over the place. Carruthers counted at least five. He walked over and picked up one of the empties, staring at it forlornly. He'd bought that beer from a newly-opened microbrewery in Skye. He'd been saving it for a special occasion. He sighed. The last thing he needed at 3am was to start tidying his living room of someone else's mess.

He climbed the stairs, walked into the bedroom, started to hunt around for a blanket in the cupboards. He found a tartan rug his mother had given him, shut the cupboard door, went back downstairs and gently tucked it round his brother. With a shake of his head he climbed back up the stairs and went to bed.

* * *

Carruthers was up and out of the house before his brother was even awake. He left him a note on the kitchen table beside a spare set of house keys. During the night his brother had thrown off the rug, which now lay abandoned on the floor. Part of him hoped that by the time he returned to his cottage his brother would be gone.

He drove the short distance to Castletown, still rubbing the sleep out of his eyes. Dawn was just beginning to break and the sky was a myriad of pink and yellow colours.

Carruthers parked up in the already busy station car park, got out of the car and rubbed his hands in the cold air. He locked up and entered the station.

Fletcher put a black coffee down for him as soon as he arrived at his desk. She pulled up a chair and sat down next to him. 'Jesus, I can't believe what happened last night, can you?'

He picked up the coffee and put it to his lips, blowing on it before he took a sip. 'Which bit? Another murder, Bingham not telling McTavish he'd authorised the release of Campbell or Rachel Abbie's finger being sent to her father?'

'All of it. McTavish must be fizzing. I know I would be. Talk about undermining her. And I wonder what the extenuating circumstances were that he mentioned. Any ideas?'

'Your guess is as good as mine.' Once again, he wondered how McTavish's meeting with Bingham had gone. 'Is Sandra in work yet?'

Fletcher shook her head. 'I haven't seen her, no.'

Carruthers put his coffee down, recalling McTavish's curt conversation with her husband on the mobile the night before. He wondered if she'd had any sleep. She really didn't need to be having a difficult time on the domestic front with everything that was going on at work. He stared at the mess on his desk and, shamefaced, searched about, shifting files and empty polystyrene cups. He picked up a pink Post-it note that he hadn't seen before and read it.

Fletcher watched him. 'God, you really need to clear that desk, Jim, before McTavish sees it. She's already made a few remarks. And I can't imagine she'll be in a good mood today after last night.'

'Don't think any of us will be, will we? Aside from another murder we've all had about three hours sleep.' He let out a sigh.

'They haven't found the murder weapon, by the way. Or the shoes. And no DNA at the scene either.'

'And no sign of the finger, I suppose?'

'Nope. Jesus, what's the betting another finger will be sent in the post – this time to Mr Torr?'

'Oh God, let's hope not. Whoever he is, he's some sadistic bastard. And like we've already said, he's always one step ahead of us. We'll just have to hope the PM throws up something we can use.'

Fletcher leant into Carruthers' desk. 'Mackie's able to fast-track it, by the way, and the parents have been located. Should be here within the hour. Thankfully, they only live in Edinburgh. Do you want me to accompany them to the mortuary, Jim?'

He ran his hands through his hair. He couldn't remember the last time he'd washed it. 'That would work for me. If you go with them to the mortuary and stay with them while they ID their daughter, I'll see if I can attend the PM.'

* * *

Fletcher stood up, grabbed her jacket from behind her chair and set out across town. She was sadly becoming all too familiar with breaking bad news to the families about the death of a loved one, but she'd never had to see a family in quite such terrible circumstances.

'It can't be Sarah. I mean, we only spoke to her on the phone a couple of days ago and she was fine.' Mrs Torr was gabbling. Fletcher recognised nerves when she saw it. Mr Torr was silent, in shock for the most part to be called at such an early hour. *All this must be like a bad dream*, she thought. *Not just a bad dream. A nightmare.*

Fletcher had picked up Mr and Mrs Torr from the train station in her own car and was driving them to the mortuary. She'd decided to use the Beetle over a station car. Most of the station cars were dirty and full of other people's rubbish. Somehow it seemed disrespectful. Her car, on the other hand, had had a good clean-out recently.

She parked up in the car park of the mortuary and led them inside, holding the door open for them. She noticed Mr Torr was gripping his wife's hand tightly. Mrs Torr was still chatting away, almost as if she'd just popped round to the neighbour's for a cup of sugar. However, once they'd walked into the mortuary, she fell silent.

Jodie Pettigrew, Carruthers' old flame, came to meet them. Fletcher never really knew how she felt about the pathologist's assistant, except that here was another woman who had broken her boss's heart.

Fletcher knew that they wouldn't have had much time to work their magic covering up the terrible wounds the attacker had inflicted. She hoped they wouldn't be too distressing for the parents.

They were led to the viewing area and Fletcher asked them if they were ready. They nodded, clinging to each other like shipwreck survivors. Fletcher noticed Mrs Torr could barely look. She was partially hiding her face against her husband's jacket, almost as if they were watching a horror movie on TV. Fletcher took a deep breath as the viewing curtain went back to reveal the dead girl. The side of the face, which was untouched by the assailant, was closest to the window and Fletcher nodded. They'd done a good job.

Almost immediately, Mrs Torr's screams filled the air. She'd torn her face away from her husband's jacket for a moment, then buried it deep in the jacket again. Mr Torr was freely crying. Finding the outpouring of grief almost too much to bear, Fletcher turned away for a moment to compose herself. She felt tears prick her eyes. This could have been her daughter in seventeen years' time, had her child lived. Often parents of dead children asked her if she had kids herself. But not the Torrs, and for that she was grateful. They were too locked in their own shock and grief to notice what was happening as Fletcher gently steered them from the viewing area to somewhere more comfortable before calling Carruthers.

* * *

Carruthers walked into the incident room. Fletcher gave him a quizzical look. After all, he was supposed to be at Sarah Torr's PM. She'd ended up leaving a message on his mobile about the Torrs having given a positive ID. He leant over and whispered in her ear, 'They've had to delay the PM. Mackie's been taken unwell. I left him having a violent stomach upset in the bathroom. Think it's something he's eaten.'

Fletcher looked concerned. 'Is there nobody else?'

'He's still insisting he'll be well enough in an hour or two. And there's nobody senior enough there, no. They could get a replacement in, but it will take a while. I get the feeling he's on a mission and needs to do this one himself.'

A hush fell as Dr Greg Ross entered the room. DS Andrea Fletcher looked at their police profiler, the lanky psychologist. They had commandeered one of the interview rooms and Fletcher, Carruthers, DS Dougie Harris and DS Gayle Watson were all present, alongside several DCs, including Willie Brown, Helen Lennox, DCI Sandra McTavish and Superintendent Bingham.

'Motivations for becoming a serial killer usually revolve around certain fears. Fears of rejection, power and perfection,' said Greg Ross. 'Serial killers tend to be insecure and irrationally scared of rejection. Often, they are terrified of being abandoned, humiliated or exposed. Many killers often have sex – the ultimate form of intimacy – with their victims, and sometimes even with the corpse.'

'Thankfully that's not going on in this case,' said McTavish quickly. 'None of the three women were raped.'

'Well, that's good to hear. Not so good, though, is the fact serial killers also enjoy prolonging the suffering of their victims as it gives them a sense of power. They get to decide whether, and how, the victim will live or die.'

Superintendent Bingham cleared his throat. 'I understand that our attacks have been quick and, mercifully, those who have sadly been killed, have been killed swiftly.'

'That's right,' said DCI Sandra McTavish. 'I know at this stage we're still not one hundred per cent sure we have one attacker or more than one. Let's go on the assumption for now though that we have one attacker and are dealing with a serial killer. The question is will he or she kill again?'

'Undoubtedly they will kill again if we are talking about a serial killer,' said Ross. 'I'm afraid they must continuously kill because they get addicted to the feelings they get when they do. They also rationalise every aspect and detail of their behaviour so there is no reason in their head as to why they should stop.'

'They know what they're doing, the consequences of their actions, and how to avoid getting caught,' said Fletcher.

'Exactly,' said Ross. 'Most serial killers, and psychopaths in general, are "consummate chameleons" who are able to hide their rage and true intentions behind a charismatic, civilized façade called "the mask of sanity". Psychopaths are amoral, and though they know the difference between right and wrong, they do not care. They lack feelings of remorse or guilt. They tend to treat other people as if they were objects. They don't know how to have sympathy for others because of their psychopathic nature, but they do know how to simulate it by observing others.'

'The killer hasn't followed the same MO though,' said Watson. 'He doesn't fit the usual profile of a serial killer. For a start the women aren't raped before being killed. Secondly, he seems to be taking trophies but not necessarily keeping them. I've never heard of a case where the trophy was sent to the victim's family.'

'I must admit I haven't come across that before. And it makes this very personal, doesn't it? You probably don't need me to tell you that the likelihood is that the killer knows the victim. These are targeted attacks. One thing to remember, though, and I think we've said it before, is that a killer learns from experience. If you don't catch him right away, he'll begin to develop his modus operandi and probably get better at the crime. Maybe he'll find a more efficient way to kill someone or a quicker way to abduct a woman from a car. He'll start showing more control over the crime.'

'What about the fact the sicko takes one of their fingers? That's clearly part of his MO.' All heads turned to DC Helen Lennox.

'There is a difference between the MO and what we call a signature, although often there's a fine line between the two. The signature is a ritual, something the subject does intentionally for emotional satisfaction – something that isn't necessary to perpetrate the crime. So, evidence of torture would be a signature. Taking a memento, like the finger, would be evidence of the signature of the perpetrator. In my experience I've found that signature is a more reliable guide to the behaviour of serial killers than an MO. That's because, as we've already said, the MO evolves, while the emotional reasoning that triggers the signature, doesn't.'

'Can you give us an example?' asked Fletcher.

'The method a killer uses to get women into his van may change, but the fact that he always tortures them once they're inside stays the same.'

'You've talked a lot about serial killers in general,' said Bingham. 'What we want to know is, what can you tell us about this one in particular?'

'Given that the attacks have all been local to Castletown it's highly likely the perpetrator lives here among the women he's attacking. All the women attacked have been students, so I think you'll find that the attacker has close connections to the university, not just the town. He may be a student himself; a former student or even a lecturer. What you've told me makes me think you are looking for just one person doing the killing, although he may be aided and abetted by a second – but it's much more likely he's working on his own. And I think, given the nature of the crimes, you're looking for a man.'

There was a low murmuring around the room and Carruthers spoke for all of them when he turned to Ross and said, 'With every attack the perpetrator's becoming more violent. He has to be stopped.'

Chapter twenty-one

Greg Ross caught up with Fletcher as she was walking up the corridor towards the canteen.

'Mind if I join you?'

She looked up at him shyly but carried on walking. She'd forgotten how tall he was. 'Not at all. I'm just wondering if there's any sausage rolls left.' Her stomach growled and they both laughed.

'Tough case you've got at the moment,' he said, shortening his stride to match hers.

They got to the canteen and stood in the short queue. They were in luck. There were two jumbo sausage rolls left. They ordered them and Greg insisted on paying for both which Fletcher found touching. He carried the tray to a table.

'Yes, I've never worked on a case with a serial killer before,' she admitted. 'I found it interesting what you said about the fact the perpetrator could be a former student. Castletown is in a beautiful part of the world and I've noticed a few former students actually end up staying here after they graduate. It hadn't occurred to me that the murderer might be a former student.'

Ross handed Fletcher her plate and they both took a seat facing each other.

Fletcher bit into her sausage roll. She gasped as it burnt her tongue. 'Ouch. You'd think I'd learn. Always burn myself.' She turned to Ross. 'You gave us a useful profile of the killer.' Fletcher chewed her sausage roll thoughtfully. She sighed. 'It's a pity Serena Davis can't remember more. We don't seem to have much to go on. We have such a vague physical description of the attacker it could be almost anyone.'

'Serena Davis, your first victim?'

'That's right.' Fletcher tried to think it through. 'We've got Serena Davis in hospital. The second victim, Rachel Abbie, was slashed, strangled, and her finger taken. When the third victim was also mutilated that's when I started seriously thinking we had a serial killer.'

'From a professional point of view, it's interesting how people end up as serial killers. In my experience a lot of serial killers start off as peeping toms.'

As soon as Ross mentioned the words 'peeping toms,' Fletcher thought once more of John Campbell. What Ross had said put Campbell right back in the frame, but then again, he'd never been out of it for her. Fletcher blew on her sausage roll. She wasn't going to burn her tongue a second time. It was still sore.

Ross took another bite. 'Why did you join the police?'

Fletcher chewed her mouthful, thinking this over. 'I wanted to make a difference, I suppose.'

'And have you? Made a difference?'

She thought back to her previous cases. Had she made a difference? She liked to think she had, that she was a real asset to the team and she'd been told as much, by Carruthers. They had a good team. Stronger now Gayle Watson had joined. When she thought of Gayle, she was embarrassed at how she'd first treated her. It had been a clear case of jealousy. She hadn't made her mind up about their new DCI though. The woman was probably okay. It's just that she was so loyal to Jim.

'You don't say much, do you?'

Fletcher looked into Ross's smiling eyes. She shook her head. 'Sorry. Was miles away. Yes, I do make a difference. Or at least I like to think I do.'

'Can I ask you a serious question?'

'Aren't all your questions serious?' She looked up, head tilted to the side, a smile in her eyes. She'd forgotten how cute he was with his smattering of freckles. What was she doing playing with him? She was on dangerous territory.

'I know it's none of my business but are you seeing anyone at the moment? I'd really like to get you know better. Outside work, that is.'

She dropped her head for a moment and looked at her plate before looking back up at him again. In his eyes she saw a mixture of hope, anxiety and something else. It might have been lust. She wasn't sure. She felt a surge of hope – of excitement. Then that feeling died, to be replaced by something else. She couldn't pinpoint what it was. Wariness maybe. What could she say to him? How did she feel about going out on a date with him? With anyone?

'Um, the thing is, Greg, I've been badly burned not that long ago. I'm still getting over the – well, what happened. I–' God, what was wrong with her? Why couldn't she get the words out?

A shadow fell across the table. Fletcher looked up, frowning. The bulky form of Willie Brown came into view. 'Sorry to spoil your date,' he said with a smirk, 'but Boy Wonder's looking for you.'

Fletcher picked up a few crumbs that had fallen on the table and put them on her paper plate. 'Tell him I'll be right there, will you. And Willie?'

He looked down.

'You've delivered your message. You can piss off now.'

He shrugged, and walked off, whistling. Fletcher stood up.

'Boy Wonder?'

'Oh, Willie and Dougie's silly joke. That's what they call Jim. It all stems from him having been a fast-track graduate.'

Fletcher hurried off, knowing she still hadn't given Greg Ross a proper answer, and at some point she'd have to decide what she wanted.

* * *

Carruthers was buried under a pile of paperwork when he heard footfall approach his desk. He was still waiting to hear news of John Mackie and kept glancing at his watch. While he had every sympathy with Mackie's predicament, he was itching to get the PM underway. He looked up to see Fletcher.

'You wanted to see me, Jim?'

'Thought you'd want to be in on this, Andie. A young woman's arrived at the front desk asking to speak with someone about the recent murder. I've put her in interview room one.'

'What's her connection?'

'Says she was out very close to where our latest victim was murdered. Thinks she heard something.'

'Does she have a name?'

'Carol Nichols. Thought you might want in.'

'I'm in. Let's go. Doesn't do to keep a witness waiting.'

Carruthers gathered his notebook up from his desk and followed Fletcher out of the office.

'You look a bit flushed. Not coming down with something, I hope? You don't have time to be ill.'

'I'm fine. Nothing like that. Greg Ross just asked me out.'

Carruthers punched the air. 'What did you say?'

'That's just it. I didn't say anything. Not really. I just babbled. To be honest I can't think of anything at the moment but these cases. Perhaps when they're over…'

Carruthers understood. When they were in the middle of a murder investigation everything else had to be put on hold. He still hadn't had a proper chat with his brother. He wondered if Alan was even still in his cottage.

Fletcher looked hopeful. 'Any news about John Mackie and the PM?'

'Not yet. I'm still waiting, but at least it means I'm here to sit in on this interview.'

Carol Nichols was sitting fidgeting with her mobile phone in the interview room. She had a bottle of water in front of her and a cup of coffee. She looked up when she heard the door open.

'Thanks for coming in, Carol. I'm Detective Inspector Jim Carruthers and this is Detective Sergeant Andrea Fletcher. I believe you wanted to speak with us about something you may have seen last night?'

Carruthers pulled up an extra plastic chair for Fletcher and sat down facing Carol Nichols. He took in the mass of blonde curls that framed a lively, oval face.

'Look, I didn't know whether to come in or not. I don't have a huge amount to tell you. It probably won't be useful.'

Fletcher smiled at the girl. 'Let us be the judge of that. Just tell us what happened last night. I believe you heard something?'

'Yes, God, I must have been so close to where that attack took place. It sends chills down my spine. I don't really know what I was doing walking home alone. It was so stupid.' The girl was rushing her words. Carruthers suspected she was still in shock at the terrible news of another murder and at how close she had been to the killing.

'Take your time.'

The girl drew in a slow, deep breath. 'We'd been drinking in the Earl of Fife and I was walking back to Edgecliffe.'

'The student halls?' asked Carruthers.

'Yes, that's right.'

'Anyway, God, I'm so stupid. I suppose I was in a bit of a mood. The thing is, I really fancy this boy called Toby, and I was just plucking up courage to make a play for him when next thing I know I turn round and that American girl is sitting on his sodding knee.'

Carruthers tried to suppress his irritation. Some people liked to give blow-by-blow accounts of a story and Carol Nichols was clearly one such person. The police waited impatiently while she got to the point.

'Anyway, look, what I'm trying to say is I wouldn't normally walk alone in these circumstances late at night, but I wasn't thinking too clearly, I'd had a fair bit to drink and I just decided to take off and get home.'

'Okay. Please carry on,' urged Carruthers.

'I wasn't far away from the halls at Edgecliffe when I heard a noise.'

Carruthers knew those halls of residence. He'd visited them on a previous case. He thought of the pretty, black-haired student, Siobhan Mathews, that he'd met during his first big case. An arresting image came to mind of the green-eyed girl wearing a green shift dress over blue jeans.

'Where exactly were you when you heard this noise?'

'Just down by the harbour. I'd passed the boats and lobster pots.'

Carruthers knew exactly where she meant. It was close to the pier. 'Can you describe the sound you heard?'

'Well, sort of a scuffling noise, I suppose. And then what sounded like a muffled shriek.' There was a pregnant pause. 'Did I hear the girl being attacked?' She shook her head. 'I thought it was just someone horsing around. I didn't realise someone was being murdered.' She put her hands to her face.

'Which direction did you hear the noise coming from?'

She thought for a moment. 'Somewhere behind the Castle.'

'Do you have any idea of the time?'

'Oh yes, I'd just looked at my watch. It must have been a few minutes after 9pm. I mean, I didn't want to be too late going back with a murderer on the loose.' She put her hand over her mouth as if she might be sick. 'Did I hear the murder? Please tell me I didn't hear that poor girl being killed?'

'Did you hear anything else?'

'Well, I did get a bit worried cos someone crept up behind me and grabbed me round the neck. Actually, I had a total fright, but it was my housemate, Hazel, who'd left the pub and caught up with me. I think she thought it was funny, grabbing me like that. Silly cow.'

Chapter twenty-two

The bags under Dr Mackie's eyes told their own story. 'I think I'm getting too old for this, Jim. Let's get this over with. I know you're needing answers.'

'Are you sure you're well enough to conduct the PM, John?'

'Aye, laddie. Whatever I had was over pretty quickly. I could have tried to get someone else in at short notice but to be honest I want to do this myself.'

So, I was right, thought Carruthers. For some reason Mackie saw this as personal. The pathologist's bespectacled assistant, Jodie Pettigrew, pulled the sheet away from the body and the post-mortem of Sarah Torr began.

Carruthers was too exhausted and anxious to think of his failed relationship with the attractive pathology assistant. All he wanted to know was how their victim had died and ultimately who had killed her. He gave Jodie a curt greeting then kept his head down.

'Another young woman who had her whole life ahead of her.' Carruthers wasn't sure if Mackie was talking to himself or addressing his comments to them. In close proximity to the old pathologist, who stank of cigarette smoke, he gazed at the slim figure of the now dead nineteen-year-old.

'The good news here, if there is good news, is that once again there's been no sexual interference. No semen or blood around the vagina or anus. A small mercy for her parents at least. This young woman died a virgin.'

Mackie made the standard incision from sternum to pubic bone. Carruthers forced himself to watch despite the inevitable nausea. Even when he'd been a DCI he'd insisted on going to the PMs of his victims. He felt it was the least he could do for them.

The throat area of the victim was a mass of congealed blood and Carruthers tried to ignore the livid knife slashings to the face. As Mackie started the inevitable task of cutting and slicing, in a bid to take out and weigh the organs, a fresh wave of nausea took the police officer. Sweat beaded his top lip, his skin started tingling and a darkness descended. He excused himself and stumbled out of the room just in time.

A grey-faced Carruthers emerged from the men's toilet sometime later. In all his years as a police officer he'd never been sick until now. The look of concern on Jodie Pettigrew's face told its own story.

Carruthers looked at her; surprised to see something resembling worry in her eyes. Their brief dalliance hadn't ended well. 'Where's Mackie?'

'Away for another smoke. You okay?'

He wiped his hand over his mouth. 'I'll survive. Don't know what came over me. Never happened before.'

'Don't beat yourself up. You're only human.' She jerked her head towards the window. 'He's out there if you want to join him. Getting a breath of fresh air and a cigarette might help.'

Carruthers nodded and stumbled out of the building. With the victim's appalling injuries in mind he was certainly more human than the bastard who had done this to that poor girl. And Carruthers realised in that moment that the resolve to catch the perpetrator and put him away had never been greater.

He shared Mackie's one remaining cigarette. Despite being an ex-smoker Carruthers could imagine it wouldn't be his only one of the day. If he didn't buy himself a pack he'd be trying to cadge cigarettes off other folk. He was still feeling queasy.

The pathologist handed him the dog-end of the fag. 'You'll get him, Jim. I know you will.'

Having taken the last drag of the pathologist's cigarette he absentmindedly flicked it on the ground and, with shoulders hunched, walked away towards his car, leaving Mackie staring sadly after his back.

Chapter twenty-three

'Well, we didn't get much from the Carol Nichols interview but at least we have a better idea of the time of death for Sarah Torr.' McTavish checked her phone. Carruthers was currently standing in her office, having brought her up to speed with the latest victim's PM. 'If you had plans for later tonight, I need you to cancel them. I want to speak to you, Jim. And I want to do it away from the station. We can do it over supper.'

Carruthers shook his head. He had no plans. He stifled a yawn. By rights, he should get home and check in on his brother, but the thought wasn't appealing.

'No, I don't have plans.' He wondered why she needed to talk to him away from the station, thinking that what he really wanted was to go back to an empty house and a hot bath. He felt too exhausted to have a heart-to-heart with a brother he felt he barely knew. Anyway, his new boss needed to speak with him, and for some reason she wanted to do it over supper. He was so used to eating fast food during a murder investigation that the thought of enjoying a meal in a restaurant was a huge luxury.

He was aware the DCI was still talking. 'Good. I want to talk about the case with you.' She leant in to him. 'There's been a development. I've got a husband and kids to get back to so I don't want to be too late. Why don't we walk to the restaurant just down the road?'

'The Italian? Fine by me. Will he mind, your husband, I mean?' Carruthers was wondering why she didn't want a meal with her husband and kids. After all, surely they could grab half an hour at the office for going over the case and whatever this latest development was. She didn't need to do it over supper.

Sandra McTavish snorted. 'No. He'll be too busy looking after the children. Anyway, his mother is coming over tonight. I can't stand her.' She started moving towards the door, hesitated, then turned round. Eyeing the empty polystyrene cups and overflowing paperwork, she said, 'I've been meaning to tell you, I think you could do with a clear up of your desk. I don't want to micromanage you, Jim, but I'm a stickler for neatness. You should take a leaf out of Andrea's book.'

Carruthers bristled. It hadn't been the first time he'd been compared unfavourably to DS Fletcher. Superintendent Bingham had done it in the past too.

They headed out of the station and walked together to the local restaurant. Carruthers had been in it a few times with work colleagues but not since it had had its current makeover. He looked around him. It could be described as a contemporary restaurant with a Scottish twist. All exposed brick, wooden tables and soft black seats. He approved. McTavish steered him to a table in the furthest corner. She took the seat facing the front door. Carruthers wondered if that was so she could keep tabs on anyone from the station coming in for a quick bite. Unlikely during a murder investigation. They usually ate little more than pot noodles and sausage rolls.

She leant into him after glancing around the restaurant to make sure nobody was listening. 'Look, there's another reason I want to speak with you.' Satisfied they weren't being overheard, she continued, 'and like I said, I want to do it away from the police station.'

Carruthers was intrigued. *What's with all the cloak and dagger stuff?*

'It's about Bingham—'

Carruthers wasn't surprised. 'Can I just say I thought he was bang out of order letting Campbell go like that without first consulting you. I don't want to talk out of turn but I thought it was completely unprofessional.' He wondered if he was being unprofessional talking about Bingham in such a way, but then, Sandra McTavish was no fool. She would know that there was no love lost between the two men, given Carruthers' demotion at Bingham's hands. And it certainly looked from the little interaction he'd seen between the two senior officers that McTavish was having her own personal struggle with Bingham. He suddenly realised he'd done it again. He'd interrupted his superior. He fell silent.

'Well, the super is the reason I needed to talk to you. I found out why he let the boy go. Do you know who John Campbell's father is?'

Carruthers wracked his brains and came up with a blank. 'No.'

'John Campbell's father is none other than a Superintendent Len Campbell. Apparently, he's friends with Bingham.'

'Shit.' Carruthers' mouth practically fell open.

Before he had a chance to speak further McTavish was continuing. 'Why wasn't I told about this, Jim?'

Good question, he thought. Come to that, why hadn't he been told? 'I wasn't in possession of this information.'

She called over a waiter to bring a couple of menus and a jug of water, before turning back to Carruthers. 'Is there some old boys' network in operation at this station that I need to know about?'

Carruthers' heart sank. Hadn't he practically accused Superintendent Bingham himself of belonging to an old boys' network with his golfing cronies during their last major case? The case that had taken him to Estonia on the trail of an art and people smuggling network? He idly wondered if Superintendent Len Campbell was a member of the same golf club as Bingham.

He'd never been a fan of Bingham, who had already been caught out by his association with one career criminal. Surely if it came to light that he was doing favours for this Superintendent Len Campbell it would herald the end of his career in the force. No wonder the boy had been so cocky under interview. He probably thought, with having a father so high up in the police force, he was untouchable.

Carruthers was trying to think fast. He was aware that McTavish was scrutinising him and more than aware that she would be looking for a fall guy. The question was – was he willing to sacrifice Fletcher or should he put his own head on the block? His thoughts turned once more to Bingham. One of the last surprisingly personal conversations he'd had with the man had been when Bingham had told him that he was no social climber and that he hated golf – that it had been his wife Irene who had made him hobnob with the great and good.

He was aware that DCI McTavish was waiting for an answer. 'I don't know what to say, Sandra. You have my word that I'll look into it. I can't understand how this information wasn't passed on. I'm as much in the dark as you.'

The waiter arrived at their table holding a couple of menus with one hand and a jug of water with the other. He put the jug down on the table and handed the police officers the menus. 'I'll be back with glasses in a moment.'

McTavish remained unsmiling. She leaned into Carruthers and hissed, 'The expression, trying to shut the stable door after the horse has bolted, springs to mind. But I do want to know why I wasn't informed. You are the DI, Jim, and as I said, I expect your support. I certainly hope you weren't throwing me to the wolves.'

Carruthers reddened. His anger was rising. He brought the menu up to his face for a moment while he pretended to read it. He wasn't just angry at the fact this vital piece of information hadn't been passed on to him. He also couldn't believe that the new DCI might even consider that he had been in possession of the facts and had deliberately intended to keep quiet in an attempt to undermine her.

He finally took the menu away from his face. 'You can't possibly think that I knew about it and kept quiet? I didn't, by the way, Sandra, but you have my word that I fully intend to conduct my own investigation into this and find out why we were both kept in the dark.'

McTavish nodded. This seemed to appease her. 'I just want to make sure we're singing from the same hymn sheet, Jim. If you have an issue with me being your DCI you need to be honest with me and tell me.'

Carruthers could see why McTavish had wanted this conversation away from the prying ears of the station. 'No, I don't have a problem with you being the station's new DCI, Sandra. In fact, I think you make a good DCI.' And he meant it. For a moment they locked eyes before she spoke again.

'Another thing which might make things rather difficult for us – John Campbell's alibi for when Sarah Torr was murdered. Bingham's told me he claims he was with his father.'

'Oh shit.' Carruthers shoulders slumped. 'Could the man be lying to protect his son?'

'Well, it's possible. Remember Campbell Junior was rattled by the end of the interview, as well he should be, and I know he did make at least one phone call. My bet's on him having called his dad.'

They studied the menus in silence. The waiter came back with the glasses and asked to take their order. Carruthers didn't have much of an appetite, but he chose the steak, like his boss, figuring that this would be the best meal he'd eat for some considerable time, given the way the investigation was currently going.

'I don't see why we should deprive ourselves. We still need to eat.' Sandra McTavish glanced at her mobile, which she'd placed on the table. 'Anyway, I'm just a phone call away.' As she spoke she sliced into her rare steak.

She looked over at him. He was pushing his food around his plate. 'Are you going to play with your food, or actually eat it?'

Carruthers looked up at his DCI but his thoughts kept drifting to his brother. It hadn't really been fair to leave him for so long, but then again, he wasn't a puppy; he was a grown man. He stared down at his steak. Between the case and his brother his appetite had all but deserted him. Given the nature of the murders perhaps steak had been a bad choice. He thought back to the PM and was still finding it hard to believe he'd thrown up.

He glanced over at McTavish to see her fork a couple of chips and pop them into her mouth. She clearly enjoyed her food. He was relieved to see that she seemed to have got over Bingham's appalling undermining of her earlier. She was making little noises of enjoyment, which, frankly, he found rather embarrassing.

Shovelling some peas into her mouth, she said, 'What do we know so far? You know the press are now calling this bastard The Student Slasher?' She picked up her glass of water and put it to her lips. 'We have to find this lunatic. And fast. Before he strikes again.'

'You think we're talking one killer, then?'

She shrugged. 'Yes, I do. I don't think it's two people.' She laid her knife and fork down carefully for a moment and locked eyes with his once more. 'I've never dealt with a serial killer before. And it's not how I envisaged starting my promotion.'

So, the rumours were true. This was Sandra McTavish's first post as a DCI. Carruthers felt really sorry for her.

'I don't want another dead student on our hands, Jim. In light of the fact there's been another murder, Serena Davis has been incredibly lucky.'

Carruthers continued to push his food around his plate. 'Doubt she'll see it that way.'

McTavish tutted. 'You make more of a mess than my kids.' She eyed his messy plate as she spoke. 'She will in time. She could have been killed.'

Carruthers thought about the severed index finger of two of the victims and how Rachel Abbie's finger had been sent to her own father. There wasn't much that was sicker than that. He wondered, not for the first time, what sort of depraved individual they were dealing with. All thoughts of food forgotten, he pushed his plate away as he said, 'I hope Serena Davis will get the help she needs and manage to put this awful ordeal behind her.'

They ate in silence for a few minutes. Or at least Sandra McTavish did. Carruthers made no effort to even try to finish his food. He threw his scrunched up paper napkin on top of his plate. A thought came into his head. 'I wonder if Rachel's father was sent his daughter's finger because he's a surgeon. Might be worth doing some research into his patients. You never know, there might be a disgruntled relative out there.'

McTavish forked some more peas. 'I hadn't thought of that.' His new boss ran a critical eye over him. 'You really should try to eat something, you know.'

Carruthers sighed. 'I know. Probably like you, I've got a lot on my mind. It often affects my appetite. And to be honest I can't get over this latest development.' Every time Carruthers looked down at his chips all he saw was severed fingers.

As soon as the words were out, he wondered why he'd just admitted to any form of weakness. It wasn't like him at all. He was aware that his new boss was still staring at him.

'You also need some sleep, by the looks of it. And a change of clothes.'

Carruthers already knew this. He couldn't understand how some people could look immaculate even after a busy day. He glanced down at himself. His white shirt was crumpled. There wasn't much he could do about that. He hastily tucked part of the bottom of his work shirt back into his trousers. He glanced up at his boss but couldn't read the expression on her face.

'Have you got problems on the home front?'

Caught unawares by her question, he didn't know what to say. Mind you, he could ask her the same. What was it about her bloody mobile ringing every two seconds? And she still hadn't said anything about why she had arrived late to the team brief. He mumbled something, hoping she wouldn't ask him to repeat it.

She was still talking. 'I know you're a very private person.'

He looked up.

'Andrea told me.'

What else has Fletcher told her?

'She's loyal to you, Jim.' McTavish managed a half smile. 'I like to get to know my staff. Despite my probing, she's actually said very little about you and your personal life.'

One thing to be grateful for then. God, he was starting to wonder where this conversation was going and whether they'd both end up naval-gazing, swapping confidences. He wasn't like that and he certainly wasn't prepared to be so open with his new boss. He couldn't imagine she was either.

'I don't need to know about your private life if you don't want to tell me,' she continued, as she put her knife and fork down. 'But I do need to know that I can rely on you and that you don't resent me. We need to be able to work together.'

Carruthers waited for the bomb to drop. He didn't have long.

'I do know why you got demoted back to DI. I assume there won't be any repeats of that sort of behaviour while you're on my watch?'

Carruthers honestly didn't know what to say to that. He wondered if that stupid incident with Alistair McGhee was going to haunt him for the rest of his police career. It most likely would. More to the point, would he ever be given a chance to rise to the rank of DCI again or was he destined to remain a DI forever?

He decided to keep his answer short but honest. 'What happened with Superintendent Alistair McGhee was a huge mistake that I bitterly regret. And as for supporting you, well, you can count on me.'

McTavish looked at Carruthers through narrowed eyes. He got the feeling she was still assessing him.

Suddenly she smiled, a genuine smile that lit up her face. It was most unexpected and totally transformed, her making her look much younger. He got an insight into how she might have been in her earlier years before kids and a demanding career had come along.

'Good. We need all hands to the pump for this case.' She chewed her steak thoughtfully. 'It can't be easy being back in contact with your ex-wife.'

Carruthers took a sip of his water. 'It isn't. He stared at the glass of water, wishing it was a beer but, like his boss, they both had their cars at the station and they both needed to drive home.

'Is this the first time you've seen her since you separated? I take it it wasn't amicable?'

Carruthers placed the glass carefully back on its coaster. He looked up. 'Yes, it's the first time, and no, it wasn't amicable.' He surprised himself by saying, 'And part of me wishes she'd never come back to Castletown.' He stood up abruptly. 'Just going to the gents.'

In the men's toilet he splashed cold water over his tired face. He looked at himself in the mirror, prodding the bags under his eyes. *I can't believe I'm sitting here having supper with my new DCI talking about my ex-wife. I need to go home and sleep.* He suddenly remembered his brother and groaned inwardly. He dried his face with a couple of hand towels and returned to the restaurant.

'Look, you might as well know, Jim, those phone calls I've been receiving…'

Carruthers looked up, interest replacing tiredness.

'I know you overheard part of the conversation.'

'Yes, I'm sorry about that. I didn't hear much, and I didn't leave the room to deliberately listen in. I needed to go to the gents.'

McTavish waved her hand dismissively in the air. 'Look, I feel I can trust you not to spread this round the station. My husband – he resents my job. We've been talking about separating.'

Carruthers shifted uncomfortably in his seat. 'I'm sorry to hear that.'

She called the waiter over and gestured that she wanted the bill. 'The problem is that with my long working hours I'm pretty sure he'd get the kids if he went for custody.'

Carruthers was now feeling completely out of his depth and in need of a drink. A proper one. He thought forlornly of his cottage and the bottle of Talisker he had in the cupboard. He hoped his brother hadn't made too much of an inroad on it. God knows he'd drunk pretty much everything else.

He suddenly realised McTavish was looking for a response. 'Oh no, surely not?' he said, quickly. 'Doesn't the ruling usually go with the mother?' He felt he was treading on a minefield. He may have had experience of separation and divorce but he and Mairi hadn't had kids.

'Do you mind me asking why your marriage failed, Jim?'

Oh God, what could he say to that? He opened his mouth to answer but just at that moment the waiter appeared with the bill. If he'd hoped he'd been saved answering an awkward question he was about to be disappointed.

'You split up when you were still a DCI, didn't you?'

He nodded, suddenly feeling miserable. And exposed. She clearly wasn't going to let it drop. He'd much rather they were discussing the cases. He wondered if he should offer to pay for the meal, but then again, she'd asked him out and was on a higher salary. He also didn't want to step on her toes, so he waited.

'It's all right. You don't have to tell me. I'm sure the job didn't help, though.' She brought out her handbag and took her wallet out, giving her credit card to the waiter. 'It's on me, Jim.'

'Thank you. No, probably not. But we didn't have kids.' He hoped she wouldn't say something trite like 'just as well,' but she was busy putting her security digits into the machine and the moment passed.

He thought about Mairi. He knew she'd wanted kids. Hadn't she said something about that? *You wouldn't have been there, Jim, not for me, not for our kids.* That remark still hurt. Probably because, in all likelihood, it was true.

McTavish suddenly stood up. 'C'mon. Enough of this navel-gazing. I can tell you're not comfortable with it – although, like I said, I'd appreciate it if you didn't mention this conversation with anyone at work. As we need to work so closely together I thought it was a good idea to put you in the picture. And about those phone calls… I keep telling him not to ring me at work.'

'They never listen, do they?'

She smiled. 'No.' She picked up her mobile from the table, and as she gathered her jacket from the back of her chair, she paused. 'Jim, I'm not sure how you're going to feel about this but I need you to do something.'

'What?' Carruthers stood behind his chair which he'd slid under the table. He wondered what on earth she was going to ask of him.

'I need to find out what's going on in that damned department. Two dead philosophy students. There must be a link.'

'What do you want me to do?' But even as he asked the question he already knew the answer.

'Get close to your wife again. Find out what's going on.'

Carruthers swallowed an uncomfortable lump. 'And when you say close, how close do you mean?'

'Dear God, I don't expect you to sleep with her if that's what you're asking.' She stood up, brushing off a few stray crumbs from her suit. 'Just close enough to find out what's going on.' She walked briskly to the door. Pulling it open, she hesitated and turned round to look at her DI. 'Put your sleuthing hat on, Jim. Find out if there's been any sort of trouble between the students; any affairs we should know of; any bad feeling between them – that sort of thing.'

Carruthers followed McTavish out of the restaurant into the night. She had no idea what she was asking of him. His feelings towards Mairi were reigniting and he had no desire to stoke them further.

Chapter twenty-four

By the time Carruthers reached his front door it had gone ten. He idly wondered whether his brother had managed to find anything to eat. As he put the key in the lock, opened the door and walked into the hall, he smelt cigarette smoke and heard music and the sound of voices coming from the living room. Frowning, he walked in.

'What the–?'

His brother was sitting in Carruthers' old battered armchair. On his lap was a red-headed woman. She had her arms around him. There were a group of people drinking and dancing in his living room. He spotted his bottle of Talisker sitting open on the coffee table. By the looks of it a good half bottle had already been consumed.

'What the hell's going on?'

Alan toasted his brother with a glass of his own whisky. 'Hope you don't mind. Invited a few folk back from the pub.' Carruthers recognised one or two faces. The woman who worked at the cash and carry was one of them. He thought her name might be Jacqueline. She at least had the decency to look embarrassed.

'We got thrown out for being a bit too rowdy.' Alan laughed uproariously. He clearly thought it was hilarious. Carruthers realised he was very drunk. He stalked over to the record player and turned it off.

'Oi! I was enjoying that.' The red-headed woman unwrapped herself from around his brother's neck. Carruthers didn't recognise her.

He walked swiftly up to her and clamped his hand round her arm. 'Grab your coat. You're leaving.'

'Get off me. You're hurting.'

Her eyes were unfocused. He wondered if drink had been the only thing they'd consumed. Surely to God his brother wouldn't have let people bring drugs into his home?

'You can't tell me what to do.' She was drunk. And belligerent.

He threw a spangly jacket at her that matched her short dress and marched her to the door. 'I think you'll find I can. This is my home. Now get out.'

* * *

When the last guest had left, Carruthers turned angrily to his brother. 'What the hell's been going on here?'

'Oh, come on, Jimmy, I just wanted to have a bit of fun.' His brother lurched, knocked into the coffee table and almost fell over it. Carruthers made a swift grab for the whisky bottle and rescued it before it fell.

'Don't call me Jimmy. You know I don't like it.'

Alan's voice took on a petulant whine. 'You weren't here. It was boring. Where have you been?'

'The station.' That wasn't strictly true, but he and his boss had still been discussing the case, even if it had been over a meal in a restaurant. And they'd had to eat at some point. Well, she'd eaten. Carruthers wondered if his brother had eaten anything at all or whether he'd started drinking on an empty stomach.

Carruthers stalked into the kitchen and came back with a black bin liner. He started to collect the empty cans. He looked around him. Thankfully, there didn't seem to have been any spillages. He might be messy at work but even he drew the line at having a dirty house. He moved around the cottage, emptying ashtrays and beer cans.

His brother seemed to have gone quiet. He was just standing, watching. At last he made a move and picked up a random empty beer bottle. Holding it by the neck, he swayed as he spoke. 'Look, I'm sorry. Okay?'

Carruthers turned on him. 'What the hell's going on, Alan?'

The drink had turned Alan emotional. His eyes filled with tears. He turned away from his brother. 'I've been staying at Mum's.'

This was news to Carruthers. 'How long for?' He briefly wondered why nobody had told him and what other secrets his brother and Mum were keeping from him. He didn't have long to wait.

'It's my heart, Jim. I'm going to need another op. I have no idea how I can tell Mum. Not with the news she's had.'

Carruthers' heart sank. He stopped tidying the living room and sat down on the couch so he was facing Alan, still clutching the black bin liner. He felt himself grow cold and his face drain of colour. 'What do you mean? With the news she's had?'

It was almost as if Alan hadn't heard him. 'This will kill her. I really don't know how she's going to cope,' he said to himself. Finally, he turned to face his younger brother. 'Look, there's something you need to know about Mum. She's been diagnosed with lung cancer.'

The former rugby player burst into tears. Carruthers felt like crying himself. Instead, he covered the space between them and for the second time in as many days hugged the life out of his brother.

* * *

In the morning Carruthers got up and made breakfast for them both. His eyes felt hot and gritty and he had a headache. He'd hardly slept and no wonder. He was quiet as he rummaged around and found some eggs, a packet of bacon that was still in date and some mushrooms. He sniffed the mushrooms before he made his almost full Scottish breakfast. He rang McTavish and told her that a situation had arisen at home and that he'd be a wee bit late in that morning. She asked him if everything was okay.

Carruthers held his mobile with his left hand as he fried the bacon with his right. He could hear his brother in the shower. 'I can't really talk now, Sandra. Can I talk to you about it later?'

'Do what you need to do, Jim,' she'd said, 'but don't be longer than necessary. We need you at the station.'

'Well, I need to be in by ten. I've got an interview set up with Rachel Abbie's father later and I want to go through my notes first. He's bringing the package and finger with him.'

'Good. Just to let you know, I want to sit in on that one.'

He cut the call and turned to his brother, who had just emerged still wet from the bathroom, naked except for a towel tucked into his waist. Carruthers handed him a strong cup of coffee, taking in the unshaven face and dull eyes. 'Why didn't Mum tell me that she'd been diagnosed with lung cancer?'

Alan shrugged, accepted the coffee, took a sip and put the mug down. Still standing, he picked up a slice of toast and tore off a bit before popping it into his mouth. At last he looked up and spoke. 'When did you last have a proper chat with Mum? And by that I mean give her more than five minutes of your time? I don't mean that to sound like a criticism, Jim. I'm just being honest.'

Carruthers felt the heat rise into his face but he knew it was a fair point. He fixed his brother with his blue eyes, assessing him as he spoke. 'I take it you and Mum had a row for you to end up on my doorstep then? Does she at least know where you are?'

Alan looked up from buttering another slice of toast and nodded. 'I called her while you were at work. She thinks it's good we're having time together. Not that we've actually had any.'

Carruthers winced.

'The thing is Jim, she didn't want you to know about the cancer.'

'Why the hell not?'

'She doesn't want to have treatment. She's too scared. That's why we rowed. Well, that and the fact she didn't want me to tell you.' He put the butter knife down. He glanced over at the sink where Carruthers had dumped all the dirty glasses from the night before. 'That's why I landed on your doorstep. I thought you had a right to know about Mum and I didn't feel it was news I could just give on the phone. By the way, I'm sorry about the state of your cottage. I'll clean up while you're at work.'

The last thing on Carruthers' mind was the state of his cottage. He just couldn't believe what his brother had told him about their mum. It dawned on him that while he was furthering his police career, real life was passing him by, and he was becoming absent from the lives of those who needed him most.

Chapter twenty-five

Monday

Carruthers walked into the police station just after nine-thirty. He'd called his mother on the hands-free on his way into work. It had been an emotional call and his mother had broken down when she had talked about her cancer diagnosis. By the end of the call though, Carruthers had achieved the result he had wanted. His mother had promised him she would at least think about seeking treatment.

Fletcher spotted him and came over. 'You missed the team brief. That's not like you. Is everything okay?'

Carruthers looked up, alarmed 'No, not really. Brief? What time was that?' He opened the desk drawer and popped a couple of painkillers out of a blister pack into the palm of his hand. He threw them down the back of his throat. He accepted the bottle of water Fletcher was carrying and took a swig.

'8:30am. McTavish asked me to fill you in. She said you had some business to take care of at home. Is this something to do with your mum and brother?'

Carruthers couldn't believe that he'd forgotten about a team brief. McTavish hadn't said anything on the phone about it. He handed the bottle of water back.

Fletcher looked at him reassuringly. 'Don't worry. I said I'd fill you in.'

Carruthers didn't know how Fletcher did it, but she was uncanny. But then again, she also knew Carruthers had no current love interest, more's the pity, so it was a case of logical deduction. Who else did he have in his life?

She continued with her probing. 'I'm right, aren't I? It is to do with your mum and brother. That was my first guess.'

'What was going to be your second?' Need he ask?

'Your ex-wife.'

Carruthers pulled a face. He wondered what Fletcher would say if she knew what McTavish had asked him to do – to become *close* to his ex-wife. He wasn't about to confide in her. The more he told her the more questions she'd ask. After all, he hadn't said much to her about his brother landing on his doorstep, but he knew he'd have to tell her something to get her off his back.

'There's some stuff going on with my brother.' He looked at her inquisitive face. 'We're working on it.' He couldn't face telling her that his mother had been diagnosed with lung cancer.

'Okay, well, I can see you don't really want to talk about it, so do you want me to fill you in on the brief?'

He suddenly remembered the conversation he'd had with McTavish about John Campbell's father. 'Before you fill me in, I need to talk to you.' Brown looked up and cast them both a quizzical look.

'In private.' He grabbed her arm. 'Let's find a quiet spot in the canteen. This can't wait. It's important.'

'Okay.' She stood up, and, looking confused, grabbed her purse and followed him out of the office. As soon as they were out of earshot of Brown, Carruthers whispered, 'Has Sandra spoken to you this morning about John Campbell's father?'

She looked alarmed. 'No. I told you she's not in yet. What's going on?'

'I know why Bingham let John Campbell go. His father is a serving police officer. A Superintendent Len Campbell, no less.'

'Shit.'

He stopped and faced Fletcher. 'Why didn't we know about this, Andie? This is basic police work. McTavish practically accused me of deliberately keeping this information from her in order to undermine her in Bingham's eyes.'

Fletcher kept her eyes downcast. 'Bugger. I gave Dougie Harris the job. I knew I should have done it myself.'

'Yes, you should have done. It's not like you, Andie.'

'Did you tell Sandra that it had been my responsibility?'

'I couldn't lie for you and, to be honest, I don't want to take the flak for someone else's mistake.' But as soon as he said that he wondered whether he was being unfair. After all, Fletcher was a DS and he was a DI. In the end he still felt the responsibility stopped with him. He wondered whether McTavish would see it that way.

What on earth had she been thinking? Harris wasn't known for his meticulous attention to detail at the best of times, and what with his wife so ill his mind clearly wasn't on the job. Thinking of Harris's ill wife got Carruthers thinking about his mother and her dreadful news. He was going to have to give a lot more support to his mother and brother despite the police work. Perhaps it was just as well he had been demoted and consequently had less responsibility. And of course, as lonely as it was, it helped having no partner. Nobody else to worry about.

'Look, let's talk about the case,' he urged.

Fletcher nodded. 'Do you mind if I get some breakfast? I haven't eaten anything yet.'

'No, carry on. Don't want you fading away on me.' For once, he'd had a proper breakfast, but he wouldn't have minded another black coffee.

They stood in the queue until they got served. Carruthers carried his steaming coffee to a table at the far corner of the canteen and waited for Fletcher, who was grabbing a knife and fork. She placed her tray opposite him and sat down. Carruthers glanced up at her. Her shoulders were slumped and she was staring miserably at her food. He knew she'd be feeling really bad and he felt for her. After all, they all made mistakes.

Silently, Fletcher forked a piece of bacon and popped it into her mouth. She chewed it thoughtfully, but said nothing.

Carruthers took a sip of his coffee. 'I take it we still haven't managed to establish a link between Serena Davis and Rachel Abbie?'

Fletcher looked up before shaking her head. 'No,' is all she said. She shrugged. 'At least it's been established that Sarah Torr was murdered at approximately 9pm but then you already knew that. What are you going to do now?'

'I need to have a quick word with Sandra, then I need to go out and speak to my ex-wife again. And, of course, we've got the meeting with Rachel Abbie's father later.'

'Oh, why are you meeting with your ex-wife again?'

'I just need to go over a couple of things we've discussed,' he said hurriedly.

* * *

As they walked back out of the canteen they saw DCI McTavish walking towards them. All was clearly not well. Her stride, purposeful and fast-paced, made her look like a ship in full sail. Her cheeks were flushed and her mouth was set like a steel trap.

'Jim, I've been looking for you. I need you in my office. Immediately.'

Carruthers pulled up. 'What's happened?'

McTavish didn't even bother to glance at Fletcher as she spoke. 'The shit's hit the fan. That's what's happened.'

The DI turned to an open-mouthed Fletcher. 'I'll see you later, Andie.'

Good luck, Fletcher mouthed to Carruthers.

Carruthers fell into line with McTavish. Impatiently, she brushed a lock of hair out of her face. 'We don't have much time, Jim. Superintendent Len Campbell is on his way up. All hell has broken loose. He wants to know on what grounds we've been interviewing his son and why he wasn't informed about it.'

'Oh Christ. Well, surely he'll know his son isn't squeaky clean from the previous incident at UEA.'

'You'd think so, wouldn't you, but that's just it.' They'd reached her office. She opened the door, ushering Carruthers inside and, following close on his heel, shut the door firmly behind her after glancing down the corridor. She didn't offer him a seat, he noticed. There was clearly no time for pleasantries.

She stepped closer to him so that she was practically whispering in his ear. 'I've been doing some digging, Jim. Called in a couple of favours, actually. What I'm going to tell you is completely off the record and in the strictest of confidence.'

'Go on,' he urged. 'You can trust me.'

'It's about the previous assault charge that was made against the super's son back in Norwich.'

'Yes, my understanding is that it all got shut down pretty quickly. I had wondered why.'

'Apparently it was the super who managed to get the case shut down. Rumour has it that it was Len Campbell who leant on the girl to change her story and retract the accusation of assault.'

'Jesus Christ. Well, he's given his son an alibi for the time of Sarah Torr's murder. What's the betting that he's lied for him? What are we facing? A bent super?'

'Well, if he is bent he has a lot of friends in high places. I've been warned off reinterviewing John Campbell – and not just by Bingham.'

'But what if he's our serial killer?'

'For all our sakes, not least Superintendent Campbell's, we'll have to hope he isn't.'

There was a knock on the door. McTavish opened it. Superintendent Bingham was standing at the threshold – with Superintendent Len Campbell.

Chapter twenty-six

The slim-built Len Campbell looked straight at Carruthers. 'DCI McTavish, I presume?' He didn't offer his hand.

Bingham cleared his throat and gestured at McTavish. 'No Len, this is DCI McTavish, DCI Sandra McTavish.' He then turned to Carruthers. 'This is DI Jim Carruthers.'

'Oh. You're the DCI? I didn't expect–'

McTavish looked at him, unsmiling. 'A woman? Why not? Thank goodness, long gone are the days of our being chained to the sink. We actually manage to leave the house once in a while nowadays.'

'What I was going to say is I didn't expect to find someone who'd made DCI so young.'

'Oh, right, sorry,' mumbled McTavish.

Carruthers, shocked at McTavish's blunt outburst, sized Len Campbell up. He didn't like what he saw. About fiftyish, crew cut, with shrewd, assessing eyes that held deep suspicion. This man was trouble with a capital T. And he was clearly a misogynist. It had been pretty obvious what he was about to say, despite being cut off before he'd said it. He didn't believe a word of the man's response.

Bingham looked almost regretful when he spoke, glancing at McTavish before his gaze settled on Carruthers. 'I'm afraid Superintendent Campbell wants you off the case, Jim, pending an investigation into your behaviour over his son.'

The look on Sandra McTavish's face said it all. She was furious. 'On whose authority? Jim's a vital member of this team and we're right in the middle of a multiple murder enquiry. I need him very much on the case.'

Campbell spoke to McTavish. 'My son says DI Carruthers has been harassing him and I believe him.'

'I haven't been harassing anyone, but what we do believe is that your son may be a danger to the public.'

'What did you say?' Superintendent Campbell gathered himself to his full height of five foot eight and rounded on Carruthers. He took a step closer to him, standing so close in fact, that the Glaswegian could smell mints on the man's breath. He wondered if here was yet another cop with a drink problem. 'Have you any idea who I am?'

Carruthers couldn't believe the man had pulled rank like that. Before he had a chance to say anything, McTavish jumped in.

'With all due respect, you're a father who refuses to believe their son is anything less than perfect. I have kids. I accept that you want to see the best in them, but unfortunately, your son is at best a serial stalker of women. And more to the point, we have proof. We understand that you're prepared to provide an alibi for your son at the time of Sarah Torr's murder?'

Campbell unleashed his fury on McTavish. 'I'm not "prepared to provide an alibi" as you put it. He *was* with me when that girl got killed.' He looked McTavish up and down. 'You were right. I'm not a big fan of women climbing the ranks and all this positive discrimination rubbish. Some good men have been left behind to fulfil these ridiculous quotas. Anyway, why should I listen to you? You don't even know my son.'

At last Bingham found his voice. 'Steady on Len. Sandra has climbed to her rank by hard work and hard work alone. Merit has got her to this position and I won't have you undermine her like this. And I certainly don't allow blatant sexism. This isn't the 1970s.'

Len Campbell took a step closer to Bingham. 'I would keep your mouth shut if I were you, Bingham. If it wasn't for me, you would have long been retired. Just remember who it was who saved your neck over the Estonia affair.'

Bingham inhaled a deep breath and now it was his turn to draw himself up to his full height. Carruthers was fascinated to see how he would handle this odious man and he also wondered about Campbell's sexist outburst. Here was a man who was very clearly on the edge.

'I won't dignify that with an answer, Len. But what I will say is this. I know your son got accused of assault at the University of East Anglia,' said Bingham slowly, 'and that the charges against him got dropped. And we all know why.' Carruthers watched Len Campbell's reaction carefully. The sneer had evaporated to be replaced with, what exactly? Fear? Anxiety?

The nervous tic that Bingham sometimes displayed when under pressure was visible. Carruthers almost felt sorry for him. Almost.

'I've seen the photos of the women he's stalking on his bedroom walls here in Castletown,' continued Bingham. 'This gives me no pleasure to say this, Len, but your son is a very disturbed young man. He's clearly an obsessive and he may well be psychologically unstable. Whether he is a serial killer, however, remains to be seen, but we've certainly got him on charges of harassment and stalking against two different women. And one of the women he has been stalking has ended up dead. The fact his father is a serving police officer will make no difference to how he gets treated, so don't even try to pull rank.'

Superintendent Len Campbell opened his mouth, but before he even had a chance to respond, Bingham silenced him. 'You've had your say. You've come into my station shouting the odds, insulting my staff. I've heard enough. I would like you to leave and I would be grateful if you didn't impede the investigation in any way.'

Campbell turned on Bingham. Carruthers stepped forward to protect his super in case it turned ugly. Bingham put his hand up to restrain Carruthers.

'This isn't over yet, and if you think you'll get away with framing him for murder, you've no idea of what I can do to all your careers,' spat Campbell.

'We don't all work by your rules, Len,' said Bingham softly. 'Some of us are honest, law-upholding officers.'

Len Campbell, spittle at the corner of his mouth, turned on his heel and walked swiftly to the door, which he opened in fury.

'And you're right,' called out Bingham. 'It isn't over. It's not over until we catch the murderer of these innocent women. You'll have to hope to God the perpetrator isn't your son, but if he is, he will be treated like anyone else.' Campbell, who'd hesitated by the door, walked through, then slammed it shut. The photographs on Sandra McTavish's desk shook.

Bingham turned to a speechless Carruthers and McTavish. 'He always was a jumped-up little shit.' He turned to McTavish. 'I'm sorry about that rampant display of sexism, Sandra. You shouldn't have had to listen to that. I'm afraid Superintendent Len Campbell is old school.'

McTavish was tight-lipped. It was pretty obvious what she thought of Len Campbell. 'Thank you for coming to my defence but I can assure you I am able to fight my own battles.'

Carruthers looked at McTavish with admiration. She really did have some guts and he was starting to like her. In some ways she reminded him of Fletcher and he remembered the way his younger colleague had stood up to the chauvinism of fellow Glaswegian, Alistair McGhee, in their first case together. He smiled. Fletcher had certainly given McGhee a run for his money. Not for the first time in his life he was thankful he was a man and didn't have to deal with this sort of sexist shit at work. He wouldn't want to put up with the sexism that he still occasionally stumbled across in the Scottish police force. They'd come a long way since the 1970s but sadly, as just witnessed, there were still chauvinistic senior police officers. He thought of a case recently in England where two male officers had been sidelined for putting their heads above the parapet and standing up for their female colleague. They'd just won a massive pay-out. Carruthers was glad, but he wondered what it had cost them on a personal level.

'Jim, Sandra, I want half an hour of your time now before we meet with Rachel Abbie's dad. We need to sit down and go through exactly what we've got on John Campbell. Our case against him needs to be watertight. I want to know every detail of why you brought him in for questioning. And it had better have been by the book. I want to be prepared before Len Campbell brings the big guns in, and bring the big guns in he will. You can be sure of that.'

* * *

After they'd had their meeting about John Campbell, an emotional Mr Abbie was led into McTavish's office. Mr Abbie was clutching a bulky, unmarked A4 padded envelope. Carruthers asked him to take a seat. The man was openly weeping. They'd decided, under the circumstances, an office was much more appropriate than an interview room. Carruthers noticed Fletcher was unusually pale-faced.

Carruthers looked at Mr Abbie. 'I'm so sorry to keep you waiting. Something came up last minute.' He thought of Superintendent Len Campbell, satisfied that they had a good case against his son, at least for the murder of Rachel Abbie. But if Campbell's father had provided an alibi for his son, did that mean the man had lied for his offspring or were they back to the possibility of it being two murderers? Carruthers didn't know.

Mr Abbie pushed the bulky package towards the officers.

'Does it contain…?' Carruthers could barely bring himself to finish the sentence.

'My daughter's finger? Yes.'

Carruthers stared at the package, noticing flecks of what looked like vomit on it, then at Mr Abbie, who had placed his hand over his mouth. The man had screwed his eyes tight shut. The detective hoped the distraught father wasn't about to be sick. But he wouldn't blame him if he were.

'Has anybody else touched it?'

Mr Abbie opened his eyes and shook his head.

'Can I take it?' Not waiting for an answer, Carruthers brought out a pair of latex gloves, put them on and carefully picked up the package. 'We'll get it sent to fingerprinting.'

'Have you found the murder weapon of the latest victim yet?'

There was hope in the man's eyes which Carruthers didn't want to extinguish. He could imagine hope was all Mr Abbie had left. Hope that they would discover the perpetrator of these terrible crimes and bring him or her to justice. But whatever they did would never bring his daughter back.

It was Bingham who spoke. 'Not yet. But we will catch whoever did this to your daughter. You have our word.'

There's something else.' Mr Abbie brought out a flowery book. 'I found my daughter's diary. She never let me read it. I can't face reading it now, it's too raw, but if you think it might help catch whoever did this to my little girl, I'm more than happy for you to have it. All I ask is that you return it to me once you're finished.'

'Thank you. This could be really helpful.' Carruthers took the diary from Rachel's father.

McTavish spoke. 'Andie, do you want to give that a read?'

Fletcher nodded and Carruthers handed the diary over to her. He could see from the look in his DS's eyes that she was itching to start reading it. He watched as her hands eagerly closed over it.

McTavish glanced around the room before continuing. 'As abhorrent as this is, the question we, as police officers, keep asking ourselves, is why did whoever killed your daughter send you her mutilated finger?'

Fletcher looked up from the diary but it was Bingham who spoke. He kept his tone low, respectful. 'It makes this very personal. In some way you're involved and we are trying to establish how and why.'

The grieving father nodded. 'I know, and I have no idea why anyone would do such a thing.'

There was a question playing on Carruthers' mind. He took his opportunity. 'We did wonder whether it could have anything to do with the fact you are a surgeon. I hate to ask this, but have you had any fatalities recently in your patients?'

'Sadly, as a surgeon, you have to be prepared for people dying under the knife. Some don't come out of the anaesthetic. You're asking if it could be the member of a bereaved family who did this? I can't think of anyone who would want to hurt me or my family in such a way. The latest victim – did they also take her finger?'

'I'm afraid so.'

'Did it get sent to the family?'

'They haven't received anything yet, no.'

'God forbid that they do. Look, if these awful murders were committed by a family member of someone who died during my surgery, why would they target other women and other women's families?'

Why indeed? thought Carruthers. That had been a question that had been baffling him.

Chapter twenty-seven

'Boss, I've made a start on the diary. I need to talk to you.' Fletcher waved the diary at Carruthers as he retreated from the DCI's office. He'd stayed on after the meeting to discuss with McTavish his imminent meeting with his ex-wife.

'What have you discovered?'

'Something pretty big. Rachel Abbie *had* slept with John Campbell. According to the diary it only happened once, and she felt it was a mistake.' Fletcher fell into step with him as he walked towards the office.

So, John Campbell had been telling the truth after all. 'An ill-conceived one-night stand then?'

'Yes, and that's probably why she didn't say anything to Will or the rest of her housemates about the fact Campbell was bombarding her with nuisance texts. She wouldn't want this to come out.'

Carruthers stopped and faced his DS. 'When did this one-night stand happen?'

Fletcher started leafing through the diary until she came to the entry. She showed Carruthers. 'That's just it. November. And according to Will they started to go out in October.'

He stroked his chin. 'So, Will and Rachel were already an item when she slept with John.'

'It would seem so.'

He looked up at her. 'Clearly, Mr Abbie didn't know.'

'It seems not, but it's not really something you'd tell your father, irrespective of how close you are.' Fletcher looked up from the diary. 'There's something else. It's about her housemate, Davey Munroe.'

'The Canadian guy?'

Fletcher nodded. 'Apparently, there's some reference to arguments they were having which she found really upsetting.'

'Interesting. Do we know what about?'

'Ayn Rand and Objectivism. It seems he was trying to convert her to Objectivism–'

'You say convert?'

'That's the word Rachel uses. Anyway, when she told him she wasn't interested he went berserk. It gets really nasty. According to what she wrote in her diary he told her she was too nice for her own good and that he was going to give her a nervous breakdown and get her kicked off the course.'

'That's pretty dreadful. And yet she was still living under the same roof as him?'

'Yes, but here's the thing. Apparently, according to Rachel's diary, Davey found out about her one-night stand with Campbell. No idea how. Looks like he was blackmailing her. In one of their arguments she told him she wanted to move out and he said that if she did, he'd expose her betrayal to Will.'

'So, he wanted her to stay under the same roof as him so he could continue to taunt her? Did her father know any of this?'

'No, she didn't tell him, but then perhaps she didn't want to worry him. In her diary she also talks about how worried she was about her dad since her mother died. She sounded like a nice kid.'

'The last couple of months must have been very stressful for her. She must have been living under intense pressure. She's living in the shadow of a massive secret being exposed, being inundated by unwanted texts from Campbell, threatened by Munroe and on top of that she knows her father's not coping well with her mother's death. Not sure how I'd handle all that at that age.'

'There's one other thing. In her diary Rachel mentions another student called Mary-Lou Gettier–'

'In what context?'

'As being a friend of Munroe's. She said that she was a bit freaked out because this girl looked the spit image of the dead writer, Ayn Rand. The thing is… I ran into a student in town. She wasn't looking where she was going and almost knocked me over. It must have been this Mary-Lou Gettier. The resemblance to Ayn Rand is uncanny. I nearly did a double take.'

They'd arrived in the office. Carruthers walked over to his desk and collected his jacket. He shrugged himself into it. 'Keep going through the diary. In particular, I want to know anything you find on John Campbell *and* Davey Munroe. I'm starting to wonder if they could be in this together. And we had better find out more about Ayn Rand and Objectivism. And Mary-Lou Gettier.'

Fletcher's eyebrows shot up. 'Do you really think Campbell and Munroe could be working as a pair? It would be unusual, wouldn't it? Most serial killers are loners. I mean, I know it happens that people do work together. There's the Moors Murderers for a start. I've never heard of two men.'

'Well, we all have the stereotypical image of the lone serial killer in our heads, don't we, but working as a pair is not unheard of. Let's just keep an open mind – it's at least a possibility. I need to be somewhere but I'll be on the mobile. I think we now need to start looking at Davey Munroe as a person of serious interest.'

* * *

Carruthers sat stiffly opposite his ex-wife. He watched her take a sip of water. Was she as tense as him? Maybe it was just the lack of sleep catching up with him and the frustration of the cases. He was now feeling well and truly exhausted. And it wasn't helping that he was working out how to tell Mairi that her naked picture was plastered all over the wall of that nutjob, John Campbell. The nutjob she just happened to teach. But could the obsessive student also be the serial killer? Somehow, he just didn't buy it.

His thoughts drifted to another student. Davey Munroe. Carruthers found what Rachel Abbie had written about him in her diary deeply disturbing. He made a mental note to find out everything he could about Objectivism and Ayn Rand. If Rand had been a philosopher then his ex-wife should be able to shed some light on her.

Between his brother descending on him with his bombshell news and the fact that they still hadn't caught the serial killer, Carruthers felt drained. But if he was honest, he also felt uncomfortable spending so much time with Mairi after such a long absence. The problem was that the more time he spent with her, the more he wanted to spend with her. That couldn't be good. For either of them.

'Jim? You're miles away. And if I may say, you look exhausted. Have you heard a word I've said?'

He looked at his ex-wife with his tired blue eyes. God, how could she chat away as if the years since she'd left him had never happened? He felt a surge of resentment as he took in her lovely face. He lifted his sagging shoulders. 'Sorry, my brother arrived on my doorstep two nights ago.' Was it two nights ago? He couldn't even remember.

'Is everything okay?'

Did he see concern in her green eyes? He wondered if she knew about Alan's shock heart attack. But then she probably didn't even know about his own demotion. Why would she? He debated confiding in Mairi and then dismissed it out of hand. It had been too long. There was nothing between them any more and in all reality he didn't want there to be anything between them. In some ways she felt like a stranger to him. But a stranger he still knew too well. It was an odd feeling.

He couldn't get his head round the fact his brother was going to need another op and his mother had cancer.

He realised he hadn't answered his ex-wife's question. He forced a smile. 'No, not really. But it's not your problem.'

'Why did you want to see me?'

He pushed all thoughts of his family and how he currently felt about his ex-wife firmly out of his mind. 'Mairi, first of all, can I just apologise for having to push this meeting back. It's been crazy back at the station.'

'Don't worry. I wasn't teaching today.'

'I've been tasked by the DCI with finding out if there's anything going on in the philosophy department that may have a bearing on the case.'

She frowned. 'I thought *you* were the DCI?'

Ouch. What can I say? Clearly, she doesn't know about the demotion, after all. 'We have a new DCI at the station,' he said carefully and a little too brightly. *Well, it's true.* He tried to smile. There was no way he was going to tell her he'd been demoted. She really didn't need to know and, to be honest, it was none of her business. Not any more.

'Is that unusual? Having two DCIs at the same station?'

God, he really didn't want to lie to her but they weren't here to talk about him. 'It can happen although it's not common.' *That would do.*

Mairi scratched her neck. 'I'm not sure how I can help. What sort of thing do you want to know about?'

He rubbed his forehead. 'I don't know, but two of the murdered students *and* two of the main suspects are registered in the philosophy department, so that's as good a place to start as any. Is there *any* information you could give me that might help with our enquiries?'

'What sort of thing?'

'Any affairs between the students? Problems between them?' Even as he said this, he wondered how this would tally with the possibility of the murderer being a serial-killing stranger.

Mairi shook her head. 'No affairs as far as I know, but then, of course, I only know what goes on in the department. I'm concerned about John Campbell, but you already know that. It looks as if he got in through the bathroom window. I'm taking no chances though. I'm getting the locks changed.'

That's a great lead in. Here goes. 'I was going to advise you to do that.' He leant in towards his wife. 'He's a bit more than just a problem, Mairi. We managed to get a search warrant for his room here in Castletown. I'm afraid my officers found pictures of you plastered all over his walls. Some of the photos were of you, naked.'

'But how?'

'He also had photographs of Rachel Abbie.'

Mairi's face drained of colour. Carruthers couldn't blame her. 'Oh my God. I thought I was being followed and I was right. But I can't believe that I was being followed by one of my own students. Am I in danger? Is he the murderer?'

'My instinct says not. But we're going to charge him with stalking. I would imagine he'll be removed from the university. And we'll certainly apply for a restraining order for him. My money would be on a stranger for the murders, if it weren't for the philosophy connection. Can you think of anyone else that you are concerned about?'

The lecturer sat in silence for a few moments. She shook her head. 'Sorry – I just can't get over what you've just told me. I'm shocked. And really worried. I mean, the man knows where I live. I just can't believe he's been taking photos of me. That's just so creepy. A real invasion of privacy.'

'I can understand you being worried but don't be. As I said, he's going to be charged.'

'You should have told me sooner,' she admonished. 'Not wait until we met up. My God—'

'I'm sorry but we are dealing with a multiple murder case, Mairi. And then with my brother just landing on my doorstep with his news about Mum.'

'Oh no, what's wrong with your mum? I really liked her.'

Shit. I'm not going to tell her about Mum. 'Look, let's not worry about my family for now. Let's just focus on what you can tell me about your students and staff.'

'Well, there's something a bit odd about Davey Munroe.'

Carruthers' ears pricked up. This was the second time the housemate of both Rachel Abbie and Sarah Torr had been mentioned. 'The Canadian guy?'

'That's right. The thing is, he just doesn't seem to be up to the mark with his studies. And he doesn't show that much interest in the subject either.'

'That in itself isn't that strange, is it?'

'Perhaps not. After all, it's not unusual for students to enrol on a course and find out it's not for them. But the strange thing is, he's on the exchange programme, that's all. I just have no idea how he got onto it, to be honest. As you can imagine, it's highly competitive. Only the most gifted of students are selected, and as I said, he just doesn't hit the mark.'

Carruthers steepled his hands and looked into the face of his ex-wife. 'See what you can find out about him, will you? Perhaps have a good look at his application form. Mairi, I was meaning to ask – there seems to be a book doing the rounds by an author named Ayn Rand. I understand she's a philosopher?'

'Was a philosopher,' said his ex-wife. 'She's been dead nearly thirty years. She started the Objectivist movement.'

'Are her books on the syllabus for undergraduates?'

'No, they're not, but I'm aware that some of my students are in an Objectivist club started by a visiting student here. Why do you ask?'

'When we searched the room of our first murder victim, Rachel Abbie, DS Fletcher found a copy of *Atlas Shrugged* on her floor. That's by Ayn Rand, isn't it?'

His wife nodded.

'The same book has also made an appearance in the room of Serena Davis and Serena is studying history of art. Not philosophy. Originally, I thought we were clutching at straws but we're desperate…'

'And now?'

'Well, now we've unearthed Rachel Abbie's diary. Not her academic diary. Her personal one. In it she says that Davey Munroe was hassling her and trying to convert her to Objectivism. That's the word she used. Is this movement a cult?'

'Well, first, can I just say it's not unusual for someone studying a subject other than philosophy to read Rand's work, although Randroids are much more common in North America than in the UK.'

'Randroids?'

'The followers of Ayn Rand. Personally, I don't like Objectivism, and starting up an Objectivist club here in the philosophy department isn't something that I would actively encourage, but I can't really stop it and nor should I. This country still has freedom of speech.'

'Is it a cult? From what Rachel Abbie had written in her diary it certainly smacks of one.'

'It's debatable. It's not a cult in the true sense of the word, but some have called it a cult. It's certainly cult-like and some believe it functions like a modified cult.'

This piqued Carruthers' interest. 'In what respect?'

'Ayn Rand's followers always believed, like a lot of cult leaders, that she was superior to everyone else. The main difference is that other cult leaders cited God as their highest power. She cited reason.'

'Why don't you like it?'

'Well look, this is just my opinion, but the thing about Objectivism is that it gives followers permission to indulge in their worst impulses. It makes a virtue of selfishness and encourages infidelity. It is cult-like in the sense that it targets a certain type of person and tells that person their weaknesses are their strengths.'

Carruthers sat, intrigued and appalled in equal measure. He was starting to build up a picture of a typical Objectivist and he didn't much like what he was hearing.

'So, somebody who is emotionally weak, who has had a past history of mental health problems or someone who is inherently selfish, could be attracted to Objectivism?'

'In a nutshell its appeal is rational self-interest so it appeals to the intelligent. It flatters their egos. In my opinion it's a very seductive simplistic philosophy.'

'Which is?'

'As I said, that unfettered self-interest is good and altruism is destructive. To be honest it's incredibly powerful stuff, especially for the young, and its appeal is far-reaching. Ayn Rand's writing has influenced a number of politicians, including Republican Ted Cruz, even Donald Trump.'

'How would Objectivists get on with each other? I mean, if they are all motivated by self-interest, how would society work if everyone was an Objectivist?'

Mairi crossed her legs at the ankle while she considered the question. A habit Carruthers had noticed when they were married. He used to love the way she would sit on the couch snuggling into him with her legs crossed.

'Another interesting question. Well, I did hear a story about two Objectivists who met at university. They moved in together.'

'What happened?' Carruthers was fascinated.

'The relationship lasted less than six months. They argued about absolutely everything. Each wanted and expected to get their own way. Both were selfish to the last. I can't see how a society that was based on Objectivist values would work, to be honest.'

Carruthers picked his next words carefully. 'How would an Objectivist treat someone else?'

'Probably with contempt, especially if they didn't think they were particularly intelligent or they didn't follow Rand's philosophy. *The Virtue of Selfishness* is the title of a collection of papers co-written by Rand. Basically, what she is arguing is that being selfish is actually good for you. What selfish person doesn't want to hear that? Some would argue she was little more than an atheist adulterer. Her ideas are clearly used to justify inequality and give credence to institutional wealth-based elitism. Well, that's my view anyway but, like I said, I don't like her philosophy, so I'm obviously biased.'

'You're not a fan then?'

Mairi arched an eyebrow and uncrossed her legs. 'Are you being facetious, Jim?'

Carruthers tried hard not to stare at his ex-wife's legs. Instead he said, 'So I can see the attraction to young people. I can also see how volatile two Objectivists living together might be if they both believe in rational self-interest. What I can't yet understand is how being an Objectivist can lead to somebody becoming a serial killer.'

'Well, if I'm truthful I don't see how it can. Objectivism is very clear on murder. They certainly don't think it morally acceptable to kill another human being. That said, it's still within the realms of possibility that there could be a serial killer out there who is an Ayn Rand fan. But no, generally as a movement, they are against murder.' She shrugged. 'I'm happy to do some further research for you if that helps?'

'Yeah, that would be good. Anything you can dig up that might be useful. One other thing. Do you have a student by the name of Mary-Lou Gettier?'

'Can't say I know the name, no.'

'We think she's the student who started the Objectivist club here.'

'She's not a philosophy student, Jim, but from what my students tell me, the university's Objectivist club was actually started by a student outside the philosophy department. They may have mentioned her name. I honestly can't remember now.'

Mary-Lou Gettier is still a mystery then.

Chapter twenty-eight

Back at the station Carruthers attempted to tidy up his desk by pushing bits of paper around. He chucked a couple of empty polystyrene cups into the recycling. A tired-looking Sandra McTavish walked into the office and up to his desk.

'Well, didn't take him long.'

Carruthers looked up, interested. 'Who?'

'Superintendent Len sodding Campbell. We've had the chief super on the phone. He wants me to file a report on what we've got on the weasel's son. Bingham was right when he said that Campbell wouldn't waste any time bringing the big guns in.'

Carruthers couldn't help but smile at the DCI's choice of words. He couldn't put it better himself. 'Do you want any help?'

'No, don't worry, Jim. Get yourself off home. You look done in. You'll be no good to me if you don't get some sleep.'

Noting the shadows under her eyes and the pale face he wondered who was the more exhausted. Looking at his watch he realised it had gone 7pm. He nodded, said goodnight and gathered his things.

* * *

As soon as he shut the front door of his cottage behind him his mobile rang. As he answered it, he walked into the kitchen, picking up a scrap of paper hastily scribbled by his brother and left by the kettle. Alan had gone down the pub. Carruthers sighed. Was he in for a repeat of last night's performance?

'Jim, it's Mairi.' A sudden intake of breath. 'Look, I know it's late. But I need to talk to you.'

He put the piece of paper down. 'Okay. Fire away.'

'There's been something bothering me about Davey Munroe. Something about him that just didn't stack up. After our meeting I asked the secretary of the department to pull his file. She was off for a half day, but I got the temp to do it. I told her I wanted a closer look at Munroe's application. You know he claims to be an exchange student from the University of Western Ontario?'

'Claims to be?.'

Mairi ignored his question. 'I'm not sure whether I should come over and talk to you in person? Are you at home right now or still at work?'

Was this a ruse to see him or did she really have important information? 'I've just got home. If it's pertinent to the case,' he found himself saying, 'which will require me to go back into work tonight, you should just tell me over the phone.' *God, why am I so bloody sensible? And so stilted?*

'Okay.' She sounded impatient. 'Look, I'll just tell you over the phone and then you can decide what you want to do. Anyway, I've got plans for later on so that suits me.'

He glanced at his watch. It was already gone eight. *Fuck. That could only mean one thing. She must have a boyfriend. Who was he?*

She continued, 'The thing is that Davey Munroe is struggling in all his courses. He doesn't even seem to have the basic knowledge, even for an undergrad, so I started to make some of my own enquiries. Apparently, he–'

The buzzer to Carruthers' cottage sounded, interrupting the conversation. Carruthers swore. Who the hell would this be at this time of night? The only person he could think of was his brother – but he'd given him the spare key. 'Hang on a sec, Mairi,' he said, walking towards the door with the phone in his hand. 'That's my doorbell.'

'Don't answer it.'

Carruthers stopped mid-stride. 'Why?'

'I really need to discuss this. Please.' She sounded scared. That wasn't like her, at least the Mairi he used to know. If what she had found out had made her feel this scared then it must be big.

The door buzzed again. Carruthers ignored it. A third time. Still Carruthers ignored it.

'Are you there?'

'I'm here. Keep talking.'

'Promise you won't answer the door?'

'Oh, for God's sake, Mairi. It's most likely my brother. I can't keep him locked outside.'

'Jim, If I'm honest I'm probably still a bit freaked that John Campbell got into my house, but I'm also scared by what I've found out about Davey Munroe.'

'Tell me what it is.' Carruthers had moved to the window and, phone still in hand, had moved the curtain aside a few inches in the vain hope of seeing who was outside. It was pitch dark. He couldn't see anyone. Disappointed, he stepped away from the curtains and walked over to the couch. He took a seat on the bucket chair, grabbing a pen and his notebook.

She spoke into the phone urgently. 'I don't know how he did it, but I think Davey Munroe managed to falsify his documents to come and study in Scotland. Like I said, I've been making some enquiries about him.'

'How did you manage that?'

'I've got contacts in academia over in Canada. Anyway, I found some stuff out. He was kicked out of university back in Ontario. He's not currently enrolled on a course over there from what I can see. Jim, there's more. The year before he got kicked out a student in his philosophy class got assaulted. The perpetrator was never caught. The student was blonde, female and slashed across the face.'

'Jesus, Mairi.' No wonder she was freaked out. What she'd found out was explosive. In all likelihood one of her own students was the serial killer. As he was contemplating how Munroe had managed to falsify his documents, he heard another doorbell sound. This one on the other end of the line.

'Jim, I've got to go. That's my… guest. He's early. Can we meet up at any point tomorrow morning? I've also found out some disturbing personal information about Ayn Rand – the woman who started the Objectivist movement.' Her bell rang again. She talked rapidly. 'Apparently, she admired a serial killer. A William Edward Hickman. If you get a chance google it.'

'Okay, I'll ring you in the morning.' Carruthers felt a knot of irritation. Mairi was happy to end the call on her terms and open her front door when it suited her.

At the same time as Mairi put the phone down, a disembodied Glaswegian voice rang through the letterbox. 'You going to open the door then, or not?'

Wearily, Carruthers climbed to his feet and slowly walked over to open the front door to his brother.

Chapter twenty-nine

Mairi opened the front door, smile on her face at the thought of seeing her lover. 'You're early. Shift go okay?' Her smile froze as she stared into the face, not of her lover, but of one of her students.

'Hello, prof.'

Mairi stared at the handsome, freckled student with the mop of reddish hair. 'How the hell did you get my address, Davey?'

The student stood menacingly in the threshold. 'Aren't you going to let me in?'

Mairi tried to slam the door on Davey Munroe but he shoved it open. Before she managed to scream, he had slammed the door shut behind him with his foot and crossed the distance between them. He clamped his hand over her mouth while he hissed in her ear. 'A little bird tells me that you've been asking questions about me. You asked how I'd got your address? Probably the same way you found out about my falsifying my documents to study in Scotland. From the obliging temp I've been shagging. Thanks to her I got the Abbies home phone number. She even told me you'd been married to a cop. I've met him, you know.'

He threw her across the hall. She fell into a table, knocking it over. A vase smashed. He looked down on her lying on the floor.

As Mairi rubbed her sore hip, she saw a knife flashing in his hand and her heart skipped a beat.

'You really shouldn't have started snooping, should you? I really liked you, too. Best lecturer I've ever had. And not bad to look at either.'

* * *

Malcolm Duggan had been staring through the net curtain at his next-door neighbour's front door.

His wife clicked her tongue in annoyance. 'Come away from that curtain, Malcolm. What will Mairi think?'

Malcolm let the curtain fall while he turned round to talk to his wife. 'I'm sure I've just seen a man force his way into Mairi's house. At least I think I did, but it's pretty dark and as you know my eyesight isnae so good.' He lifted the curtain again and peered out.

'Oh Malcolm, what if you're mistaken and it's just her boyfriend? I would come away from the window and have your cocoa. It's getting cold.'

'I heard him speak to her on the doorstep. It didnae sound like her boyfriend.' He turned to face his wife. 'I think I'm going to call the police. After all, you cannae be too careful. And she did have that intruder.'

'Don't be silly, Malcolm. You'll end up looking like a fool if you phone the police and get them out on a wild goose chase. And you'll embarrass Mairi into the bargain.'

Malcolm was bending down, taking his slippers off and putting his shoes on.

'Why are you taking those baffies off, you silly old bugger?'

'I'm going round to her house. I just want to make sure she's okay.'

'Ach, you daft old eejit. I ken you're fond of her. If you have to go round, I'll keep your cocoa warm. Don't be too long.'

* * *

Carruthers picked up his mobile and called McTavish. Even though the conversation with Mairi had been cut short he'd heard enough. There was something disturbing about Davey Munroe, and they needed to take a closer look at him.

Twenty minutes later, he was back inside the DCI's office discussing getting a search warrant for Munroe's room. He had felt hellish leaving his brother on his own once again but what could he do? And he still hadn't had time to google Ayn Rand.

There was a knock at the door. Brown put his head round. 'There's a young lady asking to see Andie. As she's not in the station at the moment I've told her you'll have to do.' He grinned.

Carruthers frowned. 'We're right in the middle of something. Who is she?'

'Annie McLeod. Girlfriend of Davey Munroe. Says it's important.'

McTavish stood up. 'Put her in interview room one. Make sure she's offered some refreshment. We'll be there in a few minutes.'

McTavish and Carruthers walked into the interview room a few minutes later. Annie was already seated; her coffee in front of her remained untouched. She was a slim, attractive girl with fine features. The girl wiped her hands on her jeans.

What does she have to be so nervous about? wondered Carruthers.

Carruthers spoke first. 'I understand you wanted to talk to the police? I'm Detective Inspector Jim Carruthers and this is Detective Chief Inspector Sandra McTavish.'

The girl wiped her hands on her thighs once again. 'I've met DS Fletcher before. Is she here? I would really like to speak to her.'

'No, I'm afraid not. She's currently out of the office, but we both work in the same team as DS Fletcher. How can we help you?'

'It's about Davey Munroe. I'm his girlfriend. Or at least I was.' She started biting her nails. They were already bitten to the quick on both hands.

Carruthers was well used to people he interviewed being nervous, even when they had voluntarily come into the station. But this girl, there was something different about her state of nervousness. She looked terrified.

Carruthers took his seat. 'Take your time. What did you want to tell us?'

'It's about Davey. I think he's seeing someone else.'

'I don't think that's a police matter, is it?' said McTavish quickly.

Annie McLeod looked from McTavish to Carruthers. It was Carruthers to whom she spoke. 'No, of course not. What I mean is that he wasn't with me when I said he was.'

Carruthers felt his stomach give a sudden lurch. This was a pivotal moment in their investigation. He spoke slowly. 'You gave him an alibi for the time Rachel Abbie was murdered. Is that what you're referring to?'

'Yes.'

The nervous girl in front of him hung her head for a few moments. She now looked embarrassed. He was desperate for her to get to the point but knew they had to be gentle with her or she would just clam up and change her mind about talking to them. Clearly what she was about to tell them was important. It was also making her very nervous.

'Are you're saying your alibi was false? You lied for him?'

Annie McLeod nodded. 'He asked me to lie. I thought he was with another girl at the time Rachel Abbie got killed, so I didn't think he had anything to do with her horrible murder, but I found out this girl, Mary-Lou, the one I thought he was with, was in a lecture. I only know this because one of my friends was in the same lecture as her and mentioned her.'

'What's this student's name? The one you thought Davey was with?'

'Mary-Lou Gettier. She's American. The thing is – Davey is obsessed with her. Hero worships her.'

An important question popped into Carruthers' mind. 'Are you sure she's American? Could she be Canadian?'

'What?' Annie McLeod seemed to ponder the question for a few moments. 'Oh yeah, that's right. She's Canadian. Think she's on some sort of exchange programme or something.'

Carruthers was starting to feel some important strands of the case were beginning to fall into place. Mary-Lou Gettier being one of them. He started to wonder if Davey Munroe and Mary-

Lou Gettier had known each other back in Canada. What was the betting that they had studied at the same Canadian university? They needed to bring her in.

'Do you know what she's studying? Mary-Lou Gettier?'

'Oh, um, some weird subject. I don't know. Zoology or anthropology or something.'

We'll find out, thought Carruthers.

'So just to confirm, are you saying that you supplied Davey Munroe with a false alibi?' McTavish's voice was curt. As well it might be. 'This is very serious, Annie.'

'Yes, I suppose I did.'

Carruthers jumped in. 'Did it not occur to you that if he had been with this other woman, like he said he was, he could have asked her for an alibi?'

'Like I said, Davey asked me to say I was with him. I wanted him back.'

'And were you with him when Sarah Torr was murdered?'

Annie shook her head.

Carruthers looked at the young woman in front of him who was so desperate to be loved that she would do anything, even lie. He exchanged a look with McTavish. This revelation catapulted Davey to the position of being most likely candidate to have murdered the two women. After all, what possible other reason did he have for asking Annie to give him a false alibi? And with Mairi's revelation about his suspect application and the assault on campus back in Canada… the man was clearly manipulative and cunning. Annie McLeod must be utterly infatuated with Davey Munroe to give him a false alibi when she already thought he was with another woman. That in itself smacked of utter desperation.

'I know what I did was wrong. I only did it because I love him. Please tell me I'm not in too much trouble? My parents will kill me.'

Carruthers considered this for a moment. Annie McLeod was in a hell of a lot of trouble if Davey was the murderer. If he was and she had told the truth earlier, there was a distinct possibility that the murder of Sarah Torr could have been prevented. If Davey Munroe had murdered Sarah Torr, Annie would come to understand the consequences of her lie and she would have to live with that for the rest of her life.

Neither Carruthers nor McTavish answered her question. She'd lied to the police investigating a series of brutal attacks and murders. Giving a false alibi often carries a prison sentence.

Annie started talking again, desperate to fill the silence. 'Since he's come under her influence he's changed. And you know what really freaks me out about this Canadian girl?'

'Mary-Lou,' interjected Carruthers.

'Yes, Mary-Lou. She looks just like Ayn Rand. The Russian émigré that started the Objectivist movement. She's the spitting image. Don't you think that's freaky? I don't like the hold she's got over him.'

Carruthers wondered if this Mary-Lou was the mastermind behind the crimes. They needed to bring her into the police station.

'He's completely obsessed with a dead woman. And a woman who is alive who looks like a dead woman.' She wrinkled her nose in disdain.

'I don't want to think this, because I loved him, but do you think he could have anything to do with the killings? Anyway, to be honest, I'm starting to wonder what I ever saw in him now. He was messy, annoying, everything had to be about him and the way he wanted it. It was like my feelings didn't matter. And then, if all that wasn't bad enough, I found out he's been sleeping with the temp in the philosophy department. Apparently, she calls him Dave. I once tried to call him Dave and he bit my head off. What is it about her? I guess you could say that was the straw that broke the camel's back. I suddenly realised what a mug I'd been.'

Well, if Davey is a true Objectivist, other people's feelings don't matter, thought Carruthers.

McTavish stood up. She'd heard enough. Carruthers followed suit. It was time to bring Davey Munroe into the station.

Chapter thirty

Carruthers punched in Fletcher's number. 'Andie, I need you back at the station. We're going to pick up Davey Munroe. His girlfriend, Annie McLeod, has just paid us a visit. She lied in her interview. He has no alibi for when Rachel Abbie or Sarah Torr were murdered. This could be our man.'

He could hear the intake of breath on the line. Fletcher was ambitious. He knew she'd want to be in. 'Jim, why don't I meet you at Strathburn Halls. It'll be quicker. I'll jump in my car now.'

'Okay. See you soon.' Carruthers finished the call. Something was playing on his mind. It was something Mairi had said about what she'd found out about Ayn Rand. Hadn't she said that the woman had admired a serial killer? He remembered that she hadn't had a chance to tell him the details because her doorbell had rung. Didn't she say he could find out himself if he googled Ayn Rand and Objectivism?

He glanced at his watch. It would take him five minutes to get across town to Strathburn Halls. It would take Andie twenty. He had fifteen minutes to play with. Following his instinct that what his ex-wife had said had been important, he booted his computer up and started googling. Within five minutes he'd found the link between Ayn Rand and an American serial killer. This was just too weird. With heart thumping he phoned Fletcher back.

She picked up on the hands-free. 'I'm five minutes away, Jim.'

'You're not going to believe what I've found out.'

'Try me.'

'Ayn Rand admired an American serial killer named William Edward Hickman.' As he said this, Carruthers felt his heart grow colder than Lake Ontario.

'Keep going,' urged Fletcher.

'In 1927 Hickman murdered a twelve-year-old girl called Marion Parker. Not just murdered, but dismembered. It shocked the nation at the time. When I first started reading about Hickman it looked like the girl was the only person he'd killed, but it appears, when he was arrested, he admitted to a couple of other murders. The murder of Marion Parker became so notorious though, that it's the only one that really gets a mention when you google him.'

'So, what's the connection between the murder and this woman, Ayn Rand?'

'Rand's early notebooks were full of praise for Hickman. It's even said that she modelled her first literary creation, Danny Renahan, the protagonist of her unfinished first novel, *The Little Street* – on him.'

'Christ.'

'There's more. Hickman was a sociopath. And that's what Ayn Rand admired about him, apparently. But it's the way in which the girl died that is important. When interviewed by police Hickman said that he had killed Marion by strangling her with a towel.'

Fletcher was silent, taking all this new information on board.

'Andie, are you still there?'

'Yes, I'm here. Carry on.'

'Hickman had knotted the towel around her throat and pulled it tightly for two minutes before she became unconscious. Once Marion was out, Hickman took his pocket knife and cut a hole in her throat to draw blood. He then took her to the bathtub and drained her body of blood. And that's just the start. I'm not wanting to tell you the rest. If you want to know the gruesome details you can read them for yourself.'

Carruthers' mind was racing. Davey Munroe had no alibi for when either Rachel Abbie or Sarah Torr had been murdered. He was by all accounts obsessed with a dead woman who herself had been in awe of a serial killer. Carruthers was now convinced Davey Munroe had lied to get on the exchange programme. The question was, why? He had no doubt that Munroe was the murderer. He just had to set about proving it. And he had the very strong feeling that the roots of the murders lay in Munroe's childhood back in Canada.

'Okay, just leaving. It's him, Andie. I'm pretty sure Davey Munroe's our man. I also want us to pick up a student called Mary-Lou Gettier.'

* * *

Within twenty minutes Carruthers and Fletcher were standing at the front door of Davey Munroe's accommodation. Fletcher was struggling to get into the stab proof vest. Carruthers was already wearing his, as were the several police officers standing behind them. Carruthers rang the students' bell and waited.

Fletcher kept her voice low. 'How did you find out the stuff about Davey Munroe?'

'It was Mairi who put me on to it. She found out Davey Munroe falsified his application to get onto the exchange programme here. She was in a bit of a state.'

Fletcher looked at him, alarmed. 'Why here, though? I mean, why would he want to come to Scotland? Are you worried about Mairi, Jim?'

He shook his head. 'No, I think her boyfriend was going round. In fact, the doorbell rang when I was on the phone to her.'

Carruthers rang the bell again and this time kept his finger down on the bell for several seconds.

'How do you feel about the fact she has a boyfriend?'

Carruthers hadn't had time to think about how he really felt so all he said was, 'It was bound to happen.'

An exhausted-looking Will Smith opened the front door. His eyes widened when he saw the line of police officers. 'What's going on?'

Carruthers kept his voice calm. 'We need to speak with your housemate, Davey Munroe. It's urgent.'

'He's not here. He's staying over with Annie McLeod tonight.'

But he isn't, thought Carruthers. *He's not with her and he's lied to his housemates.*

Carruthers and Fletcher pushed passed Will. 'We need to take a look at his room. Can you show us which one it is, please?'

'Sure, okay. What's going on?' He led the line of police officers through the hall. He stopped outside the third room on the left. 'This is it.'

Carruthers tried the door. It was locked. He gave the nod to the uniformed officer behind him. The officer took a step back and shoulder charged the room. The lock splintered. He shouted an instruction for the two officers to start a systematic search of the rest of the accommodation, and he and Fletcher walked into the boy's bedroom.

The room was tidy. Almost too tidy to be the bedroom of a student. Carruthers went over to the small writing desk in the far corner whilst Fletcher rummaged through the drawers of his bedside table.

Carruthers picked up a pad of paper that was on Davey Munroe's desk. The top page had been torn off. There were faint indentations on the next sheet.

'Have you got a pencil, Andie?'

'I may carry a lot of things in my handbag but a pencil isn't one of them.'

Carruthers searched the desk and discovered a pencil in a drawer. He picked it up and held it at an angle while he shaded the page. He held the pad up to the light. It revealed an address. A familiar address in Ceres. He gripped the scrap of paper tightly. It was Mairi's home address.

'Shit.'

Fletcher crossed the room and Carruthers handed the pad to her. His mind was racing and he was starting to feel sick.

Why on earth would Davey Munroe have Mairi's home address? Could it have been Davey Munroe who had left the rose on Mairi's bed? No, it didn't make sense. Why would he? Perhaps he had the address for an altogether more sinister reason.

He whipped his mobile out. 'I need to phone Mairi.' With sweating hands, he made the call. It just went straight to voicemail.

He cursed again. And yet he knew she would be at home. Hadn't she said that she was waiting for a visitor? Then again, if it were a visitor of the opposite sex, would she be answering her mobile to Carruthers? Perhaps she was in bed with him.

But a nagging thought pushed into the detective's mind. What if the guest at the front door hadn't been her boyfriend? What if it had been Davey Munroe? Hadn't she said her visitor had been early? *Oh God.*

With increasingly shaky hands he phoned the station. 'I want you to dispatch a unit to an address in School Hill in Ceres.'

He heard Willie Brown's voice on the other end. 'Hang on. Did you say School Hill in Ceres? We've just had a call come through from a Mr Malcolm Duggan. He was ringing about his neighbour, Mairi Beattie. I can't get a unit dispatched at the moment, Jim. We've got two men down with that stomach bug and there's been a major incident in Glenrothes.'

'Jesus. Okay. I'll go myself. Just get a unit sent out as soon as possible.' He turned to Fletcher. 'I need to leave. I want you and the officers to search Davey Munroe's room thoroughly. And I mean thoroughly. Leave no stone unturned. I'll be on the mobile if you find anything.'

Fletcher grasped his arm. 'You need to wait for back-up, Jim. It might be dangerous. You know the procedure.'

He shrugged her off. 'No time.' And with that he was gone.

Chapter thirty-one

Mairi Beattie saw the knife glinting in Davey Munroe's hand. Paralysed with fear, she could do nothing but just sit where she had fallen, rooted to the ground. Her breaths were coming fast and shallow. Just as she was about to speak there was a knock at the door. She tried to get up.

'Leave it,' Davey Munroe hissed.

He covered the ground between him and Mairi, and before she knew it, he had pulled her to her feet and unceremoniously pushed her into the shadows and was standing behind her with the cold knife against her face.

There was a noise as the letterbox was lifted and a pair of eyes and bushy eyebrows peered through. 'Mairi, hen, it's Malcolm Duggan from next door. Are you okay?'

'Tell him you're okay or I'll cut you, just like I cut the others,' he hissed.

She felt the coldness of the blade against her skin. 'Malcolm, I'm okay, thanks.' Her voice sounded shaky even to her own ears. She hoped it would be enough to concern Malcolm and for him to raise the alarm.

'Are you on your own, Mairi?'

She felt the knife digging in a bit more. 'No, I have a visitor with me.'

Munroe hissed in her ear. 'Tell him you're fine and make it convincing. We need to get rid of him.'

'We, er, can't get to the door right now, Malcolm.'

'If you're sure you're okay, hen. I don't want to disturb you. Just want to make sure you're all right.'

With a sinking heart Mairi responded. 'I'm fine, Malcolm. I'll see you tomorrow.'

Davey tightened his grip on the knife. 'Convince him.'

'Go back inside. You'll catch a chill,' was all she could think to say. She heard the letterbox clatter as it was dropped.

* * *

Malcolm's footsteps retreated as he walked back up her garden path towards his own home – and Mairi's heart sank.

'You did very well, Mairi, if I can call you that. Quite the actress.' He was still holding the knife to her face. Mairi shivered as she realised this was probably the same knife used to kill those other women. She was so close to him she could the smell the fresh sweat on him. She wrinkled her nose, wondering if he was getting off on her fear. She was determined to show none.

'The one regret I had about killing those other women was it was over far too quickly. Being in someone's house is much better. We can take our time to get to know each other. That's the problem with students. Very few of them live on their own.' He laughed. 'I should have gone after pretty lecturers instead.' He grasped a lock of her black hair and wound it around his finger.

Utterly terrified, Mairi knew enough about psychology to now know she was most probably alone with a psychopathic serial killer. She just hoped Malcolm would raise the alarm and the police would get to her in time.

'How could you murder those women? What had they ever done to you?' Mairi knew that if she kept him talking long enough the police had a greater chance of arriving before she became the next victim. She also knew from the little Jim had told her about serial killers when they had been married, that once they started talking about their killings they often wanted to talk in great detail.

* * *

Fletcher bent on her hands and knees and searched under Davey Munroe's bed. Nothing. She stood up and stripped the bed as she made a methodical search under the pillow and in the duvet. She glanced at Watson, who was riffling through the chest of drawers in the student's room.

'Nothing here, Andie,' Watson shouted over.

'Keep looking. The answer's in this room. I just know it is.' Fletcher straightened up, putting her hands on her hips. She flexed her neck, which crunched. *Time to get another massage,* she thought absentmindedly. She walked over to the bookcase and started taking each book out in turn, flicking through the pages and replacing the books on the shelves. Gayle Watson was going through Davey Munroe's wicker washing basket, picking up dirty boxer shorts and putting her hands in smelly socks. *Rather her than me,* thought Fletcher.

Fletcher walked over to Munroe's writing desk and started going through his pile of paperwork. Mostly coursework. She noticed his grades weren't that good. That tallied with what Mairi Beattie had said. She shifted the sheets of coursework, and underneath, found an unmarked file. She picked it up, puzzled, but when she opened it she got the shock of her life. There were newspaper clippings about his mother and father's death. She turned to Watson. 'I think I might have something.' She took a seat and started reading. Her hand flew to her mouth when she read the details of his mother's death. Some of the details were completely new to her. And she knew Carruthers didn't know about them either. Finally, everything started to make sense.

'What have you got?'

Fletcher tore her gaze away from the article she was reading. 'You know how his mother died from injuries received most likely from the father? Gayle, this newspaper article says his mother got slashed across the face before she was strangled. I thought she was beaten to death.'

'Same MO as our victims.'

Watson covered the space across the room quickly, looking over Fletcher's shoulder at the article. 'You saying what I think you are? That Davey Munroe murdered his own mother?'

'I think it's a possibility.' She looked around her. 'There must be more here. I feel we're so close to nailing it.' She walked across the thick rug towards the back of the room, whipping out her mobile from her bag as she did so. She couldn't sit on their find. She needed to phone Carruthers and warn him. Her thoughts were now of Mairi Beattie. She had a bad feeling about her. Her foot squeaked as it hit a loose floorboard. She hesitated. Should she phone Jim first or continue with the search? She made her decision, and crouched down on her knees, placing her mobile on the floor. Gayle Watson glanced over as Fletcher ripped the rug up.

'Anything?'

'Nothing. Can you give me a hand lifting the floorboard? It's loose.'

Watson walked over and joined her. Both her knees creaked as she squatted down. She pulled at the floorboard and it came up with not too much bother. Both women tried to peer into the darkness below.

'We're going to need a torch.' As if by magic Watson produced a torch from her pocket, switched it on and shone it down in the blackness.

Fletcher arched an eyebrow. 'Don't tell me you were in the Girl Guides?'

Watson half smiled then resumed her search. She shrugged. 'We knew we'd be searching the room so…'

'I was going to use the torch on my mobile.'

'Nothing like the real thing. There's definitely something down here.' She twisted her body so that she could get her arm at the right angle to explore the space. She yelped as she picked up nothing more than a splinter. Once more, she put her hand in the black space and resumed her search. 'I've got something.' With a flourish, she brought out a plastic bag which had been flattened to fit into the space. 'Voila.'

The two officers exchanged looks. Watson untied the bag and tipped the contents out onto the floor. Fletcher drew in a deep breath as they gazed at their booty. They had found what they were looking for. There, lying on the floor, was a clown mask, a bloodied shirt and a large matchbox. 'What's the betting the blood on that T-shirt will be a match for Sarah Torr?'

Watson picked up the matchbox. 'Does Munroe smoke?'

'I don't know. Not that I'm aware of.' Fletcher looked around her. 'There's no sign of either cigarettes or ashtray in the bedroom.'

'Do you want to do the honours, or do I?' said Watson.

Fletcher picked up the matchbox gingerly. 'I'll do it.' Anxiously, she slid open the box and recoiled when she saw its contents. A severed finger – probably from Sarah Torr. She could smell the overpowering scent of death. But there was also something else in the box, wrapped carefully in tissue paper. With a pounding heart, Fletcher picked up the object and unwrapped it. When she saw what it was she was glad to be wearing gloves. It was discoloured and shrivelled but still recognisable. A second fingertip.

Watson dropped the torch, leapt up and pulled her mobile out of her trouser pocket. 'I'll call Jim.'

Fletcher nodded before speaking. 'Gayle?'

The older woman looked down at her colleague, worry etched on her face.

'You'd better tell him we haven't found the knife.' As Watson made the call, Fletcher silently stared at the damning evidence that would hopefully help put Davey Munroe away for a very long time.

* * *

Carruthers drove like a madman on the twisting dark country roads to the village of Ceres. All he could think of was that Mairi had a serial killer in her house and that she was going to die on her own and that he would be too late to save her. He felt a lump in his throat. He took a deep breath and blinked back the tears. The car bounced as he hit a pot hole and he felt the vibration in the steering wheel. This was no good. He needed to get a grip and to get both him and his car there in one piece. He didn't want to have an accident. He took some deep breaths to steady his nerves and purposefully tried to slow down.

He arrived outside her house and jumped out of his car, leaving the door open. He noticed a curtain twitch in the next cottage and then the front door opened. A rotund, red-faced man in his seventies opened the door and beckoned him inside.

'Are you police? I made the call about my next-door neighbour, Mairi Beattie. My name's Malcolm Duggan.'

Carruthers took out his ID badge. The man nodded and continued to talk. 'There's definitely someone in the house with her but I dinnae think it's her boyfriend. I'm worried about her. She didnae sound right when I spoke to her. She sounded scared.'

'Did you try to see her?'

'Aye, but she wouldnae open the door. Said she couldnae get to the door, but somehow it just didn't feel right. That's why I phoned you lot.'

'You did the right thing. It's important to listen to your gut feeling. Have you got a spare key to her property?' As he spoke, Carruthers kept an eye on Mairi's house, but all was silent. The hall light was on but all the other rooms were in darkness. He didn't want to think about what he might find on the other side of the door. Was he already too late?

'Aye. Not to the front door though. I've got the key to the back.'

'That's even better.' Carruthers followed him inside. He was forming a plan that might just work. Malcolm was going to have to play a crucial part, though. He hoped the older man was up to it.

His mobile rang, a shrill noise. It was Watson. She sounded breathless. And excited. 'Jim, we've got it. The mask, and the fingers. There were two of them. The second is older. Could be his mother's. They were hidden in a plastic bag under the floorboards in Davey Munroe's bedroom, along with a shirt soaked in blood, but we haven't found the knife.'

While Carruthers knew that finding the fingers, mask and shirt weren't actual proof of Munroe's guilt, he knew instinctively they were one step closer to nailing him.

Watson was breathless as she spoke. 'I'm giving them to forensics ASAP. With a bit of luck, the mask might have some DNA on it from when Serena Davis tried to rip it off, and the blood's a likely match with that of Sarah Torr. Is Mairi okay?'

Was she okay? He was still to find out. 'I need to go.' He cut the call.

* * *

Carruthers took the back door key from Malcolm. He then called again for back-up, and got reassurance that there was finally a unit on its way. Carruthers knew he should wait for them to arrive and he also knew he should call DCI McTavish and touch base with her. He was breaking every rule in the book, but with a killer on the loose, and now most likely threatening his ex-wife, every second was vital.

He crept round the back of the property, cursing that he hadn't had a chance to see the layout of the house. But then again Mairi hadn't wanted him in her home.

Carefully, he unlocked the back door, and inch by inch turned the handle. A few seconds later he found himself standing in Mairi's kitchen. Silhouettes from the street lamps cast their eerie glow across the worktops. He fumbled for his mobile phone, put it to silent and shone the light on it in order to see better. He strained his ears to catch any sounds in the house. He heard a male and female voice in another room and breathed a sigh of relief. The female voice was Mairi's. She was still alive.

This was madness, being in the house without back-up, but he did have one thing in his favour: the element of surprise. Voices suddenly grew louder. They were coming his way. He heard a mobile phone ring and a male voice hissing for Mairi to leave it.

* * *

Mairi needed to keep Davey Munroe talking. It was her only hope. She couldn't bear the sound of his voice, but she had to feign interest. 'Tell me about why you killed these students? What had they ever done to you?'

'They're women. Isn't that enough?'

'Well, they were university students. Is that relevant?'

'Why would it be?'

'It's not because they're women at university taking up places that could be taken by male students?' She remembered that there was a case back in 1991 when a male student had turned a gun on women engineering students at a Canadian university. He had asked all the men to stand up and leave first. Then he'd opened fire on the women. She wondered if some of those men still suffered survivor's guilt and how their lives had turned out after witnessing such unspeakable horror.

'Women remind me of my mother. She was weak.'

Once again, a mobile phone started ringing in the house. Mairi wondered if it was Brian, her new boyfriend. He should be here by now. She hoped it wasn't him phoning to say he was going to be late, or worse, needing to cancel.

'Leave that phone,' Munroe hissed.

'So why was your mother weak? Because she didn't stand up to your father?'

'How do you know about that?'

'But why travel to Scotland and kill here?'

'My mother was Scottish.'

That explained the red hair and freckles. *But surely that couldn't be the only reason.*

There was a knock on the front door. Mairi's heart soared. It must be Brian. She then heard the sound of the letterbox being lifted. The noise startled both Mairi and Davey Munroe. 'Mairi, it's Malcolm again, hen.' As soon as she heard his voice Mairi felt a ray of hope. He obviously had picked up in her voice that something was seriously wrong. 'Can you open the door? Sorry to be a bother. I'm just a wee bit worried about you.' Keeping the knife behind his back, Davey walked Mairi closer to the door.

As Mairi and Davey were distracted with Malcolm yelling through the letterbox, Carruthers strode swiftly through the kitchen and out into the hall.

At the last moment, before Carruthers could take advantage of the element of surprise, his foot crunched on what sounded like broken glass. Davey Munroe heard the noise and swivelled round to face Carruthers. He tightened his grip on Mairi and moved the knife from behind his back to her throat.

'Don't come any closer or I'll slash her throat.'

Carruthers backed off a couple of steps, heart in his mouth. He put his hands up in a gesture of surrender as he took in the butcher's boning knife. 'Don't hurt her.'

Davey now had his back to the front door. Out of the corner of his eye Carruthers saw the letterbox flap fall. His heart sank. His plan for Malcolm to distract Davey long enough for him to unarm the student had backfired. Sick to his heart, he stood where he was. What the hell was he going to do now?

Keeping his eye on the suspect he said evenly, 'Let Mairi go, Davey. It's finished. Give yourself in to the police.'

With his back still to the front door Davey tightened his grip on Mairi. 'You won't be doing anything to me while I've got her – your ex-wife.'

Carruthers wondered if the student was on drugs. He was seriously pumped. He watched the spittle form at the side of his mouth when he talked.

'And it's pretty obvious you've still got feelings for her, otherwise why are you here?'

'I'm a police officer. That's why I'm here.' An image of DCI McTavish came into Carruthers' mind, hands on hips, wagging her finger at him, telling him quite rightly he was too close to the case. Yet again he'd gone charging in. He hadn't even kept McTavish informed of his actions. He wondered briefly if Fletcher had said anything to her.

Carruthers saw a movement behind Davey. The flap of the letterbox was being pushed back up. Horrified, Carruthers saw the barrel of a gun appear. What the hell was Malcolm doing, if it was indeed Malcolm? He couldn't see the person on the end of it.

Before Carruthers had a chance to shout a warning there was a crack, followed by a scream of pain. Davey fell to the ground, hit in the back of the leg. The knife shot out of Davey's hand and skittered across the floor. Carruthers rushed forward, seized the knife from the ground, before grabbing Mairi, who fell into his arms, sobbing.

As he hugged his shaking ex-wife close, he could see over the top of her head Davey trying to drag himself to a standing position. A well-executed kick from Carruthers brought him back to his knees. At that moment, Mairi's next-door neighbour came lumbering through her kitchen into the hall, drawing up short when he saw Davey prostrate on the floor covered in blood.

'I got him,' shouted Malcolm. 'My army training came in useful after all. That'll teach the wee shite.'

Chapter thirty-two

Tuesday

Carruthers and McTavish sat opposite Davey Munroe in hospital. Carruthers stared at the baby-faced killer. He wondered what had turned a freckle-faced boy into a monster and, ultimately, a murderer. Good looks and charm, of course, were no barrier to sadistic murder. Just look at Ted Bundy.

Carruthers considered what dark forces lay behind the veneer of respectability. 'So why did you do it? Why did you kill them?'

Davey just shrugged.

It was startling looking at the background of some of the world's worst serial killers, thought Carruthers, just how disturbed their childhoods had been. So many of them had either been abused as youngsters by their parents or had been abandoned by parents who often had drug and alcohol problems. But not all of them.

Of course, they now knew much more about Davey. How he'd been living in Canada with his family. How his father had got the young Davey involved in the Church of Scientology after the youngster had had a breakdown. And how Davey had rebelled and left the church. After that, perhaps it was inevitable he'd always be anti-religion. He wondered what Davey's experience of Scientology had been like.

'You might as well tell us,' Carruthers urged. 'Tell us your side of things. After all, you're going to prison for a very long time, Davey. And if we still had the death penalty you'd be hanging for these crimes. But answer one question first. Were you in it alone or did Mary-Lou Gettier put you up to it?'

* * *

'Why have you brought me here?' Mary-Lou Gettier looked up at Fletcher and Watson, who were conducting her interview.

As Fletcher looked at the Canadian, she critically assessed the younger woman, noting the similarities in looks between the student and the long dead Russian émigré who had started the movement of Objectivism.

Watson looked at the younger woman keenly. 'We want to know what part you've played in the deaths of Rachel Abbie and Sarah Torr and in the assault of Serena Davis.'

'None whatsoever.'

'But you do know them?' urged Fletcher.

'Sure, I met them a few times. Castletown's a small place.'

'What's your relationship with Davey Munroe?' urged Fletcher. Are you sleeping with him?'

'Not that it's any of your business but, yeah, we're having a sexual relationship, but he's not my boyfriend. It's a casual thing.'

Fletcher leant forward. 'So, you're sleeping with other people too?'

The Canadian student turned away from them and stared at the wall. 'That really is none of your business.'

'This is a murder enquiry and everything is our business.' Fletcher riffled through her little black notebook. 'We'll need to know where you were for each of the murders.'

Mary-Lou Gettier looked at Fletcher and frowned. 'I have alibis for both murders and the assault. You can't possibly think I've had a hand in them.'

'Oh, but you have, Mary-Lou, whether directly or inadvertently. What we want to know is who is the mastermind behind them? You or Davey Munroe? You know he's in love with you, don't you?'

Mary-Lou crossed her arms. 'I'm not responsible for who falls in love with me, am I?'

Fletcher tried a different tack. 'You're an Objectivist?'

'Yes, but then so's a whole heap of other folk and I don't see them being hauled in here for questioning. It's one of the fastest growing movements in North America. You're just victimising me cos I'm a follower of Ayn Rand.'

Fletcher was starting to dislike this assured young woman. 'You started a branch of the movement here at the university? Davey Munroe was a member. What about Serena Davis and Rachel Abbie? Were they ever members?'

'Having membership isn't illegal. There's a global Objectivist club network all over the world. And just for the record, neither Serena Davis nor Rachel Abbie were members, despite Davey's recruitment drive. We have twenty-five members to date and I don't recall seeing their names listed.'

'Perhaps not,' said Watson, 'but you know who they are, don't you?'

'Sure, but that doesn't make me guilty of a crime.'

Fletcher remained silent, letting Watson have her turn.

Watson jabbed her open notebook with her black pen. 'We wondered what linked all those unfortunate women who got attacked. After all, they weren't all studying the same subject. Although Rachel Abbie and Sarah Torr were studying philosophy, Serena Davis was an art student. But then we sussed there must be a connection when we found books by Ayn Rand in both the bedrooms of Rachel and Serena.'

Mary-Lou Gettier remained silent.

Fletcher took up the reins once again. 'We know becoming an Objectivist was the catalyst for Davey Munroe becoming a savage killer. He became obsessed with Ayn Rand and the movement and he became obsessed with you. In fact, he'd do anything for you, wouldn't he?'

Mary-Lou shrugged. 'If you say so.'

Fletcher leant into the table. 'What we want to know is, did he kill for you? Did you put him up to murdering these young women?'

'No, of course not. Why would I? The philosophy of Objectivism is very clear on the subject of murder. An Objectivist might kill in self-defence but murder is not compatible with the movement's ethics.'

'You say that, yet Ayn Rand, who formed the movement, was herself in thrall to a serial killer. And not just a serial killer. A child killer. Where did you meet Davey? Was it in Scotland or back in Canada?'

As Fletcher asked this question, she was coming to realise that Objectivism sounded like a philosophy full of contradictions.

* * *

'They just had to die. It's as simple as that.'

'Murder is rarely simple.' Carruthers wondered if there'd been a tipping point or had the young Davey practised on cats and dogs as he'd worked his way up to finally killing human beings, like so many serial killers.

'They were all weak.'

Carruthers glanced at McTavish, but the DCI remained silent as she listened to the conversation.

'So, you don't like weakness, but that's not a reason to kill. There must be something more. Let's start with Serena,' urged Carruthers. 'Why did you try to kill her?'

'No wait,' said McTavish, 'why did you come to the UK to do your killing? You were living in Canada. Why didn't you kill there?'

'My mother was from Scotland.'

'Yes, but that doesn't explain why you would want to do your killing here.'

'I've always wanted to come to Scotland.'

Carruthers decided to keep pushing. 'You knew Mary-Lou Gettier back in Canada, didn't you?'

'Yep. She was at the same university.'

'So, you fixed it so that you'd follow her to Scotland.' He was starting to wonder just how many stalkers there were.

Davey Munroe shrugged.

So, he had followed her over. But she must have been aware of the slashing back in Ontario, so if she was so innocent why hadn't she said anything to the Scottish police? Was she in league with Munroe, after all? Mary-Lou Gettier was more than just a person of interest. 'So, you forged the documentation needed to get onto the exchange programme.' *No mean feat. Wonder who he slept with for that?* Once again, he was reminded of the charm of Ted Bundy.

Carruthers felt utterly depressed but he had to push on. 'You were going to tell us about Serena?'

'In a way I admired Serena. She wasn't as weak as the others. But she said some very nasty things to me. They weren't very nice at all.' He pulled a face. It was obvious to Carruthers that he was reliving his experience, but to the police officer he sounded like a much younger boy.

'What did she say to you?' prompted Carruthers.

'She called me weak. *Me.* She said I was weak to be an Objectivist and that I had replaced one form of religion with another.'

From the limited knowledge Carruthers had of Objectivism, perhaps Serena Davis did have a point.

'She mocked me. She reminded me of my father. He used to call me weak.'

Once again, Carruthers wondered if the fall Davey's father had sustained that had killed him had been an accident. Had the man really tripped or had the young Davey gone and pushed him? And what about his mother's death? Had it really been by his father's hand? Or had it, as he was now suspecting, been by the son's? He thought of Fletcher's revelation and the discovery of the second severed finger that Watson and Fletcher had found in the box. It had been sent to forensics for analysis, but there was no doubting it was much older than the other digit they had discovered. He realised that he would have to tread carefully if he wanted to get the most out of this interview.

McTavish shuffled her notes. 'We understand you had a nervous breakdown back in Canada?'

'That didn't make me weak.'

'No, of course it didn't.' Carruthers spoke quickly. *So that's why Serena Davis was targeted,* thought Carruthers. No doubt the young Davey had been bullied by his domineering father.

'Anyway, they drove me to the breakdown. Always bickering. I couldn't stand it.'

'Your parents?' questioned McTavish.

Davey didn't answer. He seemed lost in his thoughts.

'You don't like weakness, do you?'

'The weak are a drain on our resources. They are like sewer rats. They should be left to die.'

Carruthers felt his blood run cold. If this was one of the tenets of extreme Objectivist ideology, then he wanted nothing to do with it.

Davey crossed his arms. 'I don't want to talk about my father any more.' A smile came over his face. 'Anyway, in the end he got what was coming to him. They all do, you know.'

This was the moment Carruthers had been waiting for. 'Did you push him down the stairs?'

Davey Munroe remained silent.

'What about your mother? Did you kill her?' Carruthers thought about the life of abuse she'd probably endured at the hands of her husband. He then thought about the manner of her death. Had it been Davey who had finally killed her or had it been the father? The MOs were so similar to the murders here in Castletown that there was clearly a connection between them.

'No comment.'

From his brief reading on the subject Carruthers knew that Munroe exhibited all the traits of an extreme Objectivist, but as odious as he found this philosophy, very few Objectivists became killers, and serial killers to boot. To Carruthers' mind he was also exhibiting many of the traits of a serial killer. He knew serial killers tended to be weak and irrationally scared of rejection. Perhaps when Serena Davis rejected Objectivism the twisted Davey Munroe saw it as a rejection of him. Serial killers were also terrified of being abandoned, humiliated or exposed. Was it possible that Munroe had embraced Objectivism to hide his own insecurities?

McTavish cleared her throat. 'Okay, well let's move on to why you killed Rachel?'

McTavish is getting impatient, thought Carruthers.

The boy's mouth turned up into a sneer. 'She was too bloody nice for her own good. Her and her father. I tried to talk to her about Objectivism and she rejected it. She *rejected* Ayn Rand's philosophy. Who the hell did she think she was?'

Carruthers could hear the anger in the young man's voice. He was reminded of what the victim had written in her diary about Munroe. As expected, once Carruthers got the student started they couldn't shut him up.

'Originally, I just set out to give her a nervous breakdown by playing mind games with her. I mean, that was a gift when I found out she'd slept with Campbell while she was seeing Will. Once I started killing, though, it was too much fun to stop.'

Davey grinned at the police officers. So, Rachel Abbie had been telling the truth in her diary. This man really had decided to try to give her a nervous breakdown. What a pathetic specimen.

Carruthers stared at this freckle-faced killer and then stole a look at his DCI. Was he mad or just plain bad? That wasn't Carruthers' place to find out. It would be left to a psychologist to work that one out. He wondered if Rachel Abbie's father being involved in the church had also played a part. The irony of Objectivism, as far as Carruthers' limited reading went, was that it rejected organised religion telling people they needed to think for themselves, yet here was a student who was incapable of thinking for himself. He was almost revering Objectivism, not so much as a cult, but more like a religion.

'Anyway, she was always helping other people. I kept telling her what she was doing wasn't rational. People need to be able to help themselves.'

McTavish leaned back in her chair. 'I take it you don't believe in a welfare state then?'

'The welfare state just allows people to be weak and reliant.'

Carruthers was just starting to understand how Objectivism held such appeal to Republicans, although there'd been an item on the news about a Republican politician who had recently distanced himself from Ayn Rand's philosophy, saying that Rand's staunchly atheistic philosophy was at odds with his own Catholicism. Carruthers suspected it was more to do with his reduced chances of winning votes rather than anything else.

'At first I decided I just wanted her to have a nervous breakdown. I wanted her to suffer. But then I decided what I actually wanted was to kill her.'

Carruthers couldn't help himself. 'But she didn't suffer, did she? Not for long anyway. Not in the way little Marion Parker did when Hickman murdered her.'

'You know about that? Impressive murder, wasn't it?'

Carruthers was disgusted. So, it wasn't just Ayn Rand who had been inspired by the serial killer. Davey Munroe had also done his research. Davey looked angry for a moment but then that charming smile returned.

'No, she didn't. But her father will. Suffer, I mean. Without his daughter. First his wife dies. Then his daughter. Touch of genius sending him the finger. Every morning his daughter's death will be the first thing on his mind. He'll be suffering for the rest of his life. And every time the post lands on his doorstep he'll be thinking of his daughter's finger.' He gave a bellow of a laugh.

Despite all his police training there were moments like this when Carruthers found it difficult to control his emotions. He was firmly against the death penalty, but just occasionally he met an individual for whom even the death penalty would be too good. Davey Munroe was one such individual. He had to fight his baser instincts in order to continue the interview.

'So that's why you sent Rachel's father his daughter's finger?' urged Carruthers. 'Because you wanted him to suffer?'

'Something like that.' Davey shrugged. 'It wasn't an easy decision to make. I wanted to keep it for myself.'

Davey, the Trophy Hunter, thought Carruthers. Yes, that was in keeping with the psychology of serial killers. And at this moment Davey Munroe looked like a little boy whose favourite cuddly toy had been taken away from him.

'But then I got to keep Sarah Torr's finger.' He smiled.

But you didn't, did you? You are now firmly in police custody.

Carruthers had another question for the student. 'Why did she have to die? I'm trying to work out how you chose your victims here, Davey. Help me out, will you?'

'By then I was enjoying killing. I enjoyed having the power of life and death over another living thing.'

Carruthers was starting to form a clearer impression of Davey Munroe. He wondered if the weak, bullied youngster had been looking for a movement that he could hide behind. If that was the case, the movement of Ayn Rand and Objectivism would have been perfect.

Davey Munroe sat back in his chair, crossed his arms and started whistling. A strange, tuneless whistling. Carruthers felt a shiver go down his spine.

* * *

'So, let me get this right,' said Fletcher. 'Davey Munroe was in thrall to a fellow student, an Objectivist, who looked the spitting image of Ayn Rand, who started the movement?'

'That's pretty much the size of it.' It was Carruthers who spoke, but the whole team was crammed into McTavish's office for a short debrief.

'He wanted to impress her so he started killing for her. He'd obviously done his research on Ayn Rand and found out she was an admirer of William Edward Hickman, the American serial killer. God, you really can't make this shit up.'

'And if you did,' put in Watson, 'nobody would believe you.'

'I've never heard of anything so demented,' cried Helen Lennox. 'Thank God he's behind bars.'

McTavish was solemn. 'Where he'll stay for a very long time.'

'Do we have reason to hold Mary-Lou Gettier?' It was to McTavish that Carruthers asked his question. 'I don't in all honesty think she had anything to do with the murders. Her alibis proved solid ones. In fact, at the time Rachel Abbie was murdered she was giving a talk on Objectivism. She's given us the names of over a dozen people who can vouch for her whereabouts. And it's been checked. There's no way Gettier could have been anywhere near the scene of the crimes. Plus, at the time of the student slashing in Ontario she was in Indonesia on some anthropology trip.'

'She might still have put Munroe up to it.' McTavish checked her mobile as she spoke. 'She doesn't have to have murdered them herself. I don't think we're finished with her yet. She still has a lot of questions to answer.'

'Apparently, she's told her department she's wanting to return to Canada and complete her studies there,' Carruthers continued. 'She was part of the exchange programme.'

'She won't be going anywhere anytime soon. Not until we're convinced she wasn't involved, although it does look as if Munroe was also stalking her if he followed her over from Canada,' conceded McTavish.

A desk phone could be heard starting to ring in another office as Helen Lennox asked a question. 'Talking about Indonesia, have the parents of Serena Davis been found?'

'Yep, they'll be in Scotland by tomorrow afternoon,' said Fletcher.

Lennox looked pleased. 'That's good news. That wee lassie needs her mum and dad.'

McTavish stood up from behind her desk. 'Okay folks. That's it. Debrief over. Good work, team. It's been a tough case but we got there in the end. I'll be buying the first round at our local if anyone wants to join me later?'

There were cheers around the office as staff started to shuffle out the door.

Fletcher caught up with Carruthers. 'What are your thoughts on Objectivism, Jim? It's not easy to be objective about it given what we've all been through.'

He smiled. 'I like the pun. For some people I can see the attraction.' He held the door open for Fletcher and Watson. 'It gives those who are inherently selfish justification for their selfishness. Personally, I think it's fundamentally flawed. And I can't really see how running a society like that would work, to be honest.'

They walked back towards their own office in companionable silence until Fletcher finally spoke. 'There wouldn't be a society, would there?'

'Well, if you cast your mind back, didn't Maggie Thatcher say there was no such thing as society, although I'm pretty sure she said later that her comment had been taken completely out of context.'

'I'm too young to know much about Margaret Thatcher, Jim. That's more your era.' She grinned. 'On a different note, what on earth was Malcolm Duggan doing with an air gun? He must be in his sixties. I always associate air guns with teenage boys somehow.'

'Funny you should say that. He actually took the air gun off his grandson.'

'What will happen to Malcolm now? After all, he might have prevented two murders, even if he did discharge a firearm.'

'We've taken a statement from him. The courts will bear in mind that he acted to prevent a crime being committed, but he did fire a potentially lethal weapon. However, in the circumstances, I don't think they'll prosecute.'

'So now we've cracked the case and Munroe is going to be behind bars what do you want to do? Like Sandra said, some of us are going for a drink to celebrate.'

Carruthers shook his head. Ordinarily he knew he would have joined the team but, on this occasion, he would have to give it a miss. Some things were more important.

'No, not this time. I didn't tell you, but my brother turned up on my doorstep on Friday night.'

'Oh, I didn't know. Is he okay?'

'No, he's not. He's in bad shape. He's needing another op. I'm going to invite him to stay with me during his recovery. I'm going to try to get to know him properly at last.' He still wasn't ready to tell Fletcher about his mother's lung cancer, although he had decided to talk to McTavish about it. He was wanting to take some time off to chum his mum to her first appointment. And he had spoken with his mother's GP. He had been reassured that having the diagnosis of lung cancer wasn't necessarily a death sentence. With a bit of luck, it might be of the slow growing variety. After all, they had found it when they were investigating something else.

The door burst open and Watson, Lennox and Brown stood there. 'You guys ready?'

'Go on, urged Carruthers. 'Go and have a drink with your colleagues. You've earned it.'

'If you're sure?'

He nodded.

She leant into him as she whispered, 'Greg Ross is coming out with us.'

Carruthers winked at her. 'Go and have a bit of fun.'

Still in a whisper she said, 'What happened to Mairi's boyfriend? Wasn't he on his way to see her when it all kicked off with Munroe?'

Carruthers pulled a face. 'Apparently, he had a flat tyre. That's why he was running late. I heard a mobile ringing when I was in her cottage. It was him leaving her a message.'

'So, they're still together then?'

'Apparently so.'

'Not to worry, Jim. In the end it was you who rescued her. Not him. That has to count for something. If you want her back, that is,' she added. She skipped out of the office with a wink of her own and a final backward glance.

He smiled affectionately at her back, wondering about the truth of her last comment. Was there a chance he could win Mairi back? Did he want to? He walked back to his desk, grabbed his jacket and car keys, and walked out of the building towards his car in the knowledge Castletown was a much safer place.

THE END

Acknowledgements

When I signed with Bloodhound Books in October 2016 I could never have envisaged the success of this series. In October 2018, two years after the publication of my debut novel, *Robbing the Dead* and three books into the series, to my amazement I became a UK Amazon Top 10 bestseller, with 100,000 sales behind me, which was wonderful.

Much of this success is due, in no small part, to a wide variety of people. First, the team at Bloodhound for taking a chance on me and for their amazing promotional skills; my editor, Clare Law and proof reader, Ian Skewis and all the book bloggers and online book clubs who work tirelessly to promote authors' work simply for the love of books. A huge thank you must go to Dr Jacky Collins for her encouragement, support and friendship and also to the readers who have bought the books.

Massive thank yous also go to Alison Baillie and Sarah Torr for being my first readers (in fact, Sarah has a character named after her in this book) and to my partner, Ian Brown, for his invaluable comments and support. Thank you also to my niece, Rachel Abbie, who also allowed me to use her name as a character in the novel, and the student friends of another of my nieces, Louise Pettigrew, especially Alex, Akaash, Deepikaa, Trini, Joanna and Mairi. On police matters, Andy Carlin and Kerry Richardson must get a mention for keeping me right.

My novels deal with contemporary themes and I'm a passionate believer in social justice. During the writing of this book I ran a raffle to try to support Jacqueline Culleton, who started a fund to help Albert Thompson, a child of the Windrush generation, get his much needed cancer treatment. The winner of the competition, Amanda Selway, became a character in the book and she makes a great PC! I would also like to mention Kathleen Sweeney, who works so hard to make the Pensioners' Wee Xmas Do in Springburn, Glasgow, a success every year – a lovely Irish lady called Mary McPhee won a cameo appearance in this book, so I hope she enjoys being a young librarian for the day.

Lastly, thank you to all my family and friends for their support, in particular my mum; my brother Rob; Kelly Lacey; Jackie McLean and Ally Brady. I'm busy writing Book 5 so hopefully we won't have too long to wait to see Jim Carruthers and the team again.

Printed in Great Britain
by Amazon

82634140R10161